ESTABLISHED
1986

A SOUTHERN ORIGINAL

CANNIBAL

70 cl e

40% Vol.

VOLUME ONE

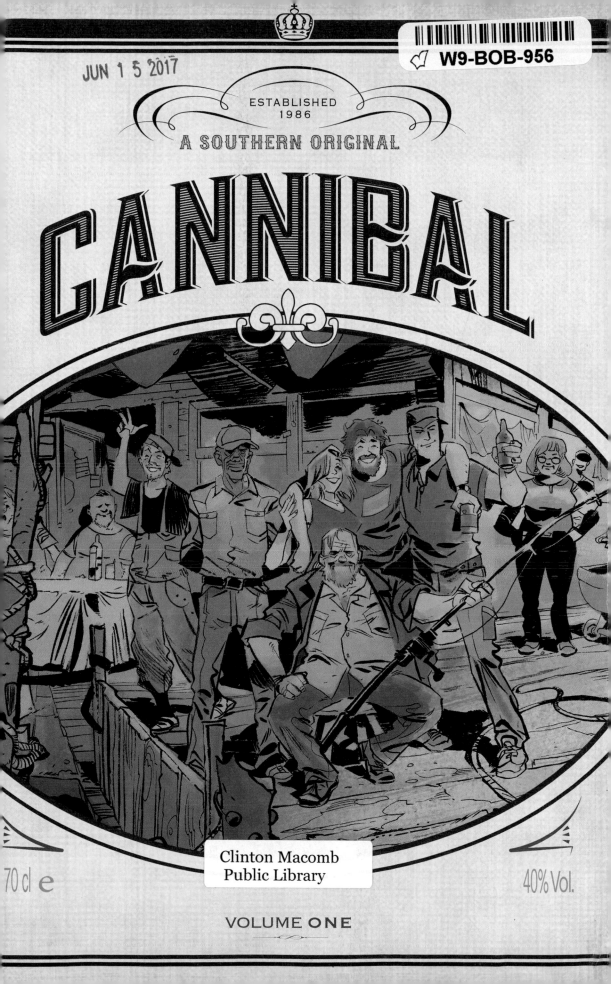

GOVERNMENT WARNING:(1) ACCORDING TO THE SURGEON GENERAL, WOMEN SHOULD NOT DRINK ALCOHOLIC BEVERAGES DURING PREGNANCY BECAUSE OF THE RISK OF BIRTH DEFECTS. (2) CONSUMPTION OF ALCOHOLIC BEVERAGES IMPAIRS YOUR ABILITY TO DRIVE A CAR OR OPERATE MACHINERY, AND MAY CAUSE HEALTH PROBLEMS.

IMAGE COMICS, INC

Robert Kirkman — Chief Operating Officer
Erik Larsen — Chief Financial Officer
Todd McFarlane — President
Marc Silvestri — Chief Executive Officer
Jim Valentino — Vice-President
Eric Stephenson — Publisher
Corey Murphy — Director of Sales
Jeff Boison — Director of Publishing Planning & Book Trade Sales
Chris Ross — Director of Digital Sales
Kat Salazar — Director of PR & Marketing
Branwyn Bigglestone — Controller
Susan Korpela — Accounts Manager
Drew Gill — Art Director
Brett Warnock — Production Manager
Meredith Wallace — Print Manager
Briah Skelly — Publicist
Aly Hoffman — Conventions & Events Coordinator
Sasha Head — Sales & Marketing Production Designer
David Brothers — Branding Manager
Melissa Gifford — Content Manager
Erika Schnatz — Production Artist
Ryan Brewer — Production Artist
Shanna Matuszak — Production Artist
Tricia Ramos — Production Artist
Vincent Kukua — Production Artist
Jeff Stang — Direct Market Sales Representative
Emilio Bautista — Digital Sales Associate
Leanna Caunter — Accounting Assistant
Chloe Ramos-Peterson — Library Market Sales Representative

IMAGECOMICS.COM

PRODUCT OF USA
HAND MADE
PROUDLY DISTILLED
IN EVERGLADES, FLA

CANNIBAL, VOL. 1. ISBN: 978-1-5343-0054-5. First printing. March 2017. Published by Image Comics, Inc. Office of publication: 2701 NW Vaughn St., Suite 780, Portland, OR 97210. Copyright © 2017 Brian Buccellato & Jennifer Young. All rights reserved. Contains material originally published in single magazine form as CANNIBAL #1-4. "Cannibal," its logos, and the likenesses of all characters herein are trademarks of Brian Buccellato & Jennifer Young, unless otherwise noted. "Image" and the Image Comics logos are registered trademarks of Image Comics, Inc. No part of this publication may be reproduced or transmitted, in any form or by any means (except for short excerpts for journalistic or review purposes), without the express written permission of John Layman or Image Comics, Inc. All names, characters, events, and locales in this publication are entirely fictional. Any resemblance to actual persons (living or dead), events, or places, without satiric intent, is coincidental. Printed in the USA. For information regarding the CPSIA on this printed material call: 203-595-3636 and provide reference #RICH–726450. For international rights, contact: foreignlicensing@imagecomics.com.

ESTABLISHED
1986

A SOUTHERN ORIGINAL

CANNIBAL

BRIAN BUCCELLATO

&

JENNIFER YOUNG
STORY

MATIAS BERGARA
ART

BRIAN BUCCELLATO
COLORS

TROY PETERI
LETTERS

VOLUMEONE

ISSUEONE

ESTABLISHED
1908

A SOUTHERN ORIGINAL

CANNIBAL

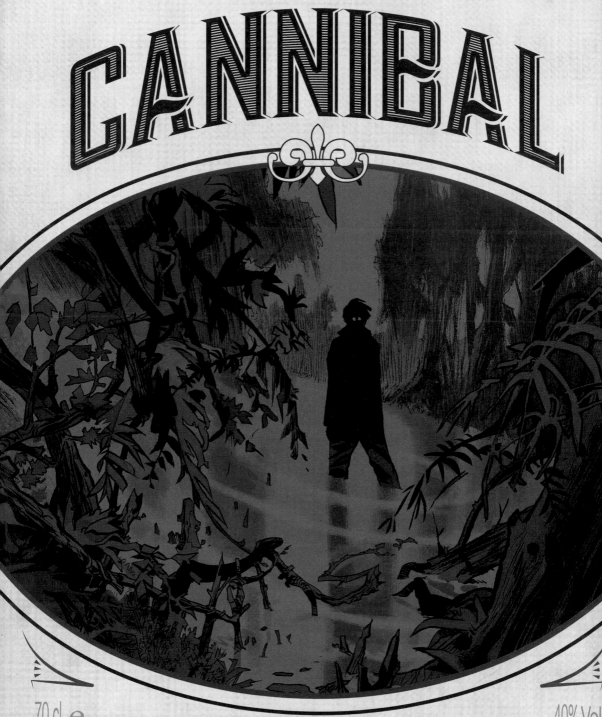

70 cl e

40% Vol.

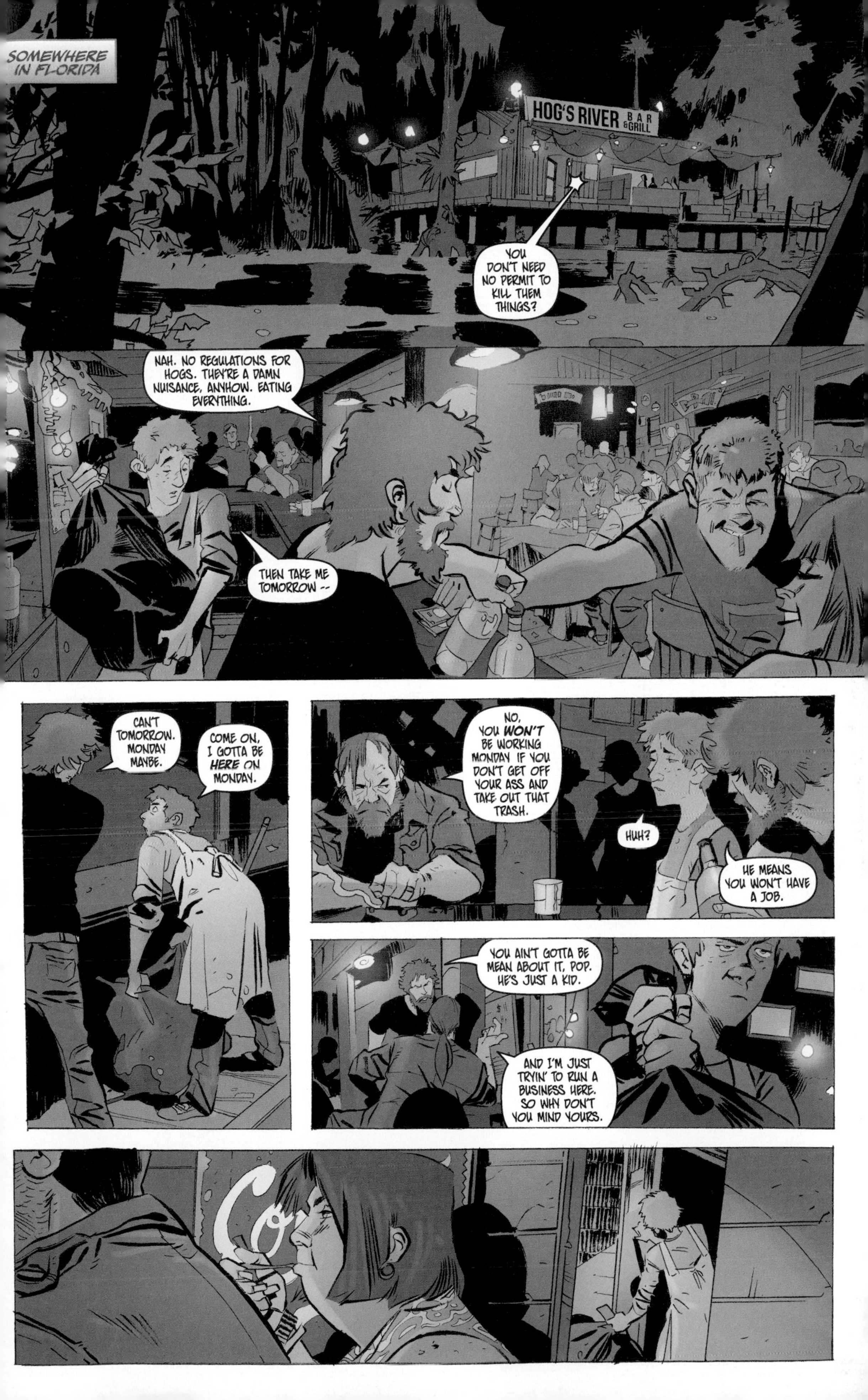
SOMEWHERE IN FLORIDA
HOG'S RIVER BAR & GRILL
YOU DON'T NEED NO PERMIT TO KILL THEM THINGS?
NAH. NO REGULATIONS FOR HOGS. THEY'RE A DAMN NUISANCE, ANYHOW. EATING EVERYTHING.
THEN TAKE ME TOMORROW --
CAN'T TOMORROW. MONDAY MAYBE.
COME ON, I GOTTA BE HERE ON MONDAY.
NO, YOU WON'T BE WORKING MONDAY IF YOU DON'T GET OFF YOUR ASS AND TAKE OUT THAT TRASH.
HUH?
HE MEANS YOU WON'T HAVE A JOB.
YOU AIN'T GOTTA BE MEAN ABOUT IT, POP. HE'S JUST A KID.
AND I'M JUST TRYIN' TO RUN A BUSINESS HERE. SO WHY DON'T YOU MIND YOURS.

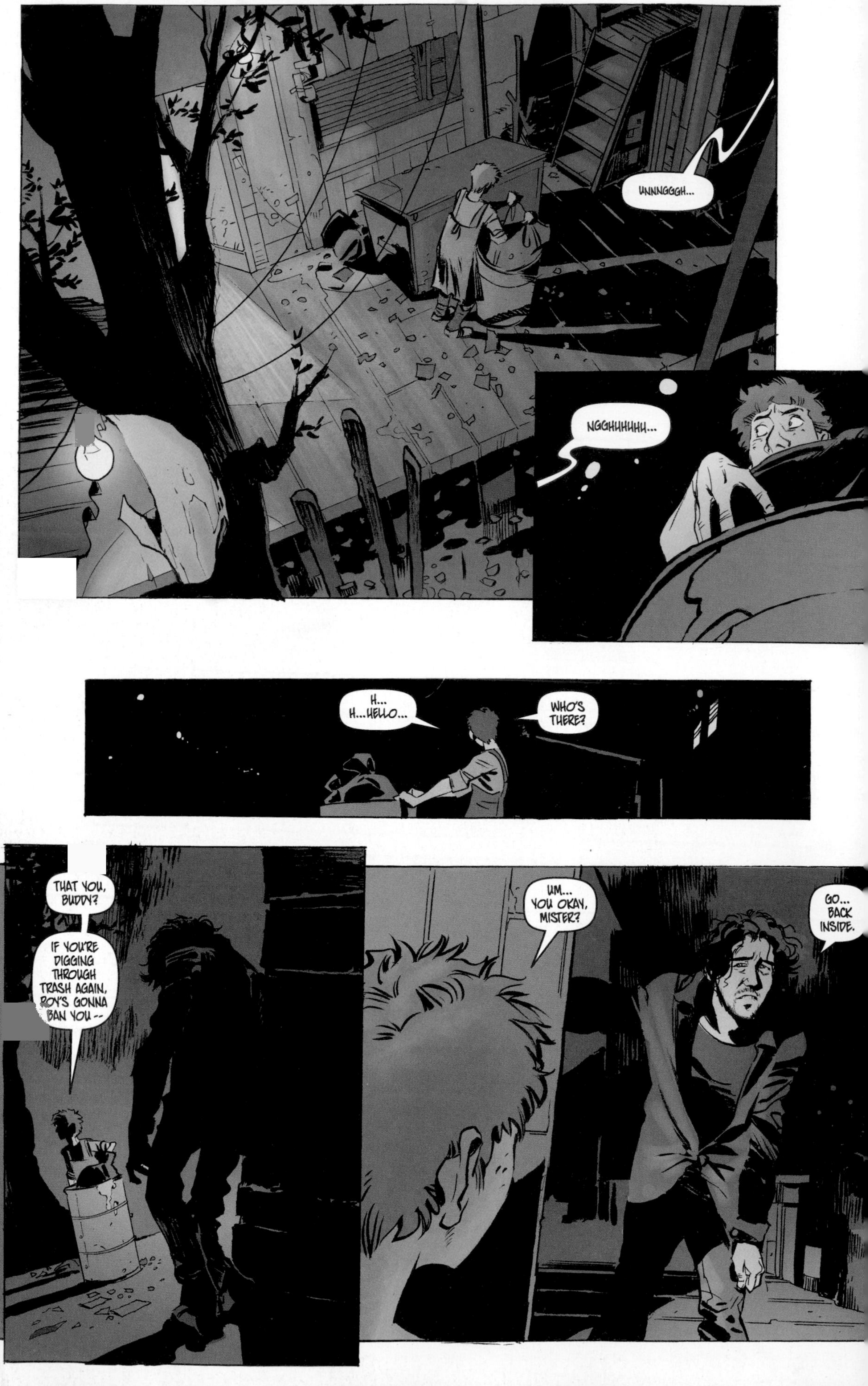
UNNNGGGH...
NGGHHHHHH...
H...
H...HELLO...
WHO'S THERE?
THAT YOU, BUDDY?
IF YOU'RE DIGGING THROUGH TRASH AGAIN, ROY'S GONNA BAN YOU --
UM... YOU OKAY, MISTER?
GO... BACK INSIDE.

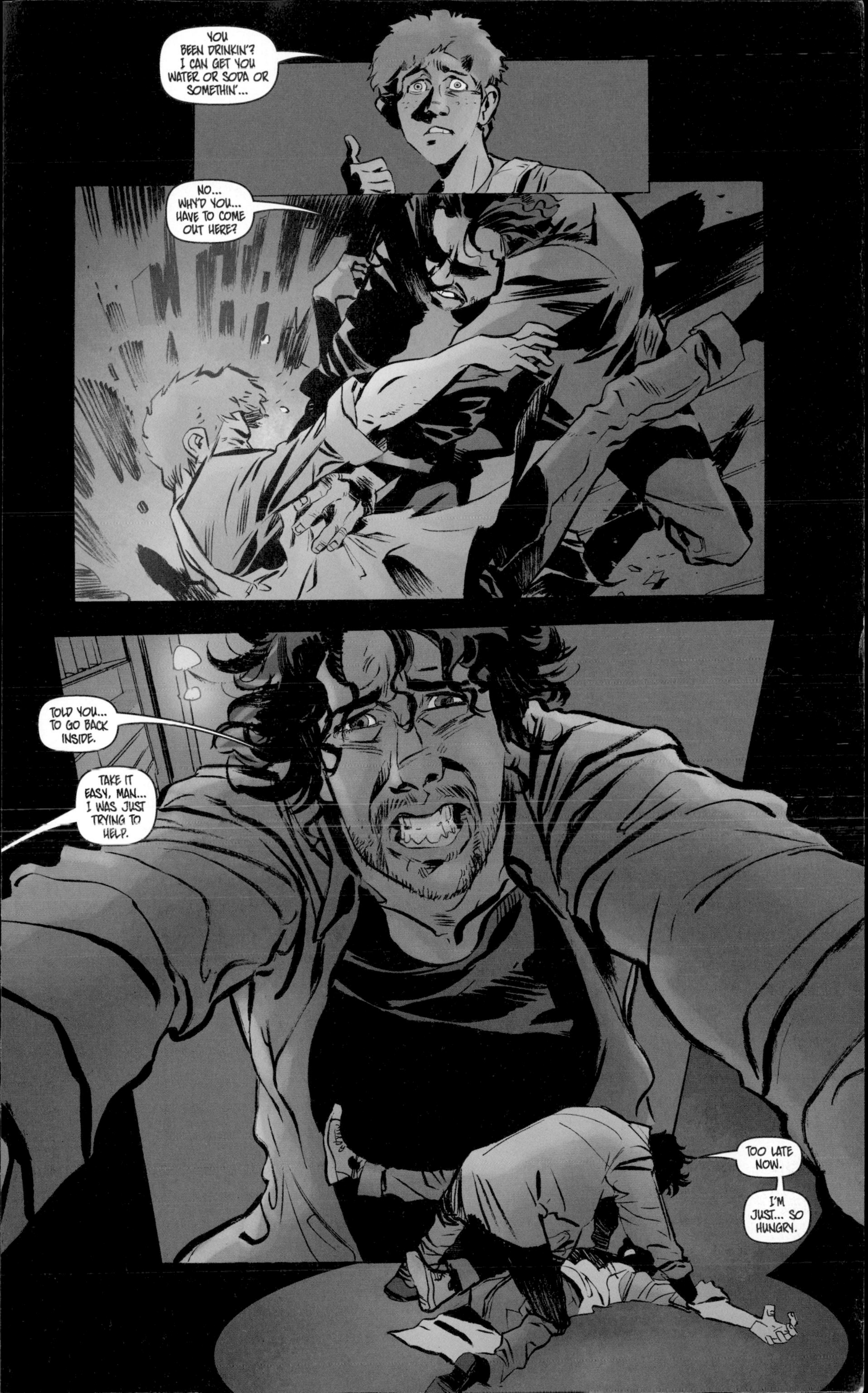

YOU BEEN DRINKIN'? I CAN GET YOU WATER OR SODA OR SOMETHIN'...
NO... WHY'D YOU... HAVE TO COME OUT HERE?
TOLD YOU... TO GO BACK INSIDE.
TAKE IT EASY, MAN... I WAS JUST TRYING TO HELP.
TOO LATE NOW.
I'M JUST... SO HUNGRY.

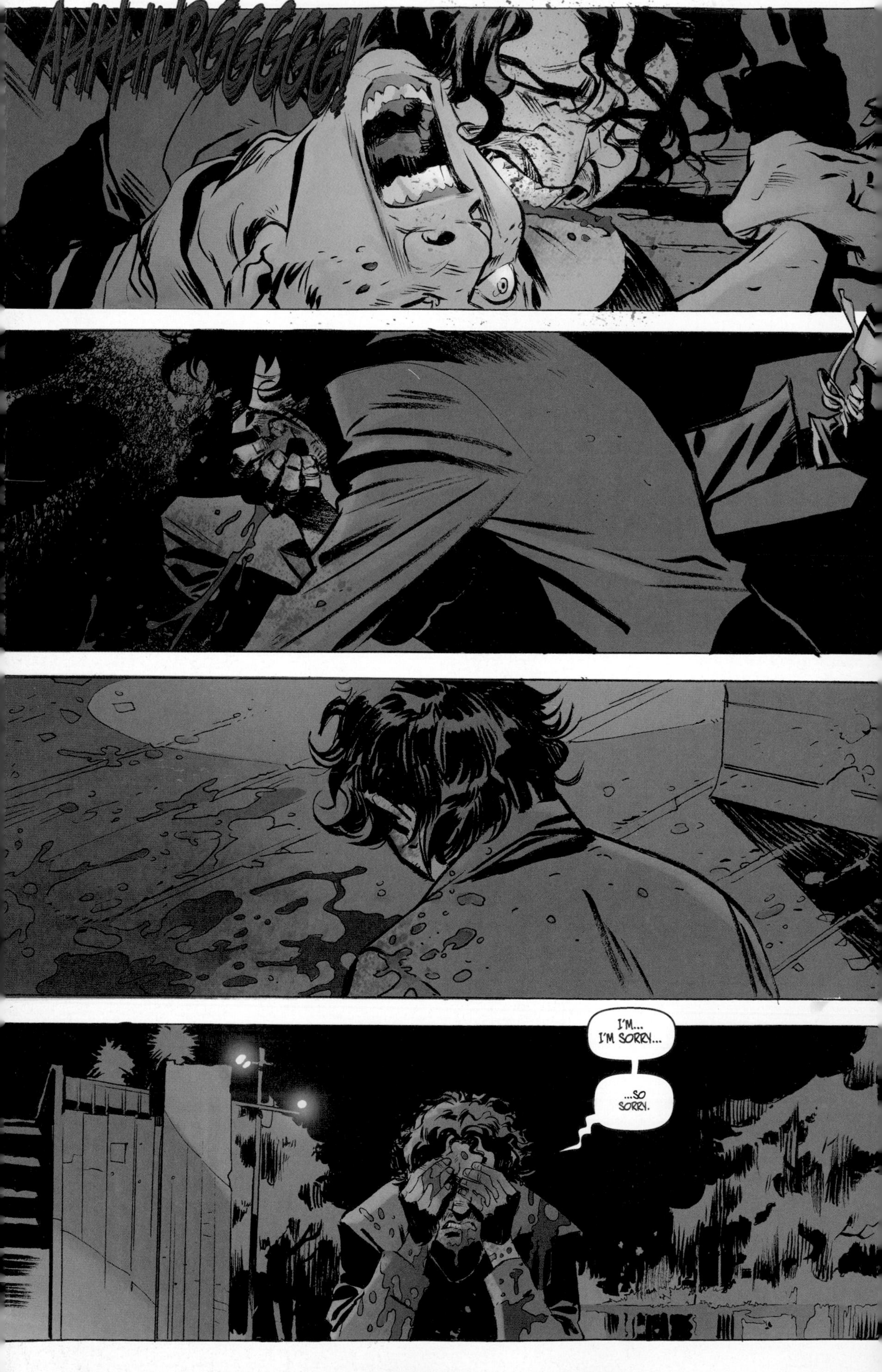
AHHHHRGGGGGG!
I'M... I'M SORRY...
...SO SORRY.

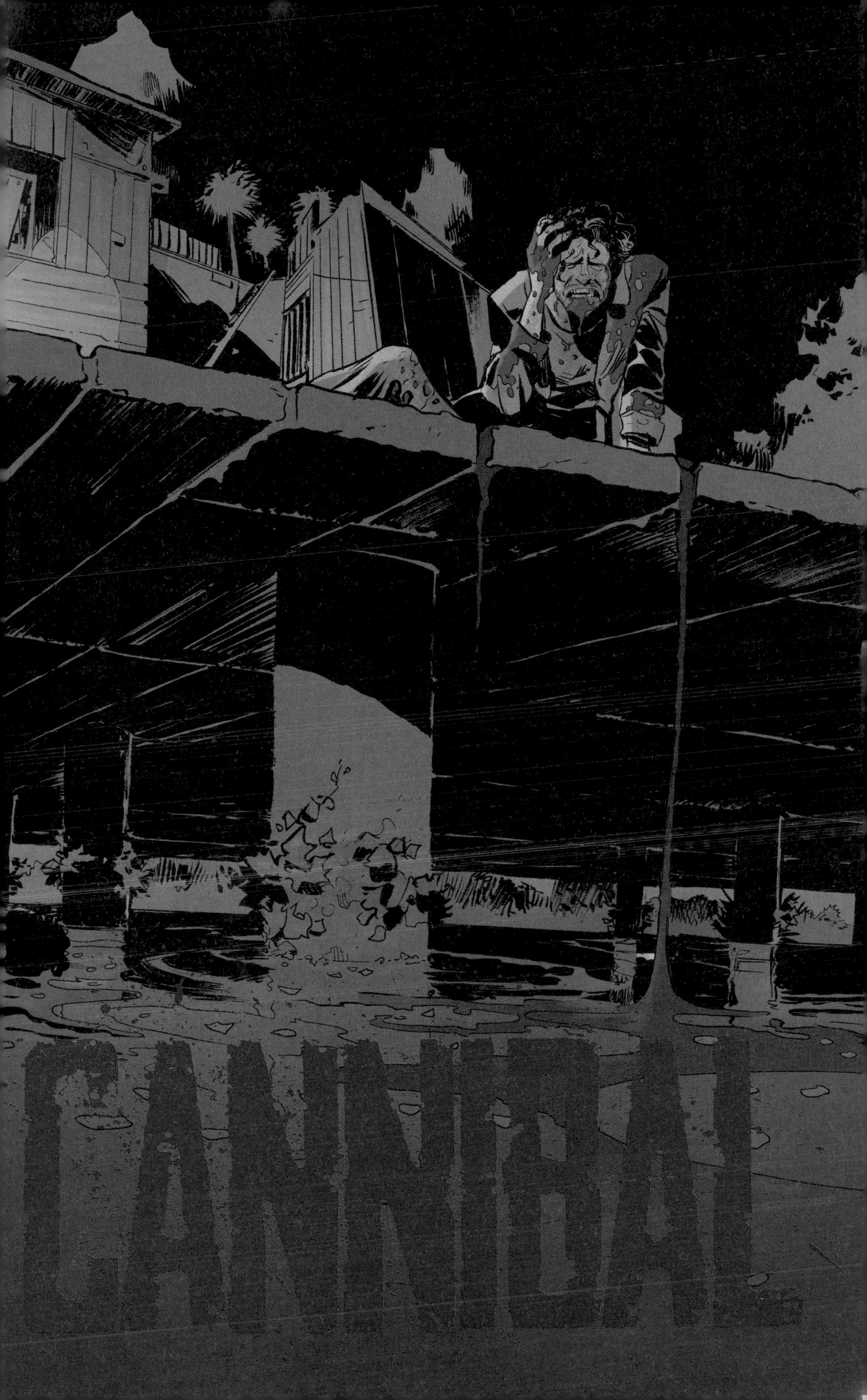
CANNIBAL

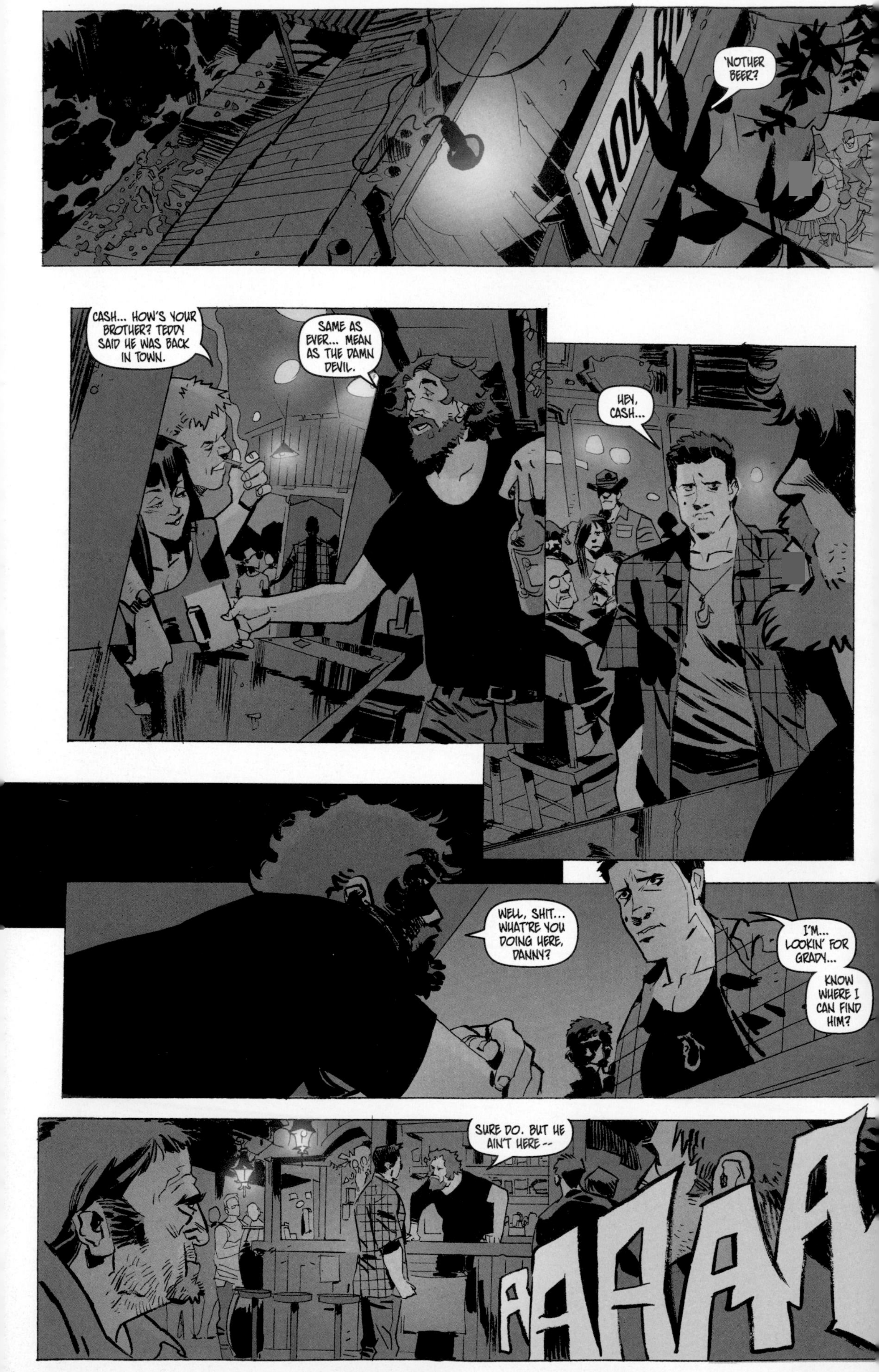
'NOTHER BEER?
CASH... HOW'S YOUR BROTHER? TEDDY SAID HE WAS BACK IN TOWN.
SAME AS EVER... MEAN AS THE DAMN DEVIL.
HEY, CASH...
WELL, SHIT... WHAT'RE YOU DOING HERE, DANNY?
I'M... LOOKIN' FOR GRADY...
KNOW WHERE I CAN FIND HIM?
SURE DO. BUT HE AIN'T HERE --
AAAAA

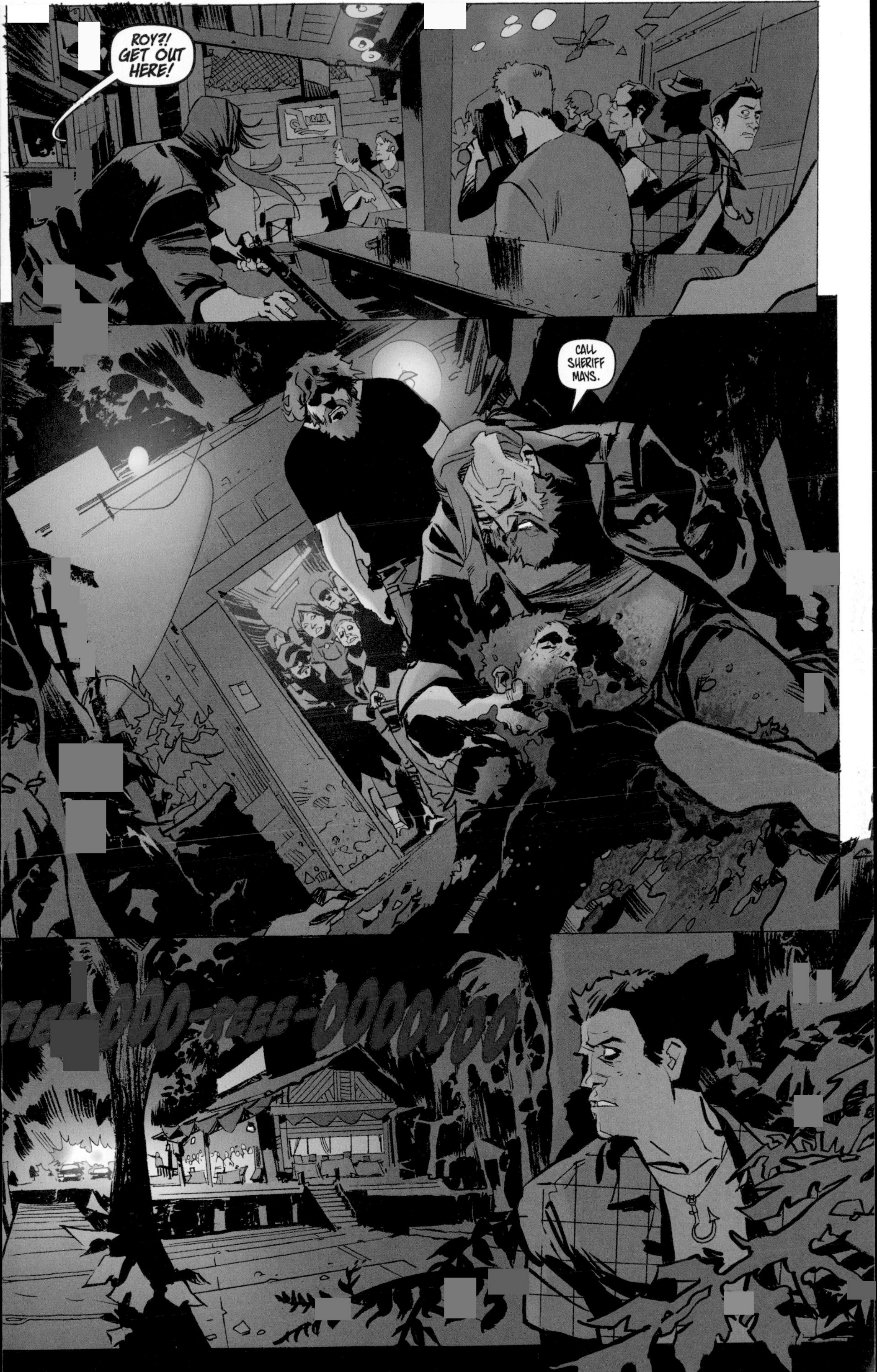
ROY?! GET OUT HERE!
CALL SHERIFF MAYS.

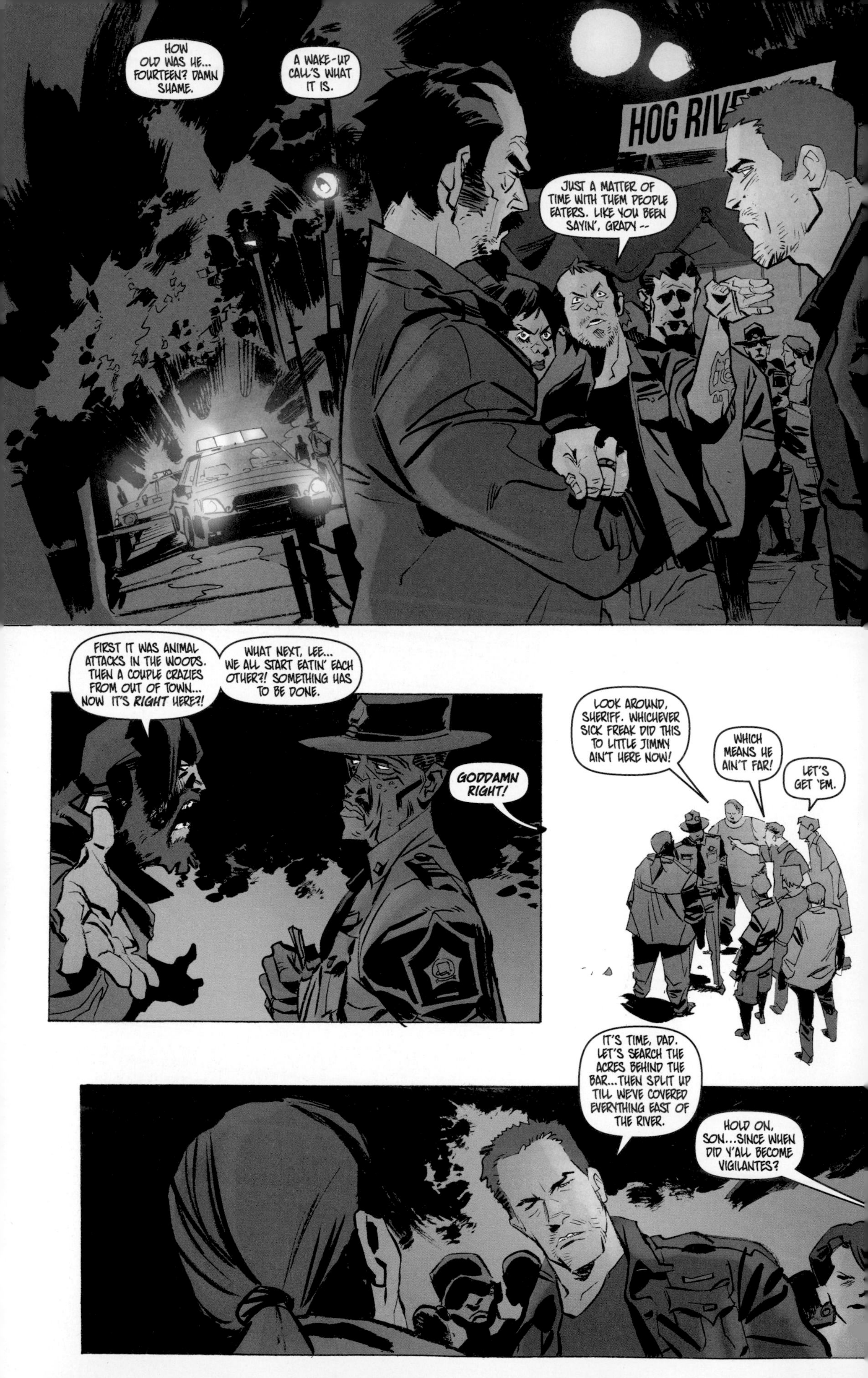
HOW OLD WAS HE... FOURTEEN? DAMN SHAME.
A WAKE-UP CALL'S WHAT IT IS.
HOG RIVE
JUST A MATTER OF TIME WITH THEM PEOPLE EATERS. LIKE YOU BEEN SAYIN', GRADY --
FIRST IT WAS ANIMAL ATTACKS IN THE WOODS. THEN A COUPLE CRAZIES FROM OUT OF TOWN... NOW IT'S RIGHT HERE?!
WHAT NEXT, LEE... WE ALL START EATIN' EACH OTHER?! SOMETHING HAS TO BE DONE.
GODDAMN RIGHT!
LOOK AROUND, SHERIFF. WHICHEVER SICK FREAK DID THIS TO LITTLE JIMMY AIN'T HERE NOW!
WHICH MEANS HE AIN'T FAR!
LET'S GET 'EM.
IT'S TIME, DAD. LET'S SEARCH THE ACRES BEHIND THE BAR...THEN SPLIT UP TILL WE'VE COVERED EVERYTHING EAST OF THE RIVER.
HOLD ON, SON...SINCE WHEN DID Y'ALL BECOME VIGILANTES?

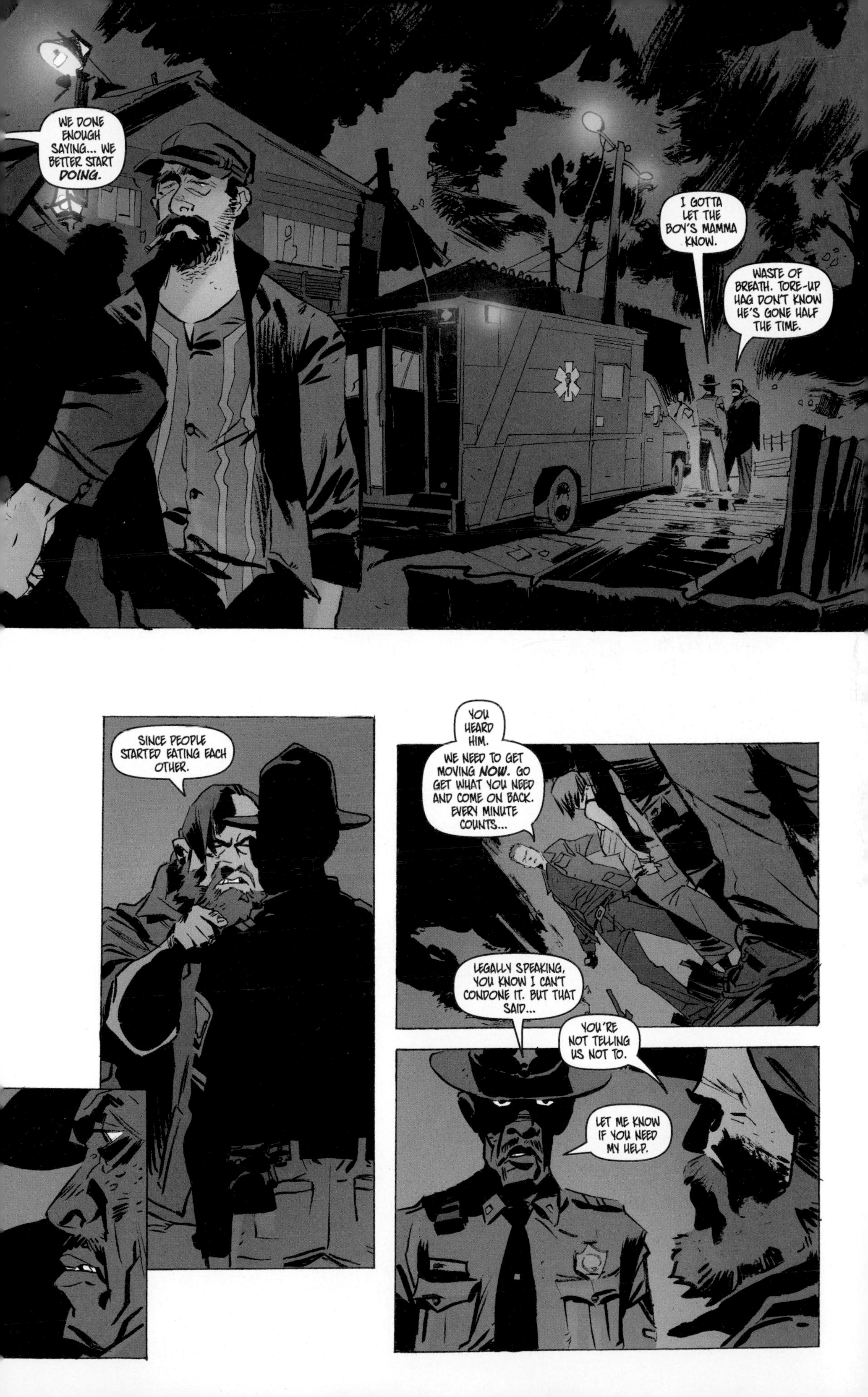

WE DONE ENOUGH SAYING... WE BETTER START DOING.
I GOTTA LET THE BOY'S MAMMA KNOW.
WASTE OF BREATH. TORE-UP HAG DON'T KNOW HE'S GONE HALF THE TIME.
SINCE PEOPLE STARTED EATING EACH OTHER.
YOU HEARD HIM.
WE NEED TO GET MOVING NOW. GO GET WHAT YOU NEED AND COME ON BACK. EVERY MINUTE COUNTS...
LEGALLY SPEAKING, YOU KNOW I CAN'T CONDONE IT. BUT THAT SAID...
YOU'RE NOT TELLING US NOT TO.
LET ME KNOW IF YOU NEED MY HELP.

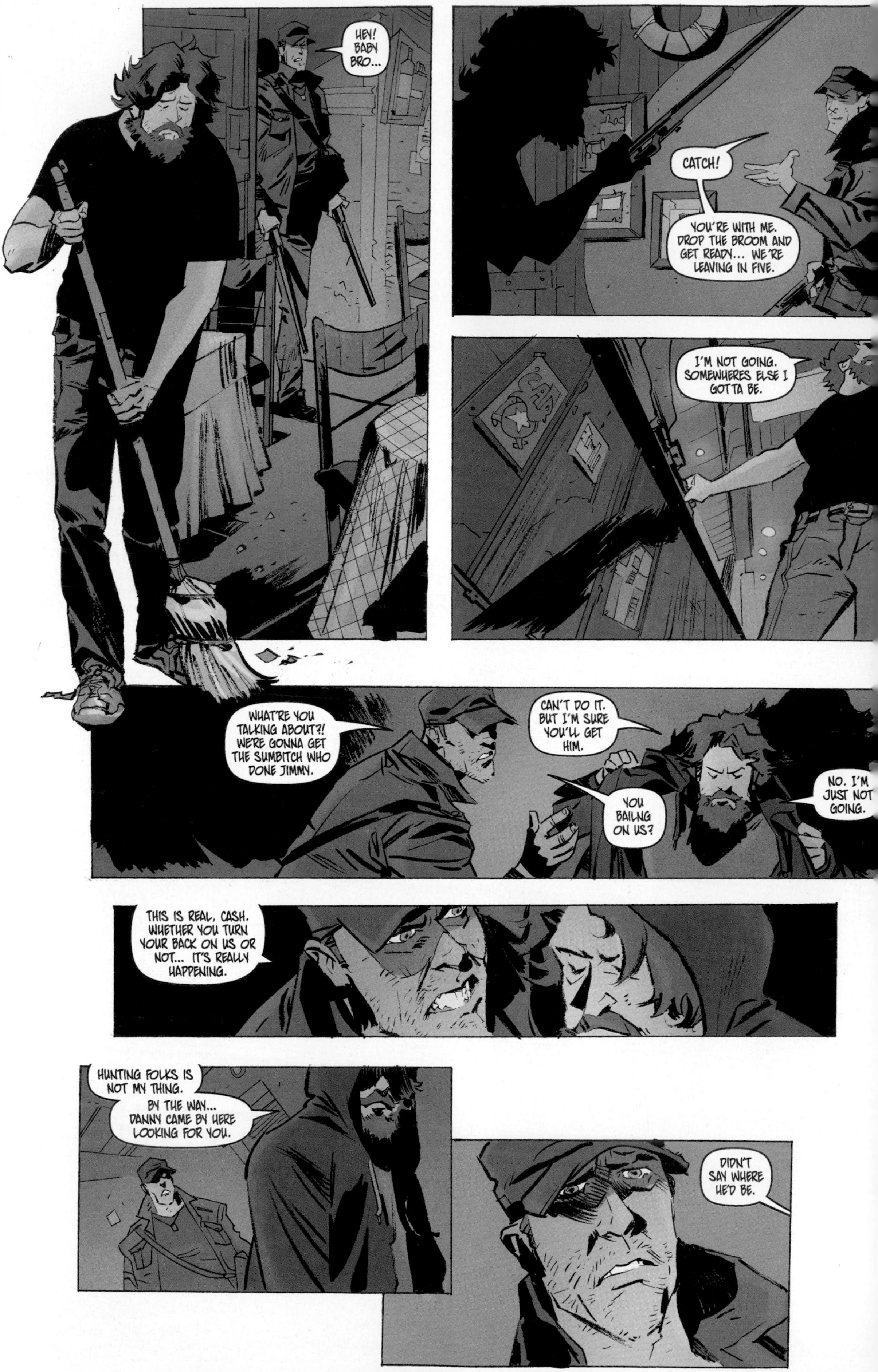
HEY! BABY BRO...
CATCH!
YOU'RE WITH ME. DROP THE BROOM AND GET READY... WE'RE LEAVING IN FIVE.
I'M NOT GOING. SOMEWHERES ELSE I GOTTA BE.
WHAT'RE YOU TALKING ABOUT?! WE'RE GONNA GET THE SUMBITCH WHO DONE JIMMY.
CAN'T DO IT. BUT I'M SURE YOU'LL GET HIM.
YOU BAILING ON US?
NO. I'M JUST NOT GOING.
THIS IS REAL, CASH. WHETHER YOU TURN YOUR BACK ON US OR NOT... IT'S REALLY HAPPENING.
HUNTING FOLKS IS NOT MY THING.
BY THE WAY... DANNY CAME BY HERE LOOKING FOR YOU.
DIDN'T SAY WHERE HE'D BE.

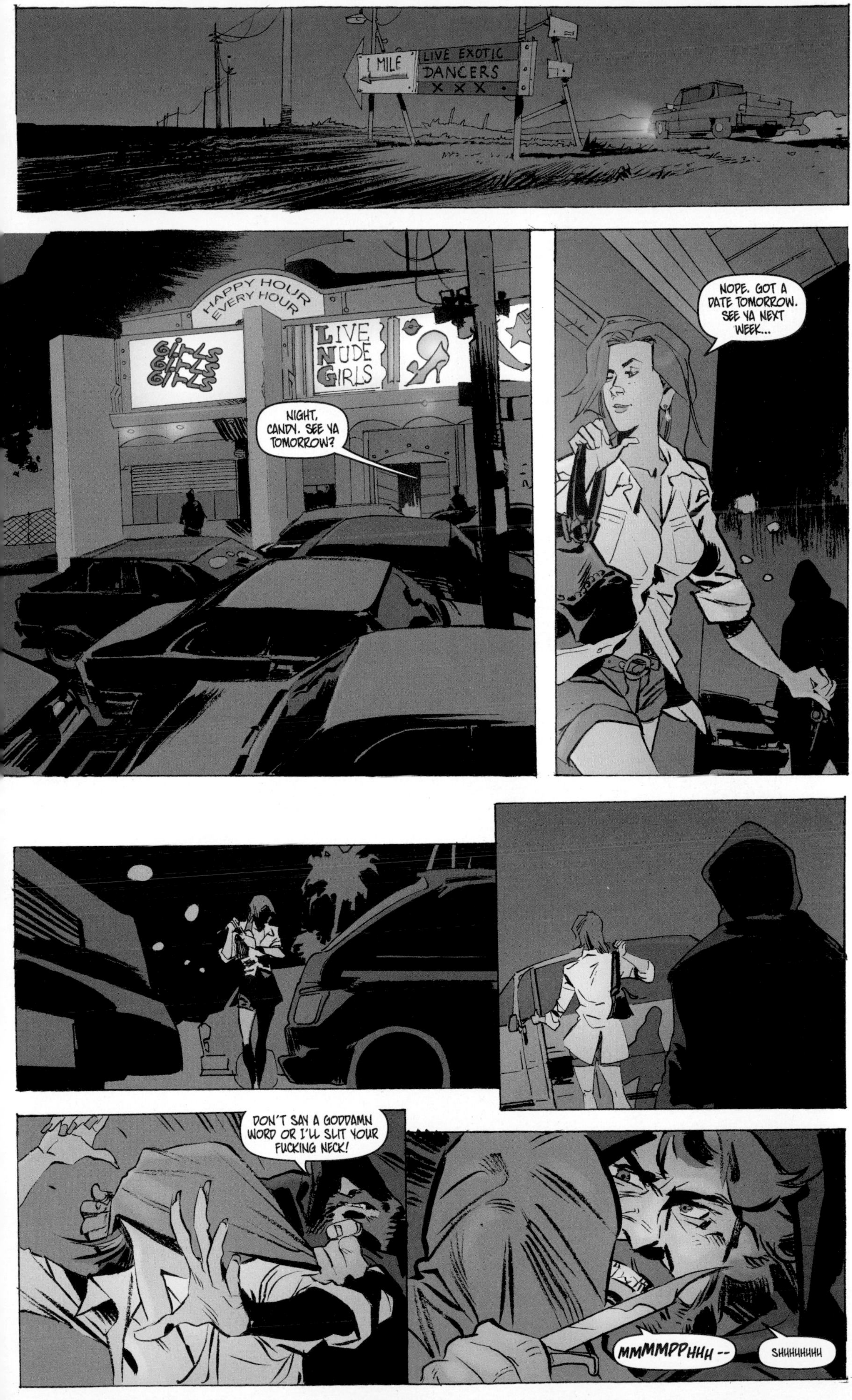
1 MILE
LIVE EXOTIC DANCERS XXX
HAPPY HOUR EVERY HOUR
GIRLS GIRLS GIRLS
LIVE NUDE GIRLS
NIGHT, CANDY. SEE YA TOMORROW?
NOPE. GOT A DATE TOMORROW. SEE YA NEXT WEEK...
DON'T SAY A GODDAMN WORD OR I'LL SLIT YOUR FUCKING NECK!
MMMMPPHHH--
SHHHHHHH

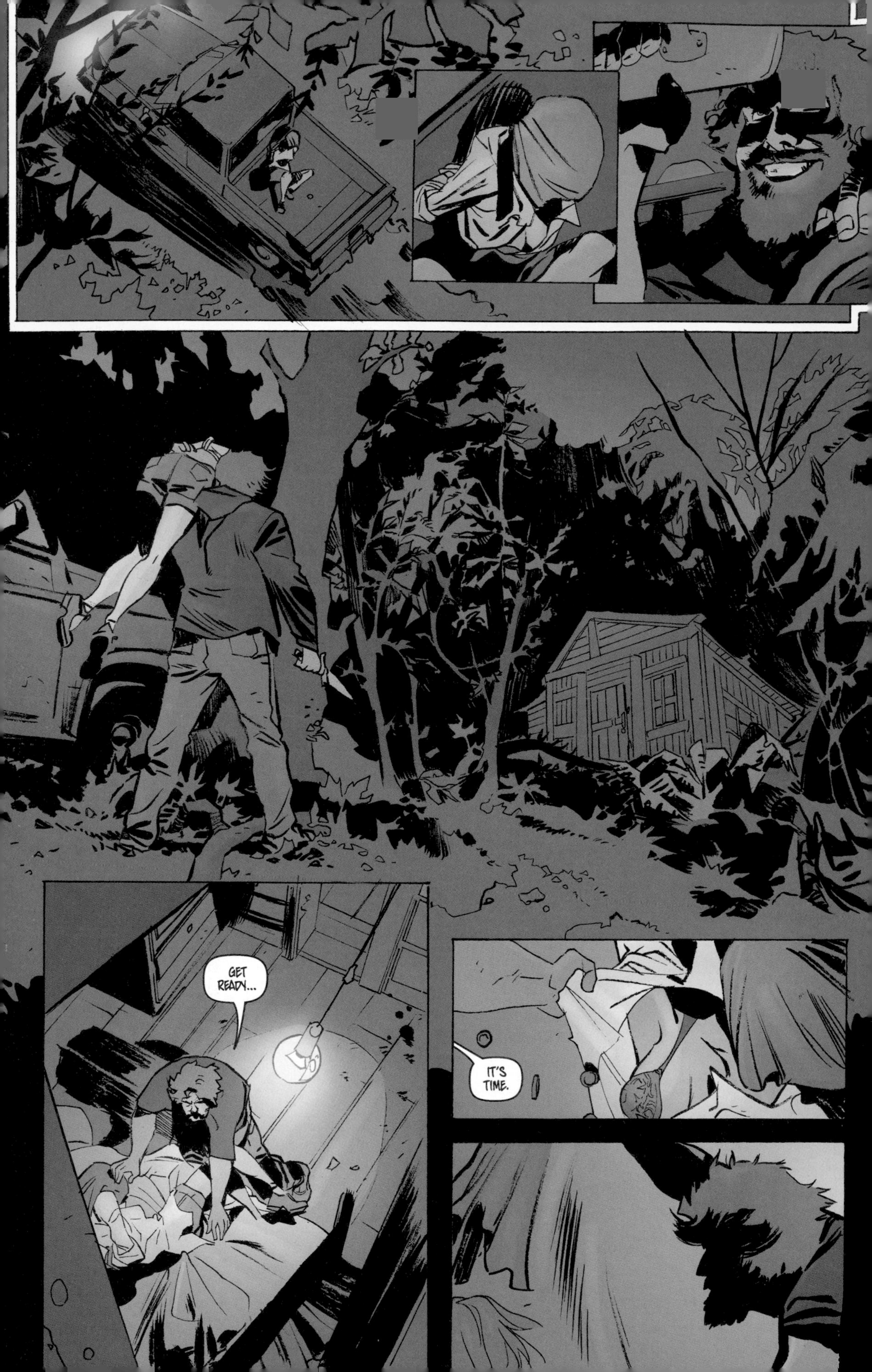
GET READY...
IT'S TIME.

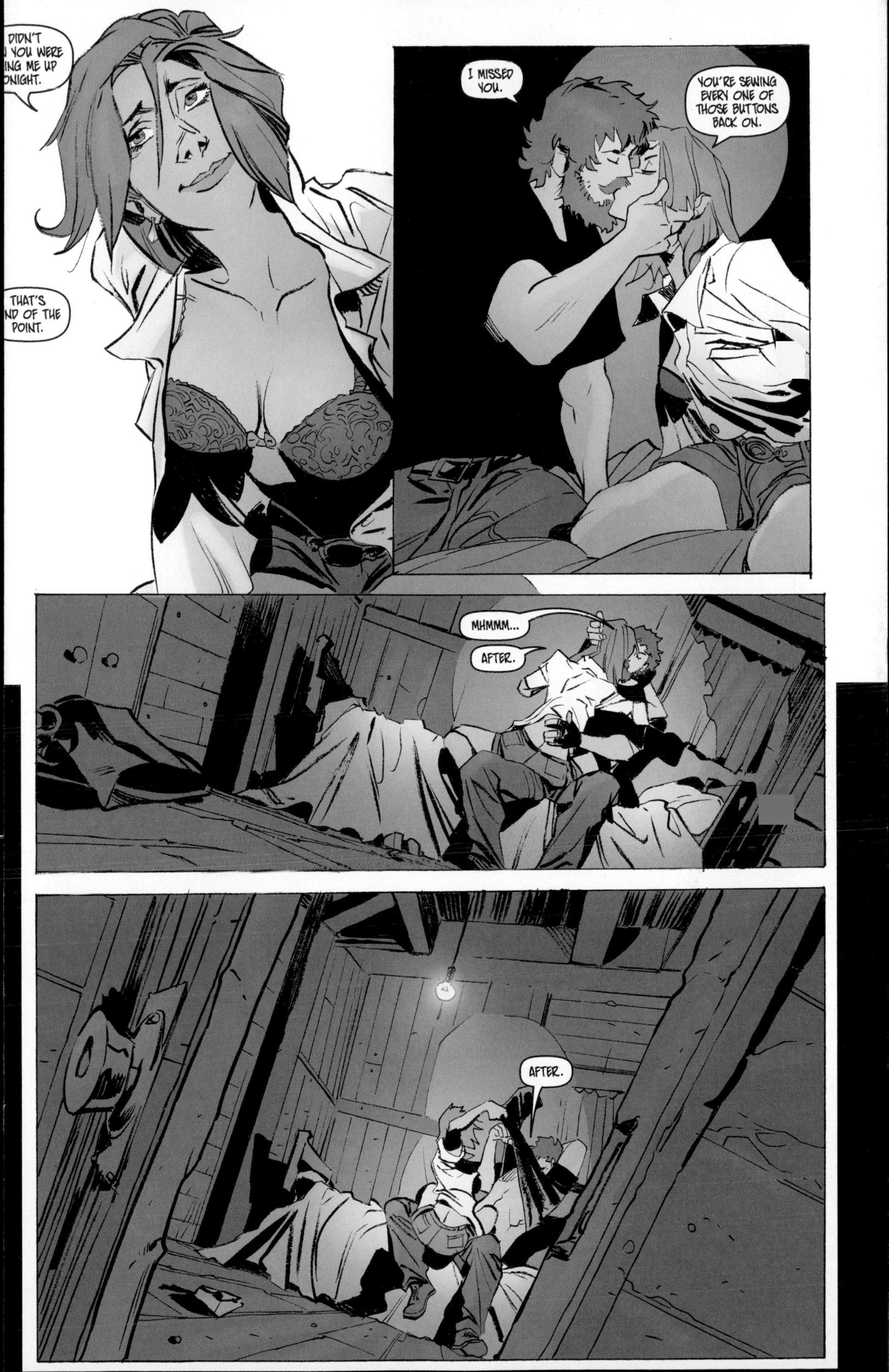
DIDN'T N YOU WERE ING ME UP ONIGHT.
THAT'S ND OF THE POINT.
I MISSED YOU.
YOU'RE SEWING EVERY ONE OF THOSE BUTTONS BACK ON.
MHMMM...
AFTER.
AFTER.

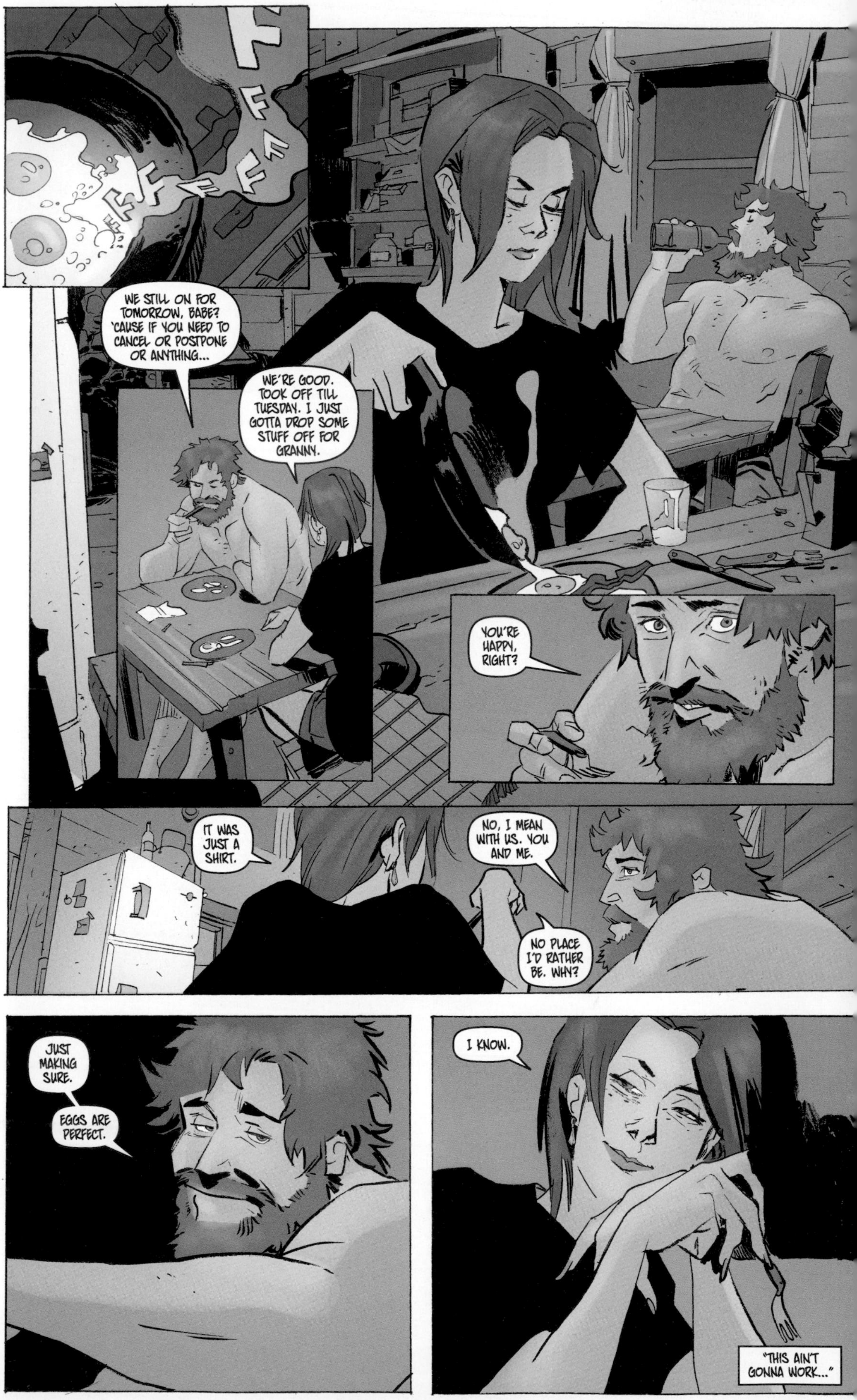
FFFFF
WE STILL ON FOR TOMORROW, BABE? 'CAUSE IF YOU NEED TO CANCEL OR POSTPONE OR ANYTHING...
WE'RE GOOD. TOOK OFF TILL TUESDAY. I JUST GOTTA DROP SOME STUFF OFF FOR GRANNY.
YOU'RE HAPPY, RIGHT?
IT WAS JUST A SHIRT.
NO, I MEAN WITH US. YOU AND ME.
NO PLACE I'D RATHER BE. WHY?
JUST MAKING SURE.
EGGS ARE PERFECT.
I KNOW.
"THIS AIN'T GONNA WORK..."

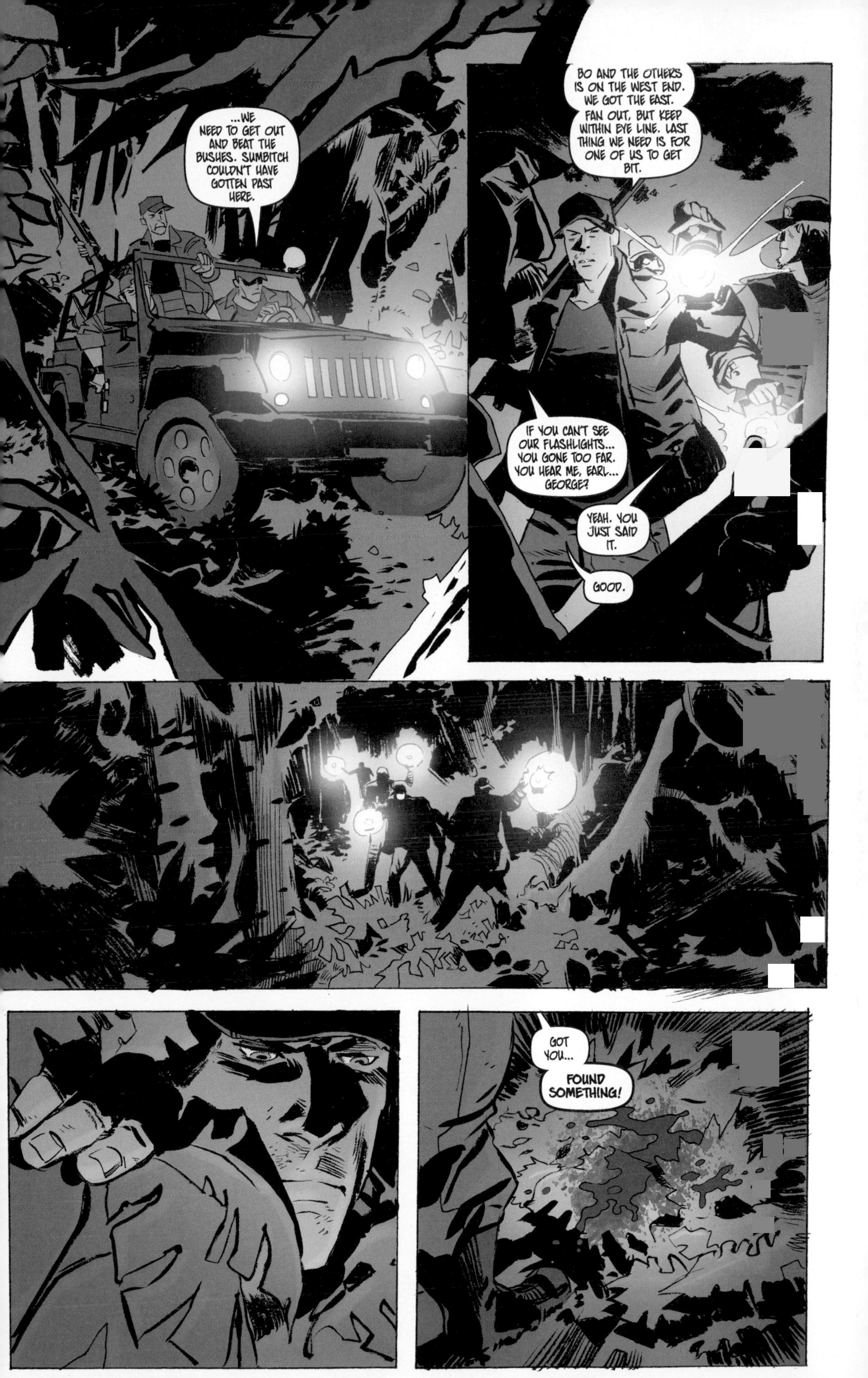
...WE NEED TO GET OUT AND BEAT THE BUSHES. SUMBITCH COULDN'T HAVE GOTTEN PAST HERE.
BO AND THE OTHERS IS ON THE WEST END. WE GOT THE EAST. FAN OUT, BUT KEEP WITHIN EYE LINE. LAST THING WE NEED IS FOR ONE OF US TO GET BIT.
IF YOU CAN'T SEE OUR FLASHLIGHTS... YOU GONE TOO FAR. YOU HEAR ME, EARL... GEORGE?
YEAH. YOU JUST SAID IT.
GOOD.
GOT YOU...
FOUND SOMETHING!

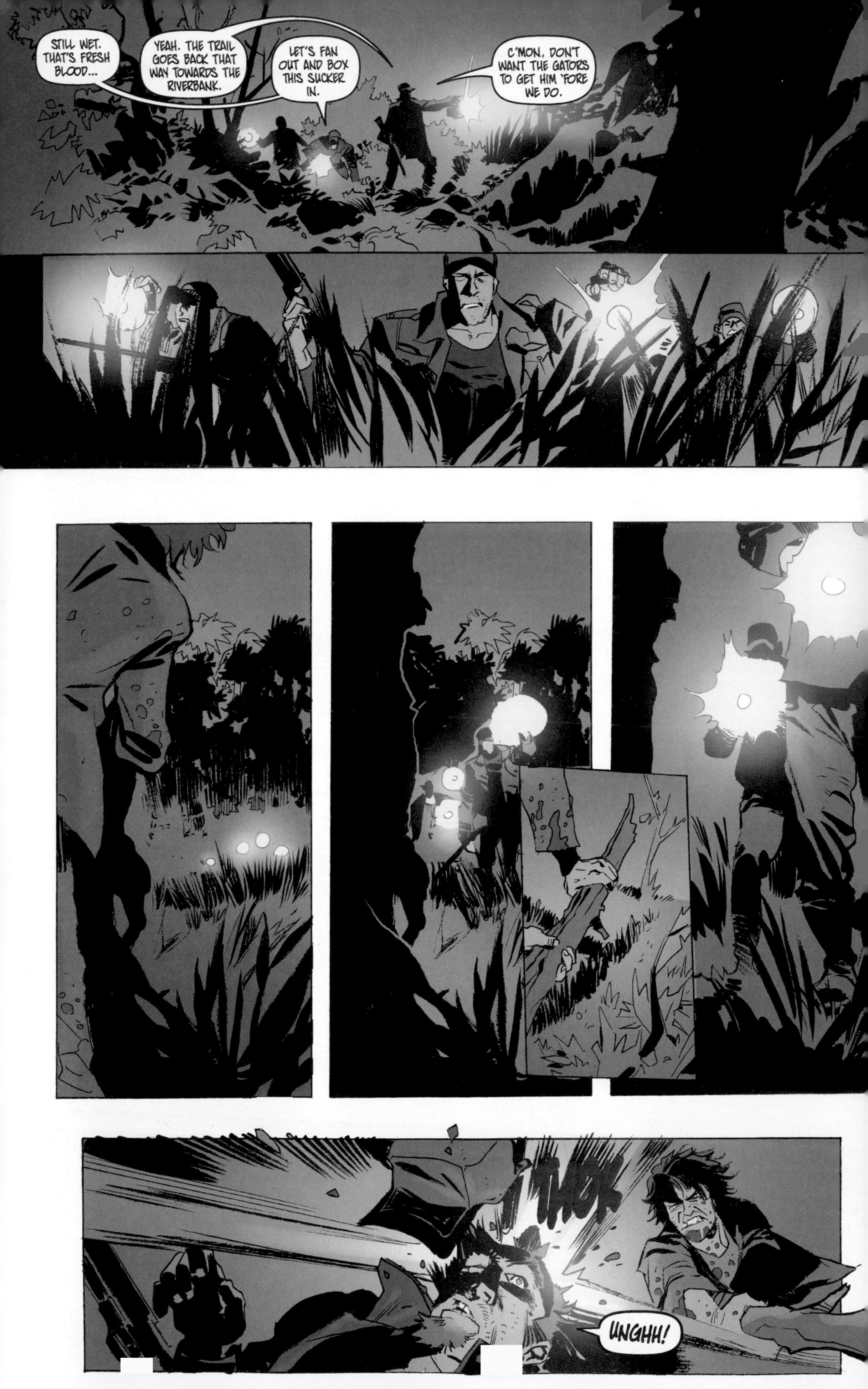
STILL WET. THAT'S FRESH BLOOD...
YEAH. THE TRAIL GOES BACK THAT WAY TOWARDS THE RIVERBANK.
LET'S FAN OUT AND BOX THIS SUCKER IN.
C'MON, DON'T WANT THE GATORS TO GET HIM 'FORE WE DO.
THOK
UNGHH!

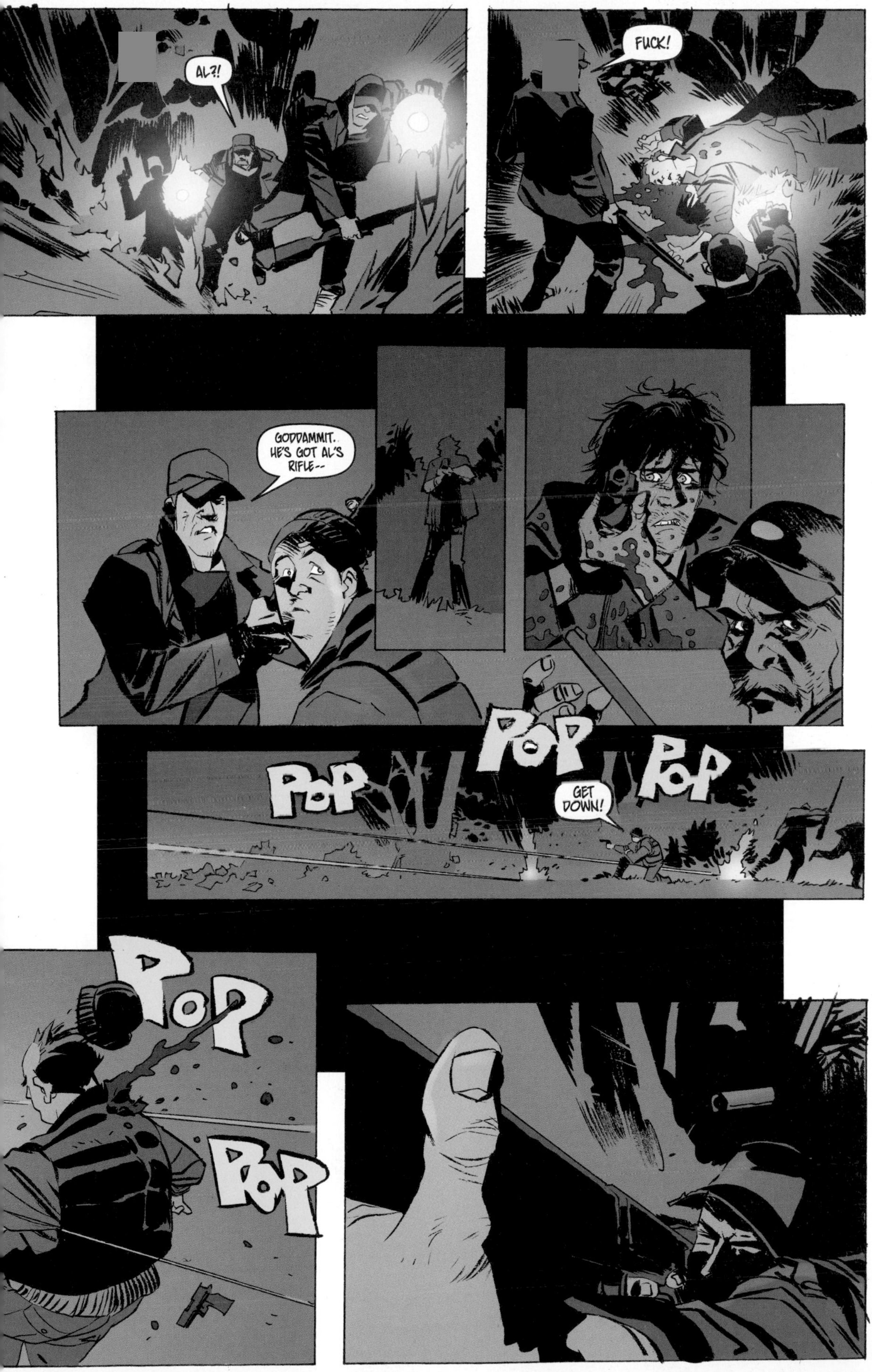
AL?!
FUCK!
GODDAMMIT. HE'S GOT AL'S RIFLE--
POP
POP
POP
GET DOWN!
POP
POP

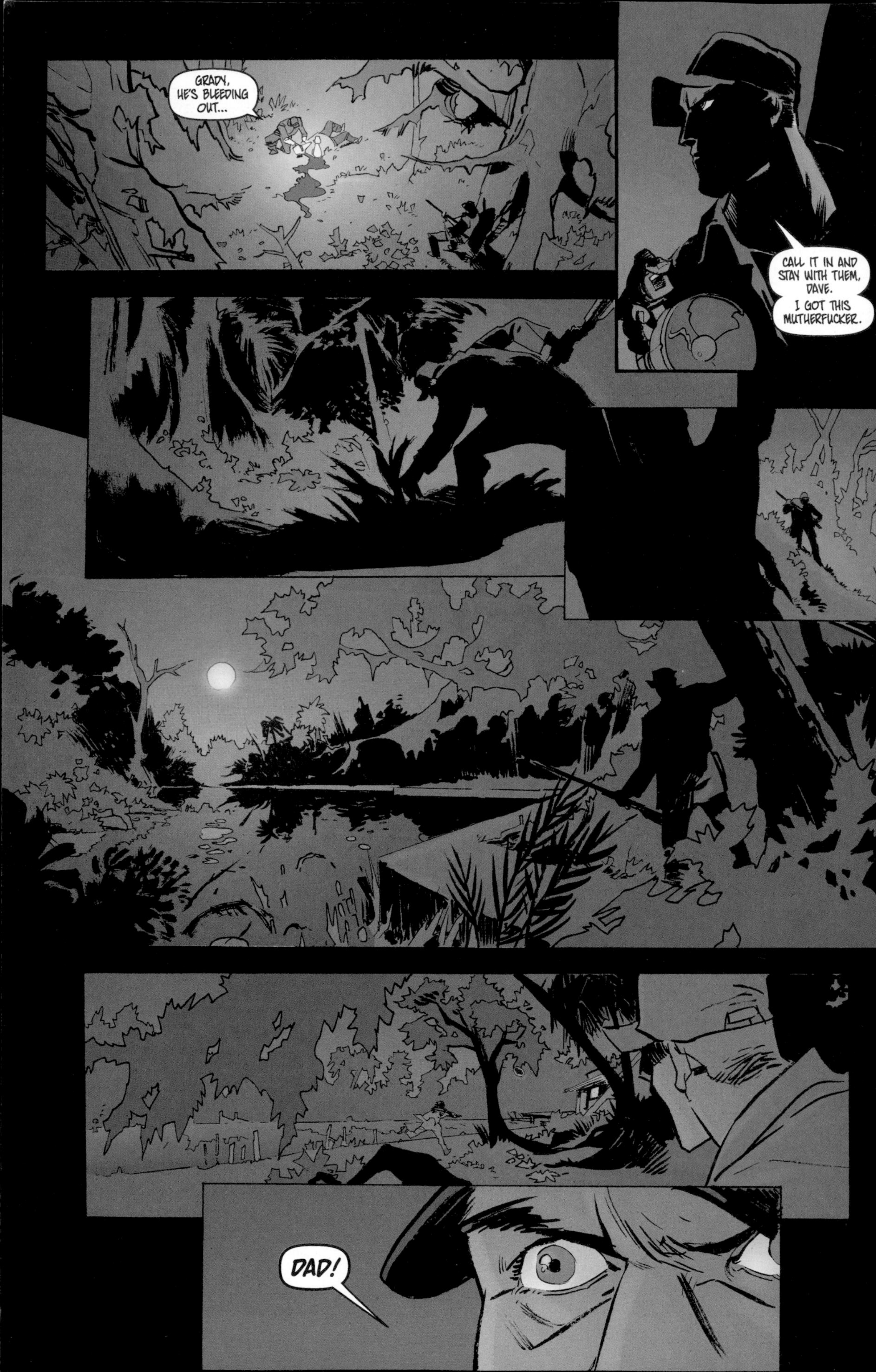
GRADY, HE'S BLEEDING OUT...
CALL IT IN AND STAY WITH THEM, DAVE. I GOT THIS MUTHERFUCKER.
DAD!

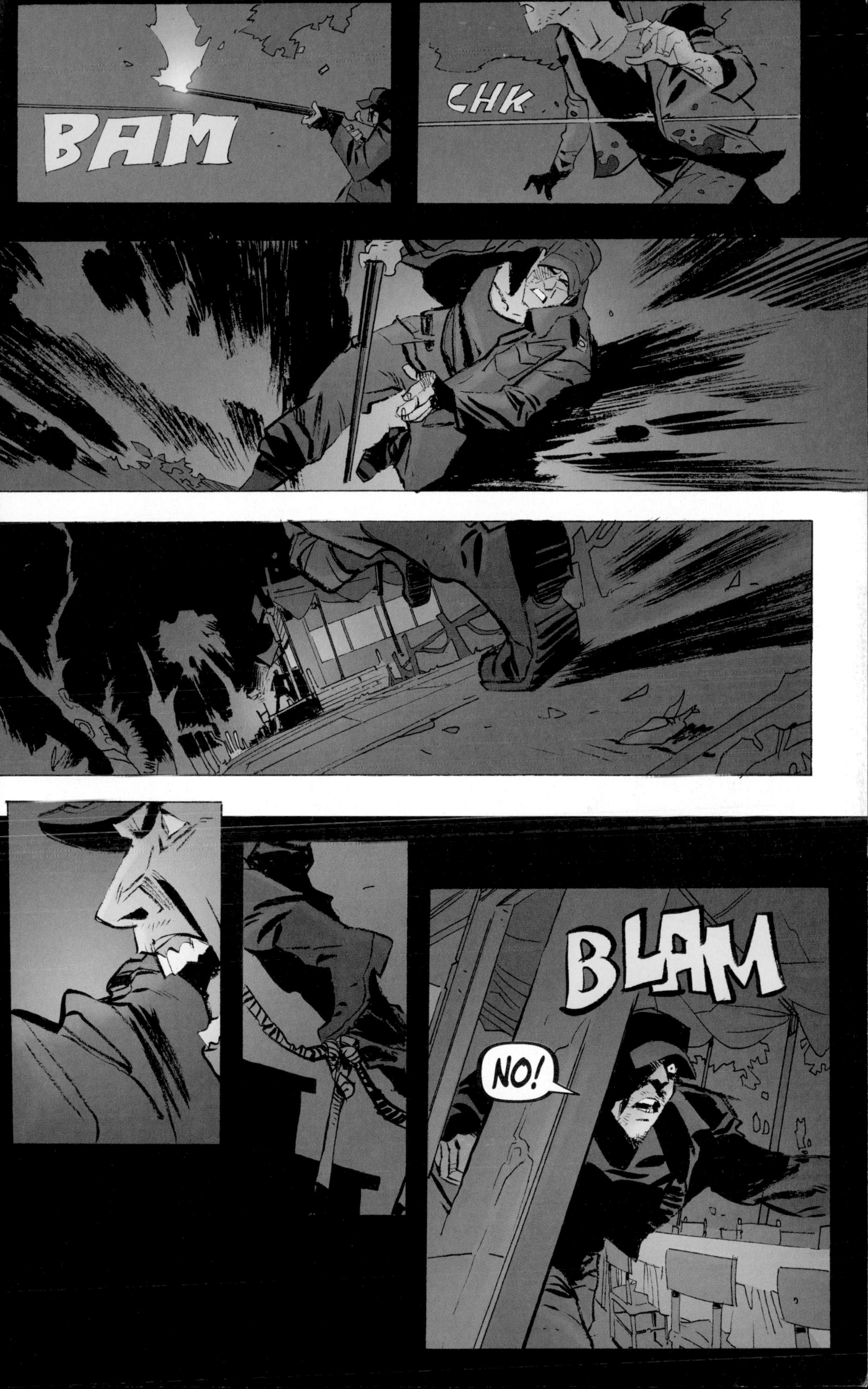
BAM
CHK
BLAM
NO!

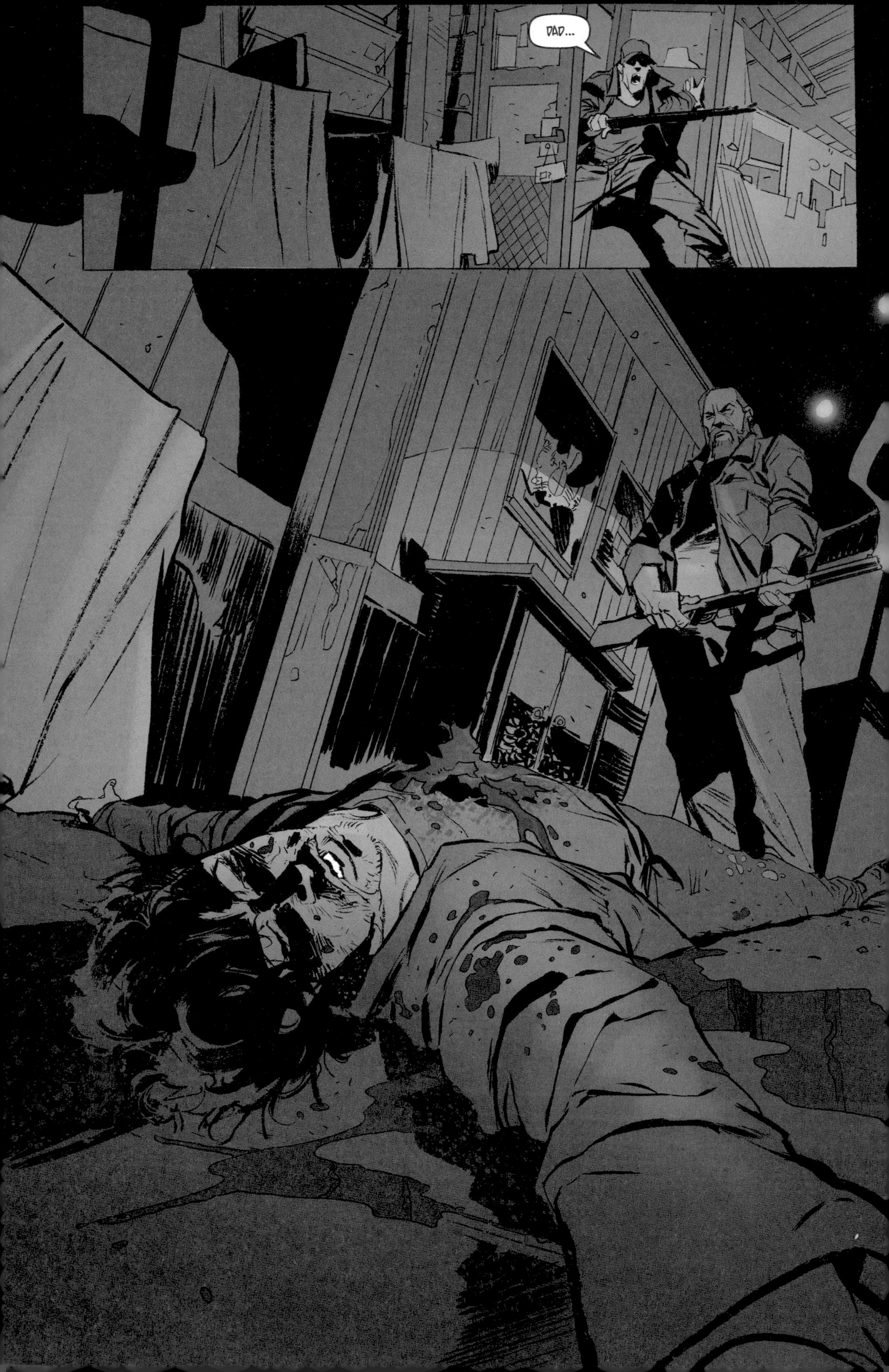
DAD...

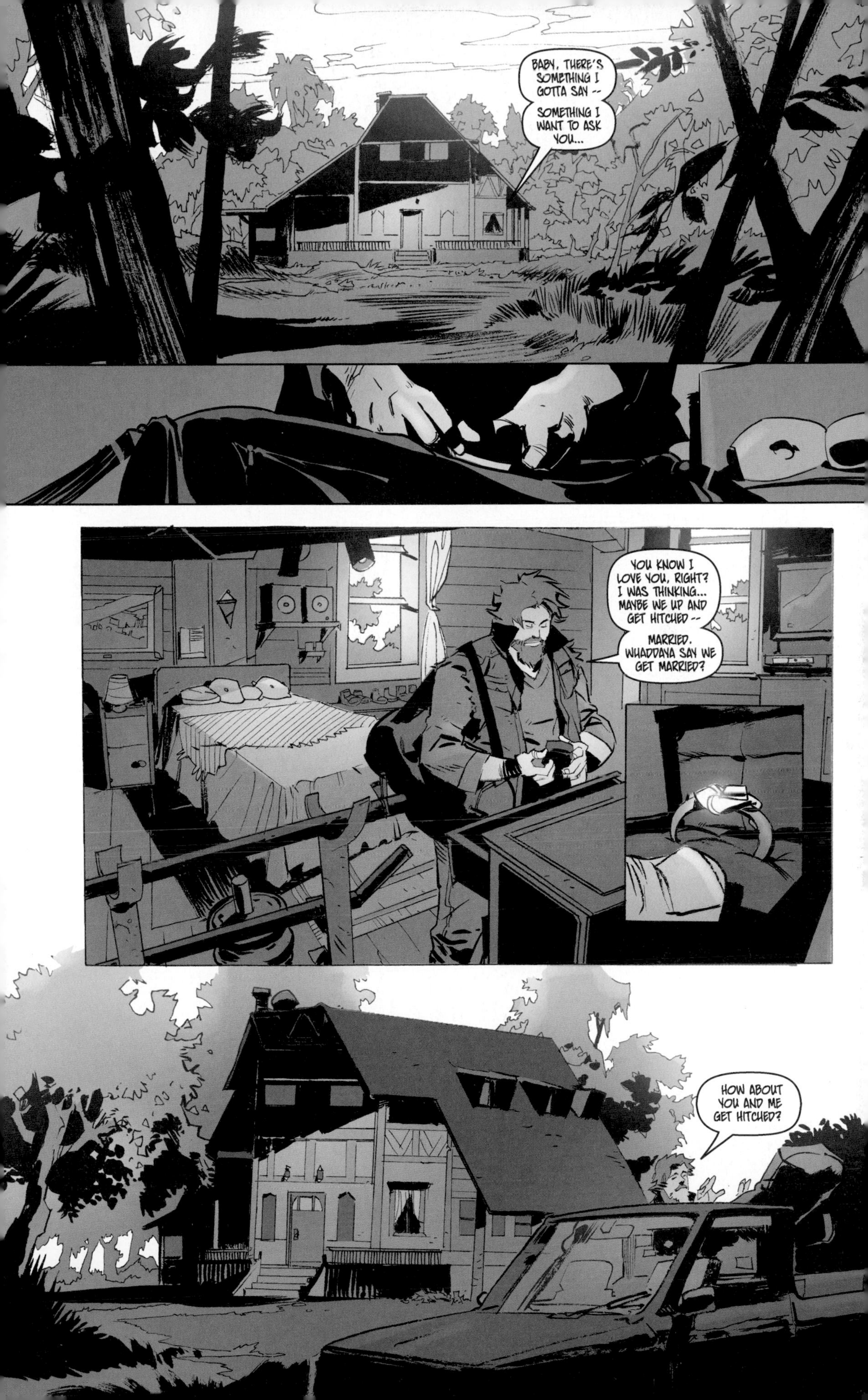
BABY, THERE'S SOMETHING I GOTTA SAY --
SOMETHING I WANT TO ASK YOU...
YOU KNOW I LOVE YOU, RIGHT? I WAS THINKING... MAYBE WE UP AND GET HITCHED --
MARRIED. WHADDAYA SAY WE GET MARRIED?
HOW ABOUT YOU AND ME GET HITCHED?

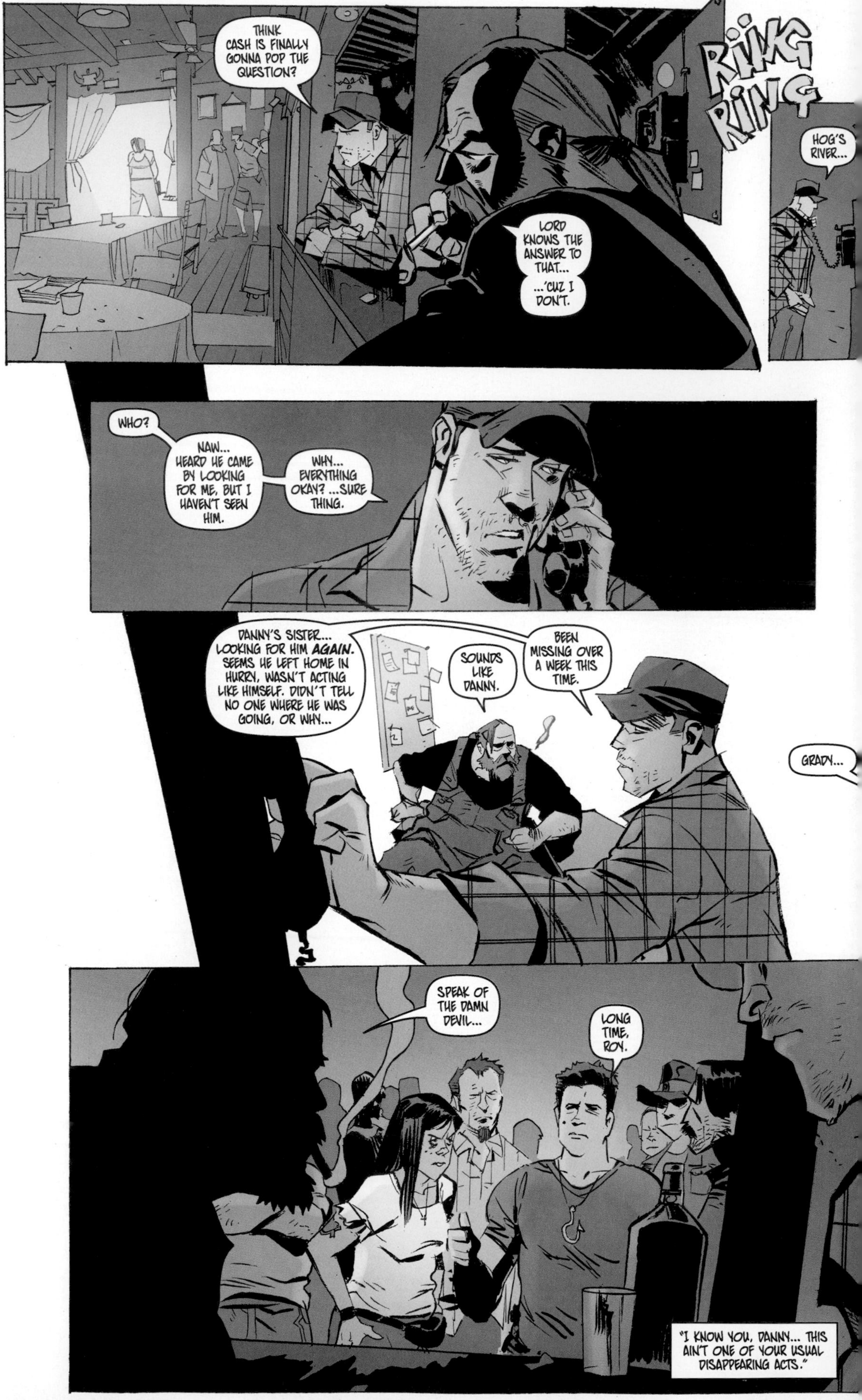
THINK CASH IS FINALLY GONNA POP THE QUESTION?
RING RING
LORD KNOWS THE ANSWER TO THAT...
...'CUZ I DON'T.
HOG'S RIVER...
WHO?
NAW... HEARD HE CAME BY LOOKING FOR ME, BUT I HAVEN'T SEEN HIM.
WHY... EVERYTHING OKAY? ...SURE THING.
DANNY'S SISTER... LOOKING FOR HIM AGAIN. SEEMS HE LEFT HOME IN HURRY, WASN'T ACTING LIKE HIMSELF. DIDN'T TELL NO ONE WHERE HE WAS GOING, OR WHY...
BEEN MISSING OVER A WEEK THIS TIME.
SOUNDS LIKE DANNY.
GRADY...
SPEAK OF THE DAMN DEVIL...
LONG TIME, ROY.
"I KNOW YOU, DANNY... THIS AIN'T ONE OF YOUR USUAL DISAPPEARING ACTS."

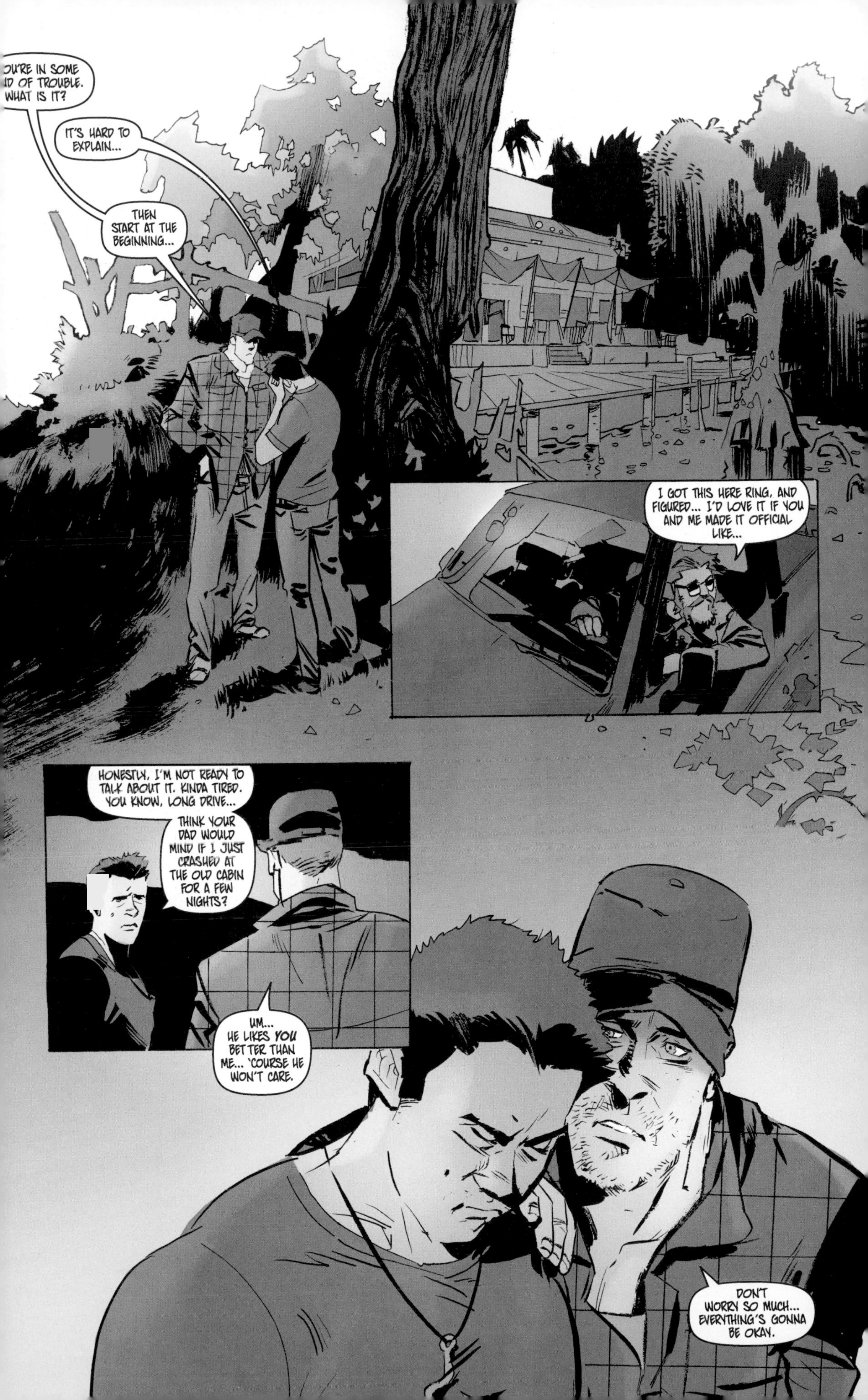
OU'RE IN SOME
ND OF TROUBLE.
WHAT IS IT?
IT'S HARD TO EXPLAIN...
THEN START AT THE BEGINNING...
I GOT THIS HERE RING, AND FIGURED... I'D LOVE IT IF YOU AND ME MADE IT OFFICIAL LIKE...
HONESTLY, I'M NOT READY TO TALK ABOUT IT. KINDA TIRED. YOU KNOW, LONG DRIVE...
THINK YOUR DAD WOULD MIND IF I JUST CRASHED AT THE OLD CABIN FOR A FEW NIGHTS?
UM... HE LIKES YOU BETTER THAN ME... 'COURSE HE WON'T CARE.
DON'T WORRY SO MUCH... EVERYTHING'S GONNA BE OKAY.

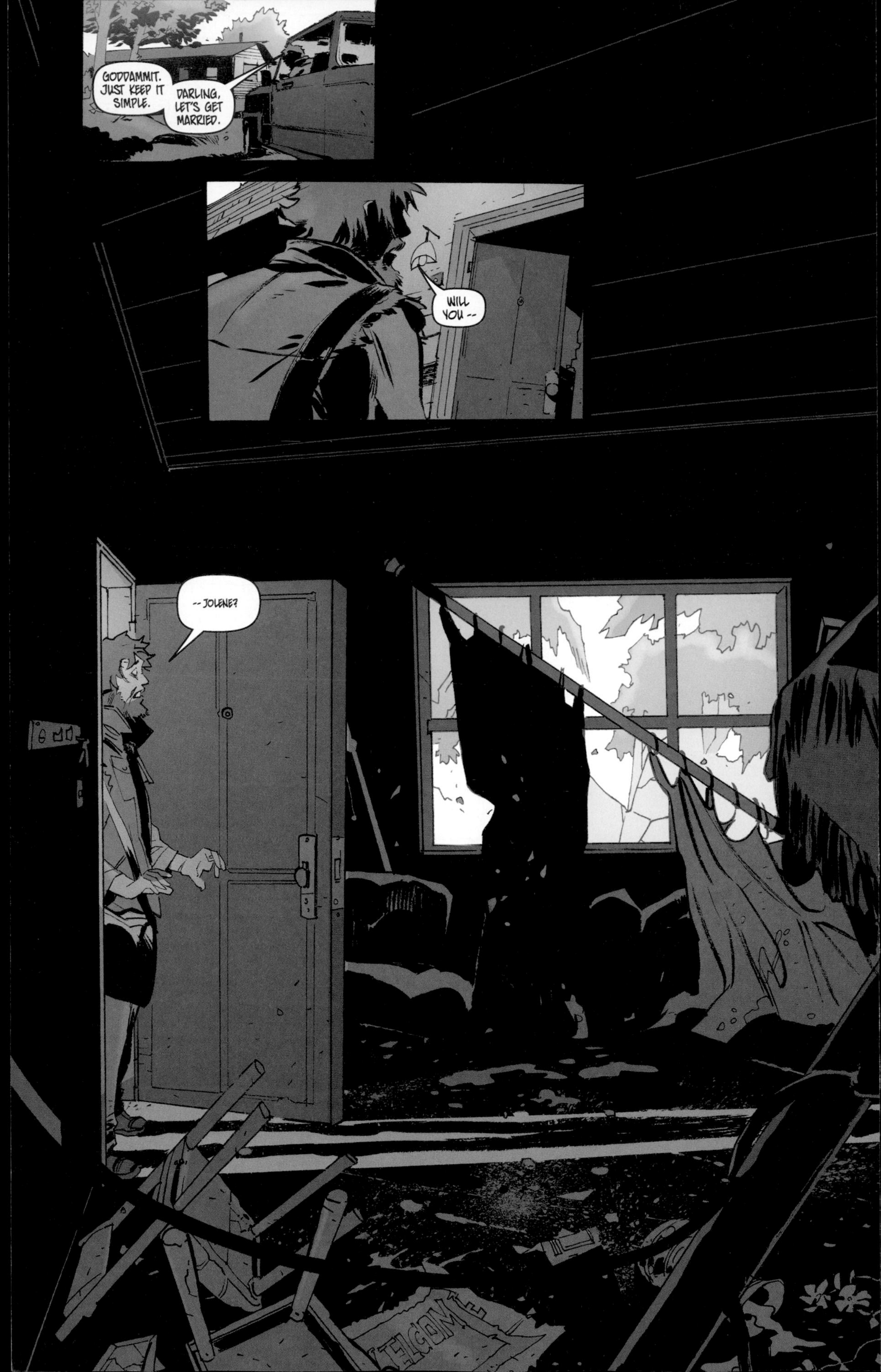
GODDAMMIT. JUST KEEP IT SIMPLE.
DARLING, LET'S GET MARRIED.
WILL YOU --
-- JOLENE?
TELCOM

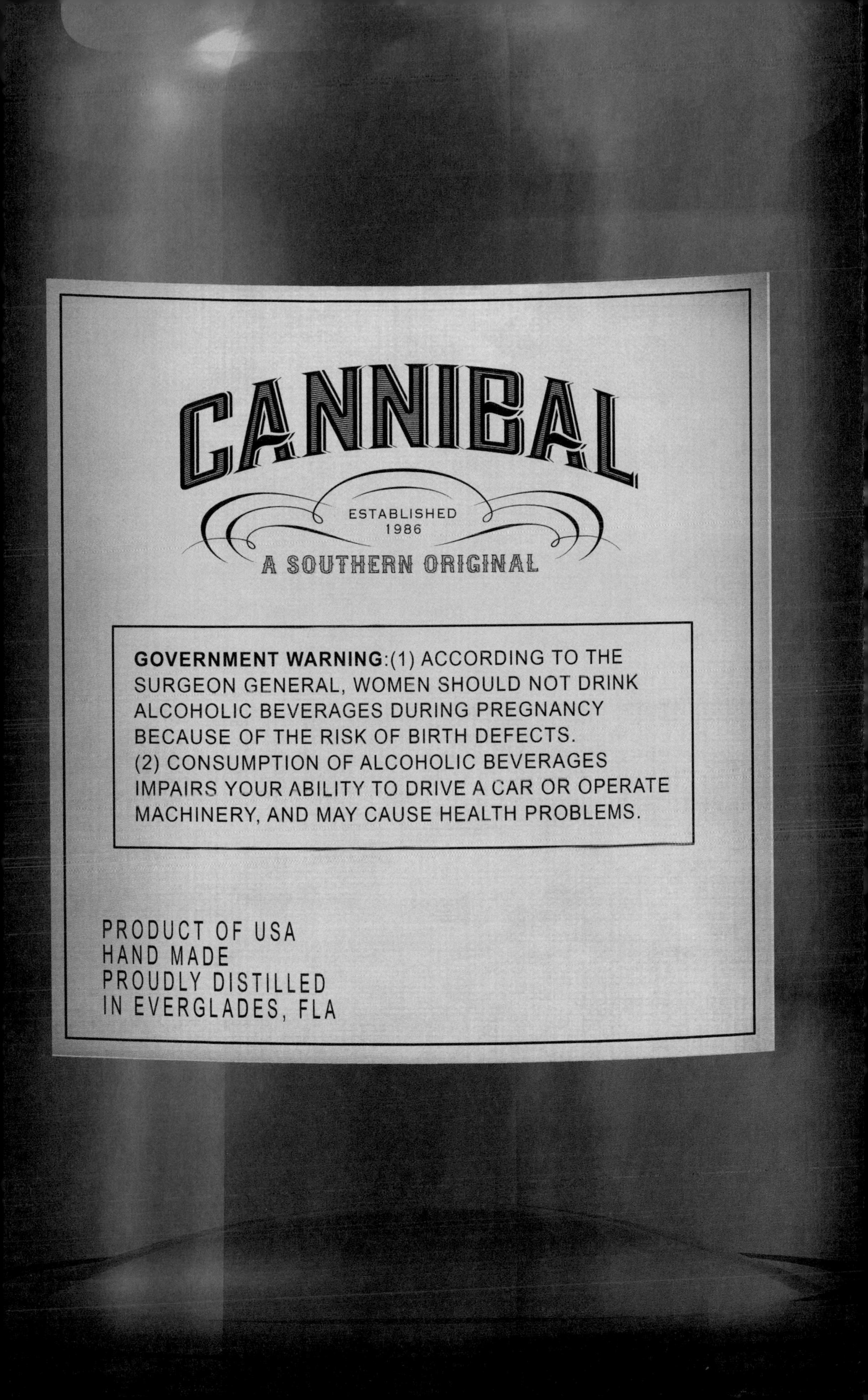
CANNIBAL
ESTABLISHED
1986
A SOUTHERN ORIGINAL
GOVERNMENT WARNING:(1) ACCORDING TO THE SURGEON GENERAL, WOMEN SHOULD NOT DRINK ALCOHOLIC BEVERAGES DURING PREGNANCY BECAUSE OF THE RISK OF BIRTH DEFECTS. (2) CONSUMPTION OF ALCOHOLIC BEVERAGES IMPAIRS YOUR ABILITY TO DRIVE A CAR OR OPERATE MACHINERY, AND MAY CAUSE HEALTH PROBLEMS.
PRODUCT OF USA
HAND MADE
PROUDLY DISTILLED
IN EVERGLADES, FLA

ISSUETWO

ESTABLISHED
1908

A SOUTHERN ORIGINAL

CANNIBAL

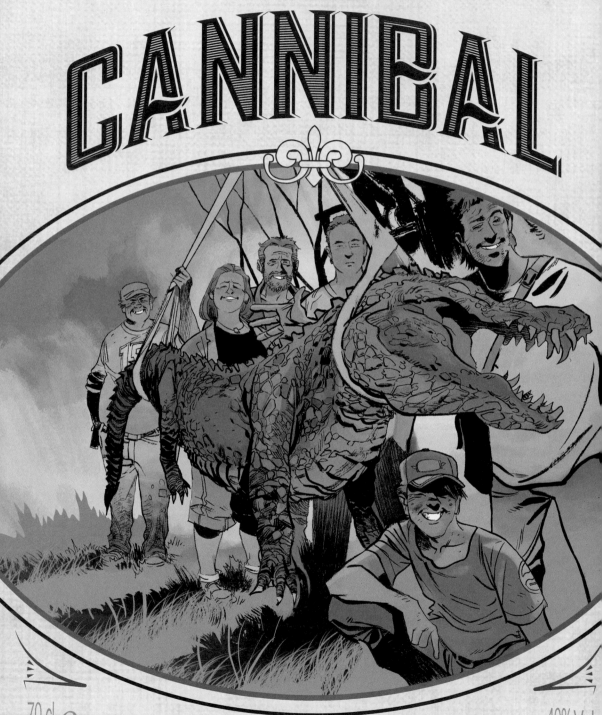

70 cl e

40% Vol.

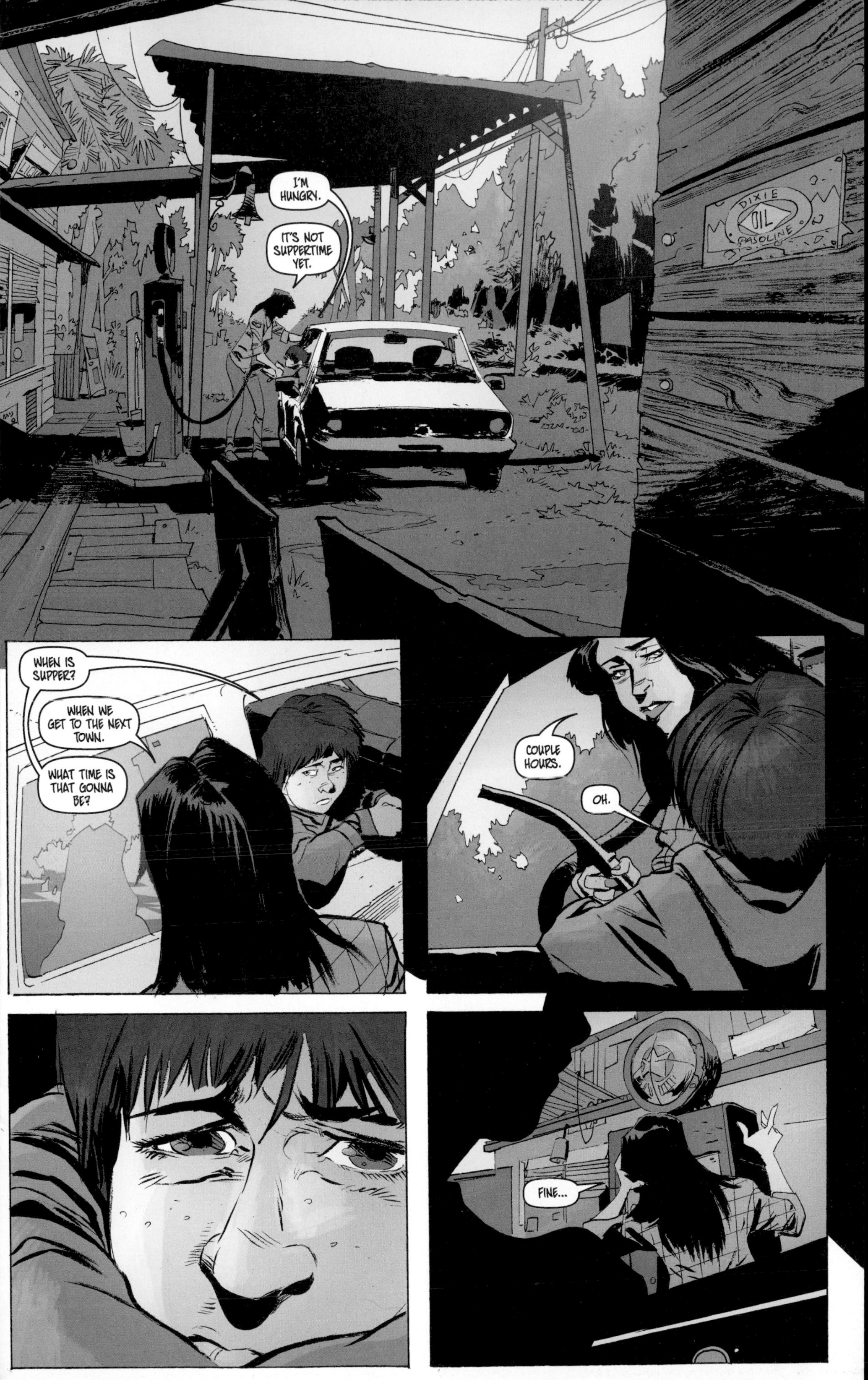
I'M HUNGRY.
IT'S NOT SUPPERTIME YET.
DIXIE OIL GASOLINE
WHEN IS SUPPER?
WHEN WE GET TO THE NEXT TOWN.
WHAT TIME IS THAT GONNA BE?
COUPLE HOURS.
OH.
FINE...

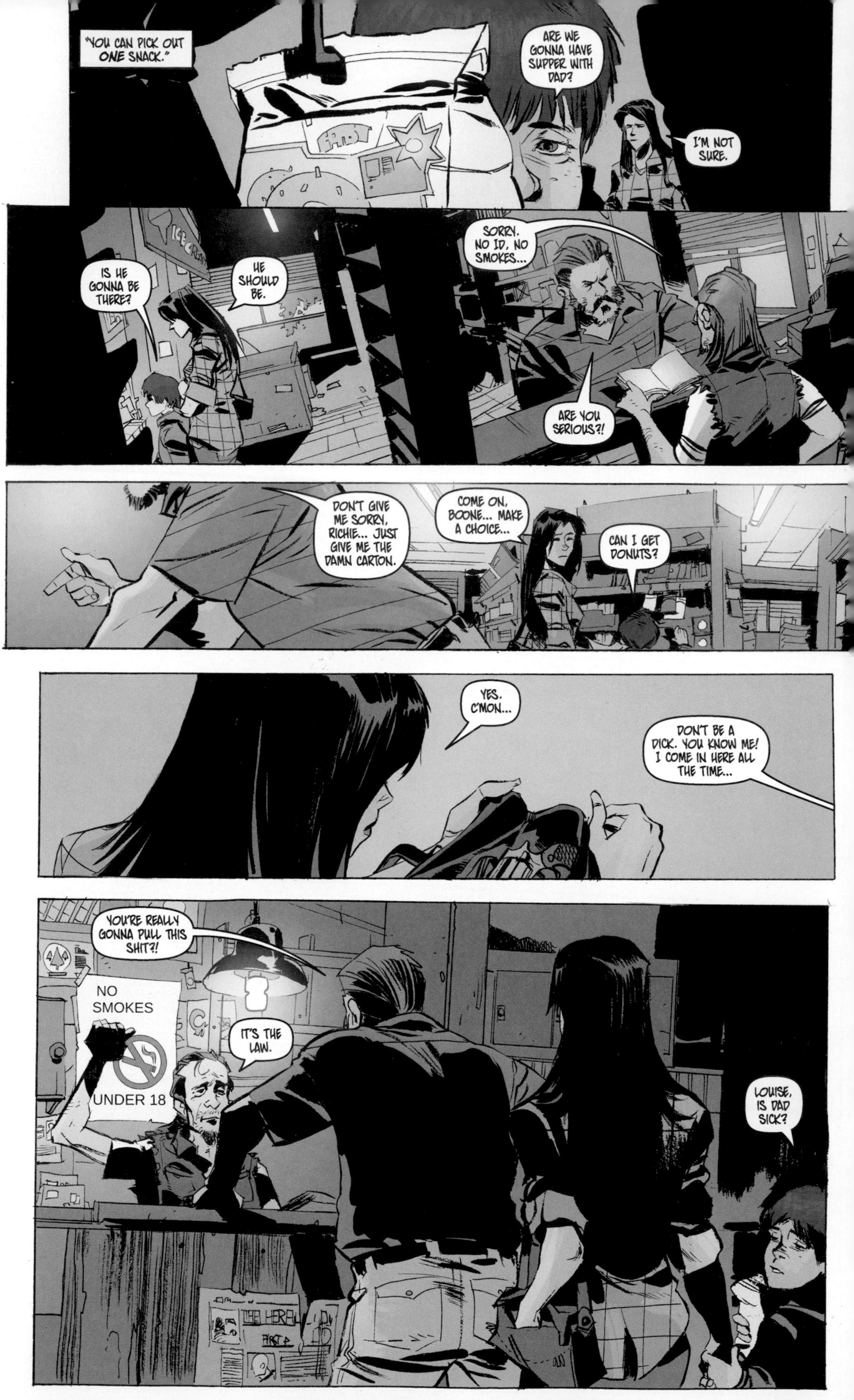
"YOU CAN PICK OUT ONE SNACK."
ARE WE GONNA HAVE SUPPER WITH DAD?
I'M NOT SURE.
IS HE GONNA BE THERE?
HE SHOULD BE.
SORRY. NO ID, NO SMOKES...
ARE YOU SERIOUS?!
DON'T GIVE ME SORRY, RICHIE... JUST GIVE ME THE DAMN CARTON.
COME ON, BOONE... MAKE A CHOICE...
CAN I GET DONUTS?
YES. C'MON...
DON'T BE A DICK. YOU KNOW ME! I COME IN HERE ALL THE TIME...
YOU'RE REALLY GONNA PULL THIS SHIT?!
NO SMOKES
UNDER 18
IT'S THE LAW.
LOUISE, IS DAD SICK?

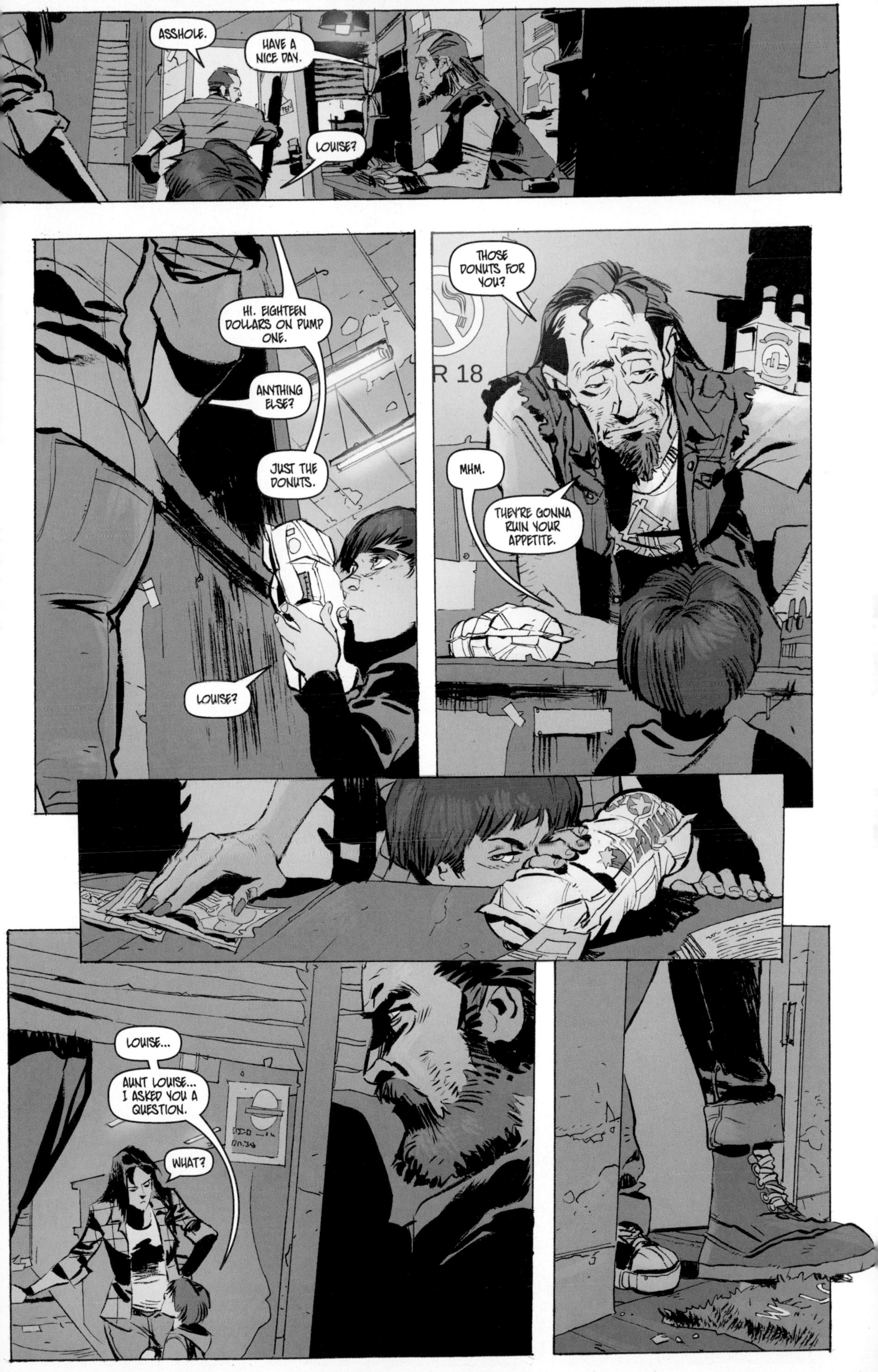
ASSHOLE.
HAVE A NICE DAY.
LOUISE?
HI. EIGHTEEN DOLLARS ON PUMP ONE.
ANYTHING ELSE?
JUST THE DONUTS.
LOUISE?
THOSE DONUTS FOR YOU?
R 18
MHM.
THEY'RE GONNA RUIN YOUR APPETITE.
LOUISE...
AUNT LOUISE... I ASKED YOU A QUESTION.
WHAT?

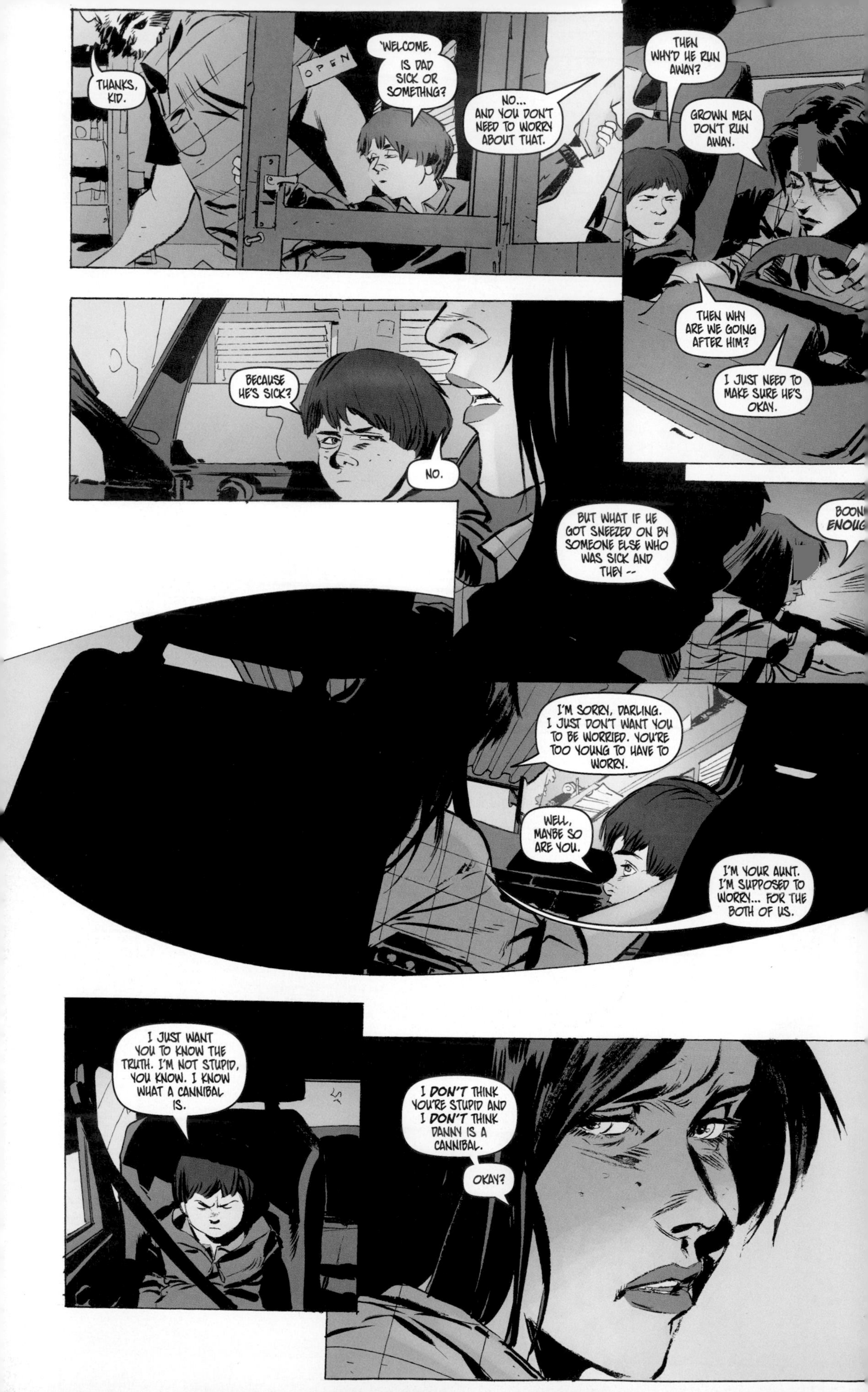
THANKS, KID.
'WELCOME. IS DAD SICK OR SOMETHING?
NO... AND YOU DON'T NEED TO WORRY ABOUT THAT.
THEN WHY'D HE RUN AWAY?
GROWN MEN DON'T RUN AWAY.
THEN WHY ARE WE GOING AFTER HIM?
I JUST NEED TO MAKE SURE HE'S OKAY.
BECAUSE HE'S SICK?
NO.
BUT WHAT IF HE GOT SNEEZED ON BY SOMEONE ELSE WHO WAS SICK AND THEY --
I'M SORRY, DARLING. I JUST DON'T WANT YOU TO BE WORRIED. YOU'RE TOO YOUNG TO HAVE TO WORRY.
WELL, MAYBE SO ARE YOU.
I'M YOUR AUNT. I'M SUPPOSED TO WORRY... FOR THE BOTH OF US.
I JUST WANT YOU TO KNOW THE TRUTH. I'M NOT STUPID, YOU KNOW. I KNOW WHAT A CANNIBAL IS.
I **DON'T** THINK YOU'RE STUPID AND I **DON'T** THINK DANNY IS A CANNIBAL.
OKAY?

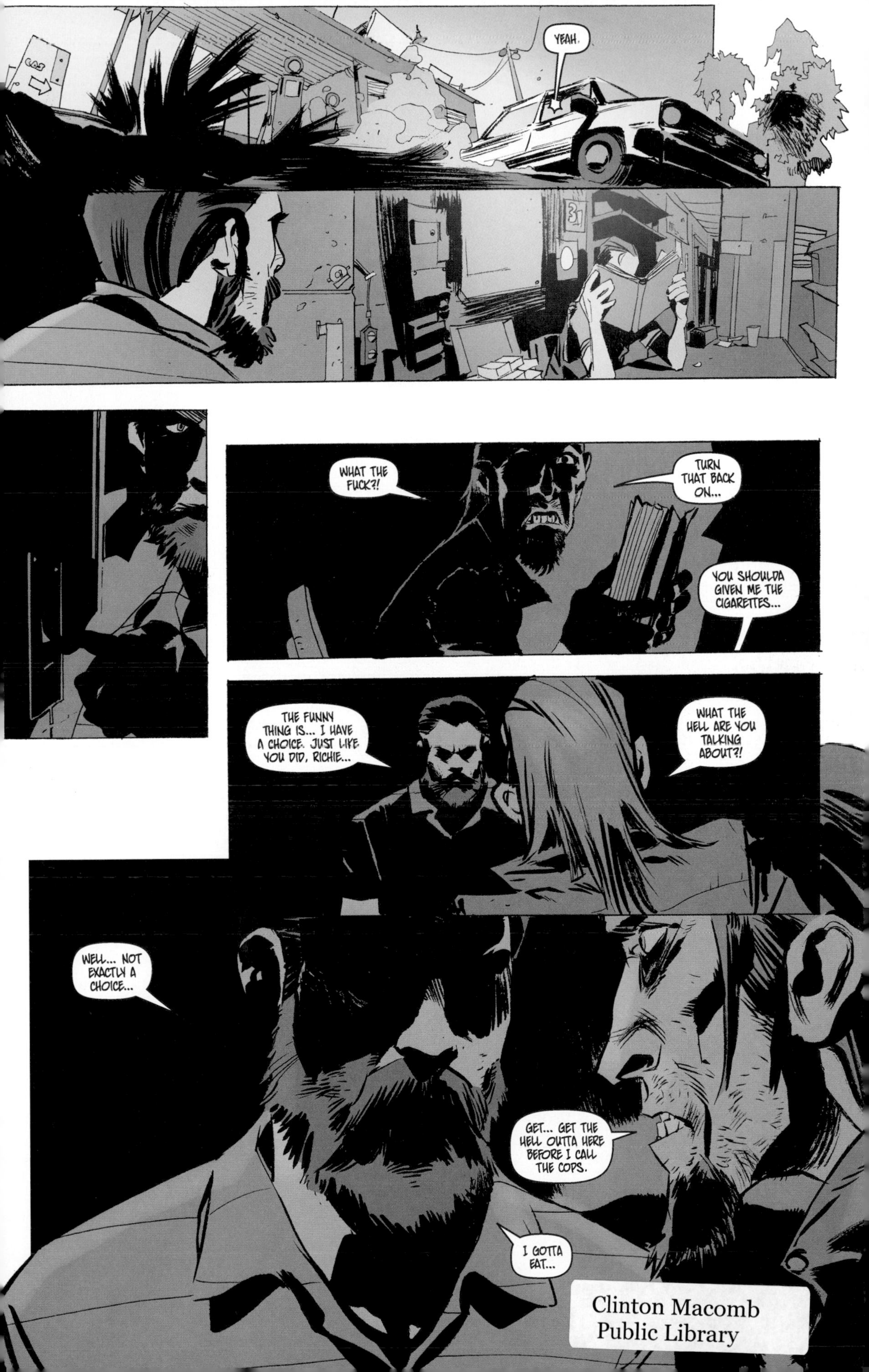

YEAH.
WHAT THE FUCK?!
TURN THAT BACK ON...
YOU SHOULDA GIVEN ME THE CIGARETTES...
THE FUNNY THING IS... I HAVE A CHOICE. JUST LIKE YOU DID, RICHIE...
WHAT THE HELL ARE YOU TALKING ABOUT?!
WELL... NOT EXACTLY A CHOICE...
GET... GET THE HELL OUTTA HERE BEFORE I CALL THE COPS.
I GOTTA EAT...

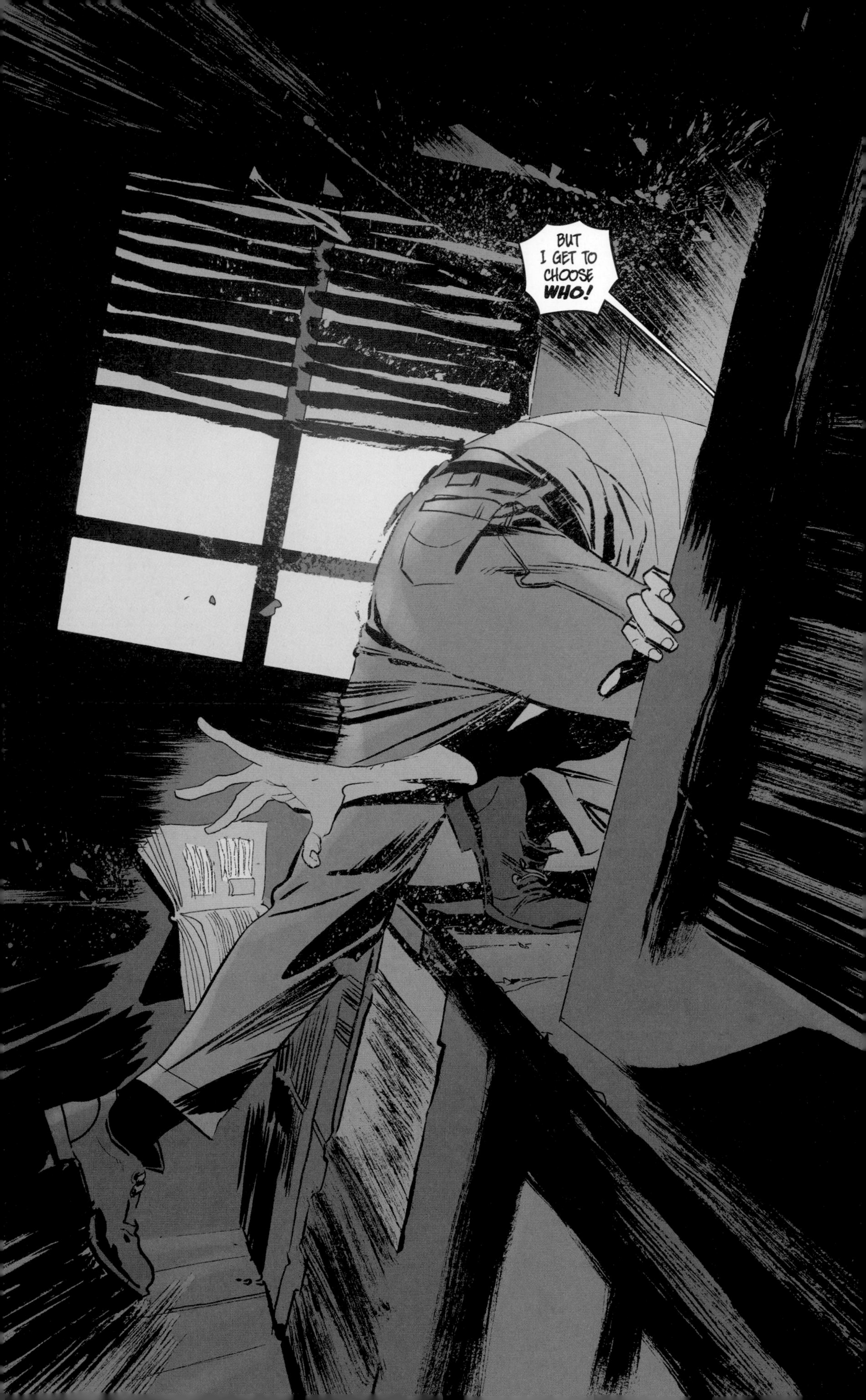
BUT I GET TO CHOOSE **WHO!**

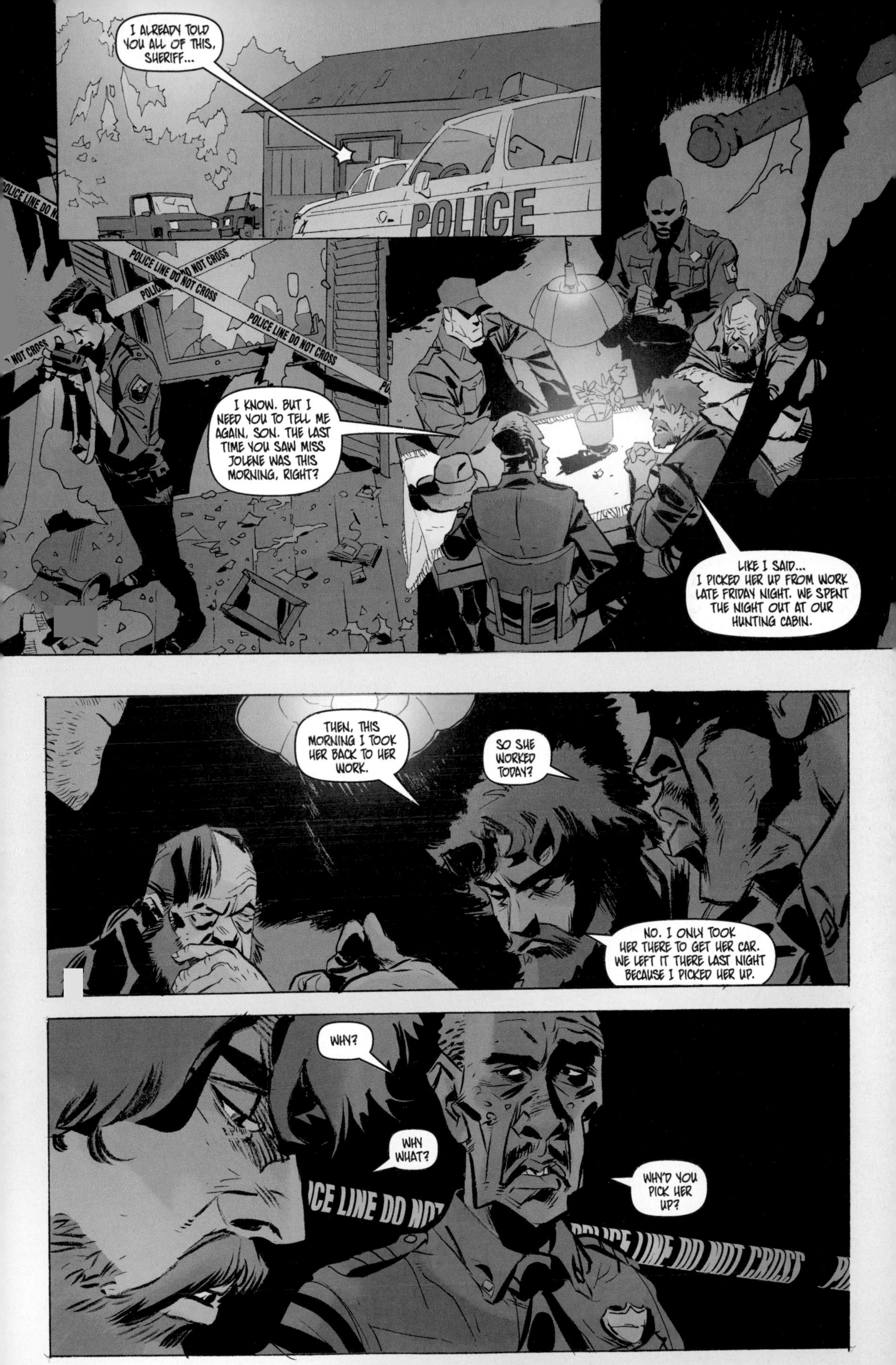
I ALREADY TOLD YOU ALL OF THIS, SHERIFF...
POLICE
POLICE LINE DO NOT CROSS
I KNOW. BUT I NEED YOU TO TELL ME AGAIN, SON. THE LAST TIME YOU SAW MISS JOLENE WAS THIS MORNING, RIGHT?
LIKE I SAID... I PICKED HER UP FROM WORK LATE FRIDAY NIGHT. WE SPENT THE NIGHT OUT AT OUR HUNTING CABIN.
THEN, THIS MORNING I TOOK HER BACK TO HER WORK.
SO SHE WORKED TODAY?
NO. I ONLY TOOK HER THERE TO GET HER CAR. WE LEFT IT THERE LAST NIGHT BECAUSE I PICKED HER UP.
WHY?
WHY WHAT?
WHY'D YOU PICK HER UP?

BECAUSE A KID JUST GOT EATEN OUTSIDE OUR BAR AND I THOUGHT SHE COULD USE AN ESCORT.

DID YOU SEE HER LEAVE? THIS MORNING WHEN YOU DROPPED HER OFF?

DID YOU ACTUALLY WATCH HER GET INTO HER CAR AND DRIVE AWAY?

I'M NOT SURE.

I KNOW THIS AIN'T EASY, CASH, BUT I NEED ALL THE DETAILS WHILE THEY'RE FRESH IN YOUR MIND. IF WE DON'T FIND HER INSIDE OF TWO DAYS, THE ODDS --

LET'S JUST SAY THEY GET LONGER AFTER TWO DAYS.

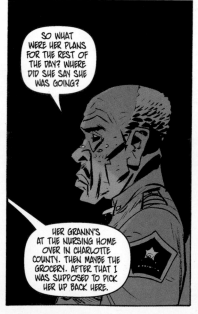

SO WHAT WERE HER PLANS FOR THE REST OF THE DAY? WHERE DID SHE SAY SHE WAS GOING?

HER GRANNY'S AT THE NURSING HOME OVER IN CHARLOTTE COUNTY. THEN MAYBE THE GROCERY. AFTER THAT I WAS SUPPOSED TO PICK HER UP BACK HERE.

WHICH IS HOW YOU CAME UPON THE BUSTED DOOR AND SIGNS OF STRUGGLE.

YES, SIR.

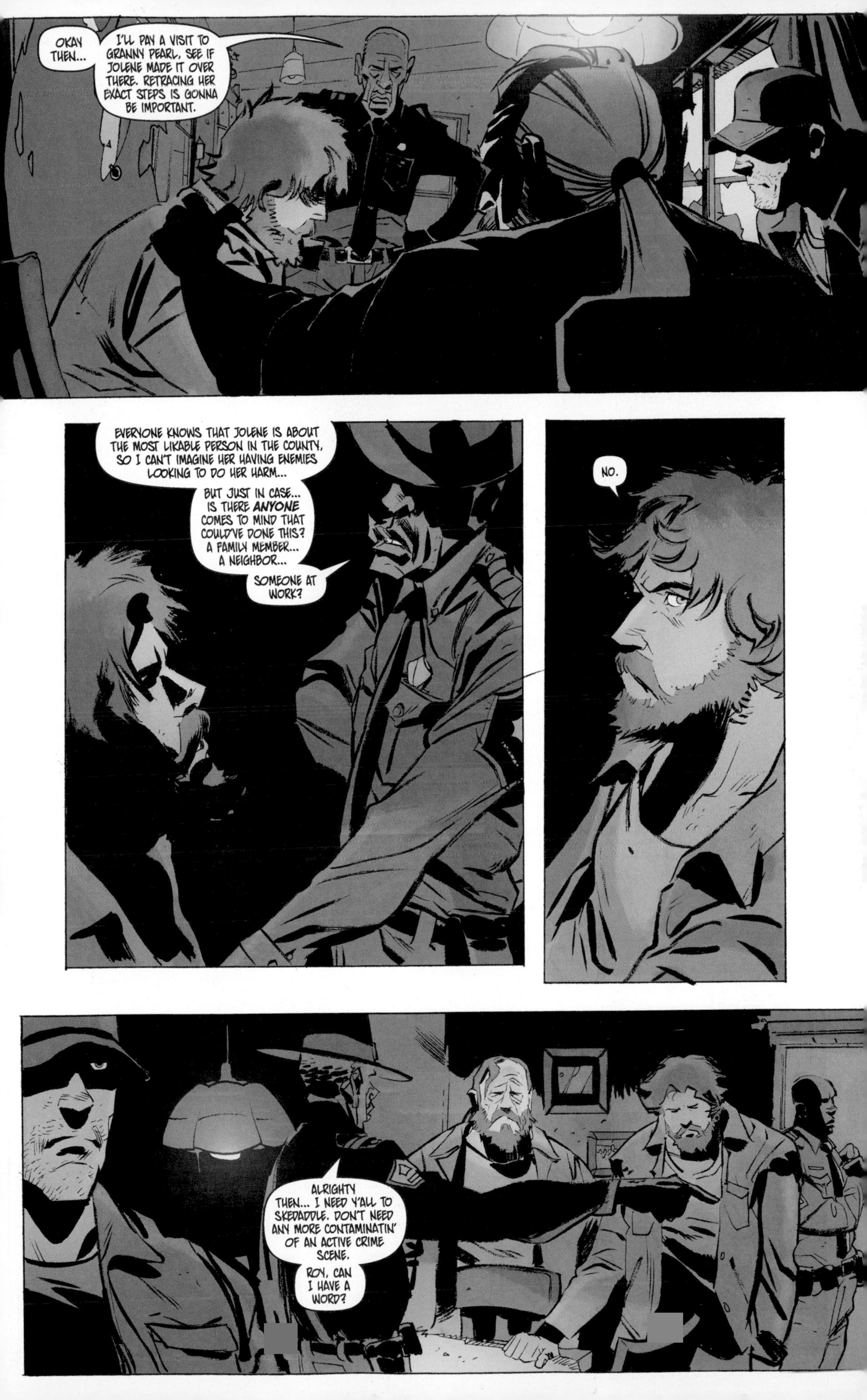
OKAY THEN...
I'LL PAY A VISIT TO GRANNY PEARL, SEE IF JOLENE MADE IT OVER THERE. RETRACING HER EXACT STEPS IS GONNA BE IMPORTANT.
EVERYONE KNOWS THAT JOLENE IS ABOUT THE MOST LIKABLE PERSON IN THE COUNTY, SO I CAN'T IMAGINE HER HAVING ENEMIES LOOKING TO DO HER HARM...
BUT JUST IN CASE... IS THERE ANYONE COMES TO MIND THAT COULD'VE DONE THIS? A FAMILY MEMBER... A NEIGHBOR...
SOMEONE AT WORK?
NO.
ALRIGHTY THEN... I NEED Y'ALL TO SKEDADDLE. DON'T NEED ANY MORE CONTAMINATIN' OF AN ACTIVE CRIME SCENE.
ROY, CAN I HAVE A WORD?

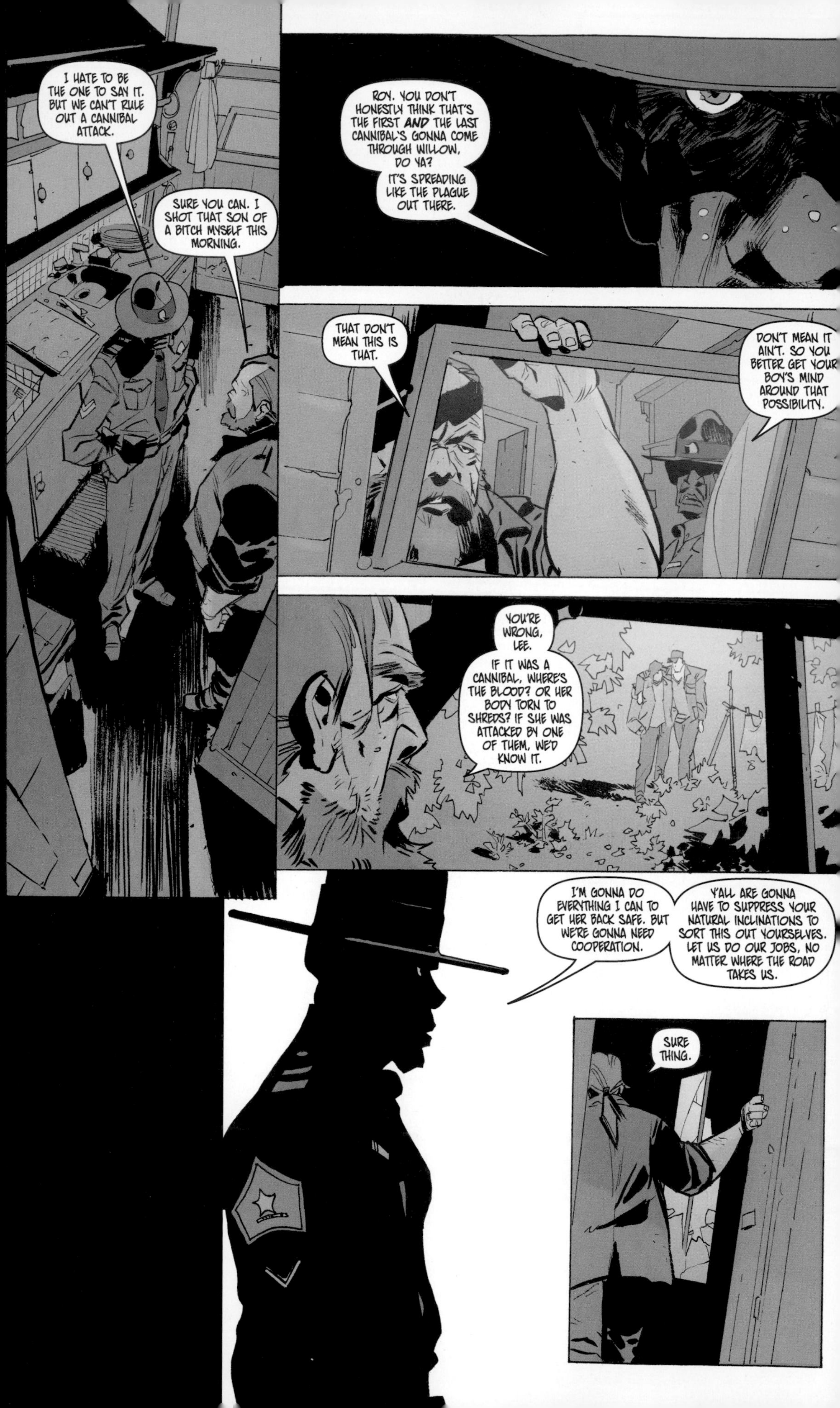
I HATE TO BE THE ONE TO SAY IT. BUT WE CAN'T RULE OUT A CANNIBAL ATTACK.
SURE YOU CAN. I SHOT THAT SON OF A BITCH MYSELF THIS MORNING.
ROY. YOU DON'T HONESTLY THINK THAT'S THE FIRST AND THE LAST CANNIBAL'S GONNA COME THROUGH WILLOW, DO YA?
IT'S SPREADING LIKE THE PLAGUE OUT THERE.
THAT DON'T MEAN THIS IS THAT.
DON'T MEAN IT AIN'T. SO YOU BETTER GET YOUR BOY'S MIND AROUND THAT POSSIBILITY.
YOU'RE WRONG, LEE.
IF IT WAS A CANNIBAL, WHERE'S THE BLOOD? OR HER BODY TORN TO SHREDS? IF SHE WAS ATTACKED BY ONE OF THEM, WE'D KNOW IT.
I'M GONNA DO EVERYTHING I CAN TO GET HER BACK SAFE. BUT WE'RE GONNA NEED COOPERATION.
Y'ALL ARE GONNA HAVE TO SUPPRESS YOUR NATURAL INCLINATIONS TO SORT THIS OUT YOURSELVES. LET US DO OUR JOBS, NO MATTER WHERE THE ROAD TAKES US.
SURE THING.

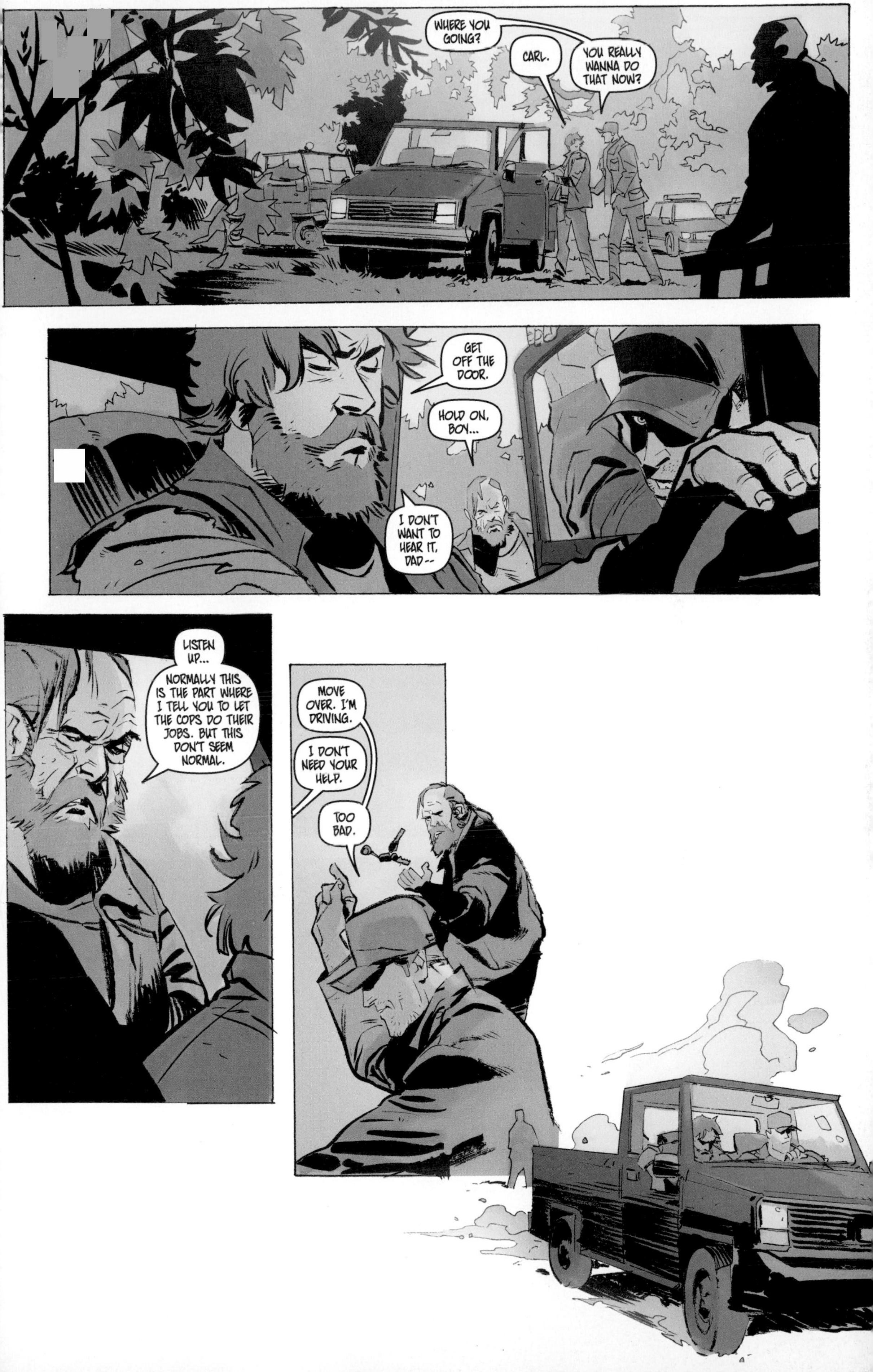
WHERE YOU GOING?
CARL.
YOU REALLY WANNA DO THAT NOW?
GET OFF THE DOOR.
HOLD ON, BOY...
I DON'T WANT TO HEAR IT, DAD--
LISTEN UP...
NORMALLY THIS IS THE PART WHERE I TELL YOU TO LET THE COPS DO THEIR JOBS. BUT THIS DON'T SEEM NORMAL.
MOVE OVER. I'M DRIVING.
I DON'T NEED YOUR HELP.
TOO BAD.

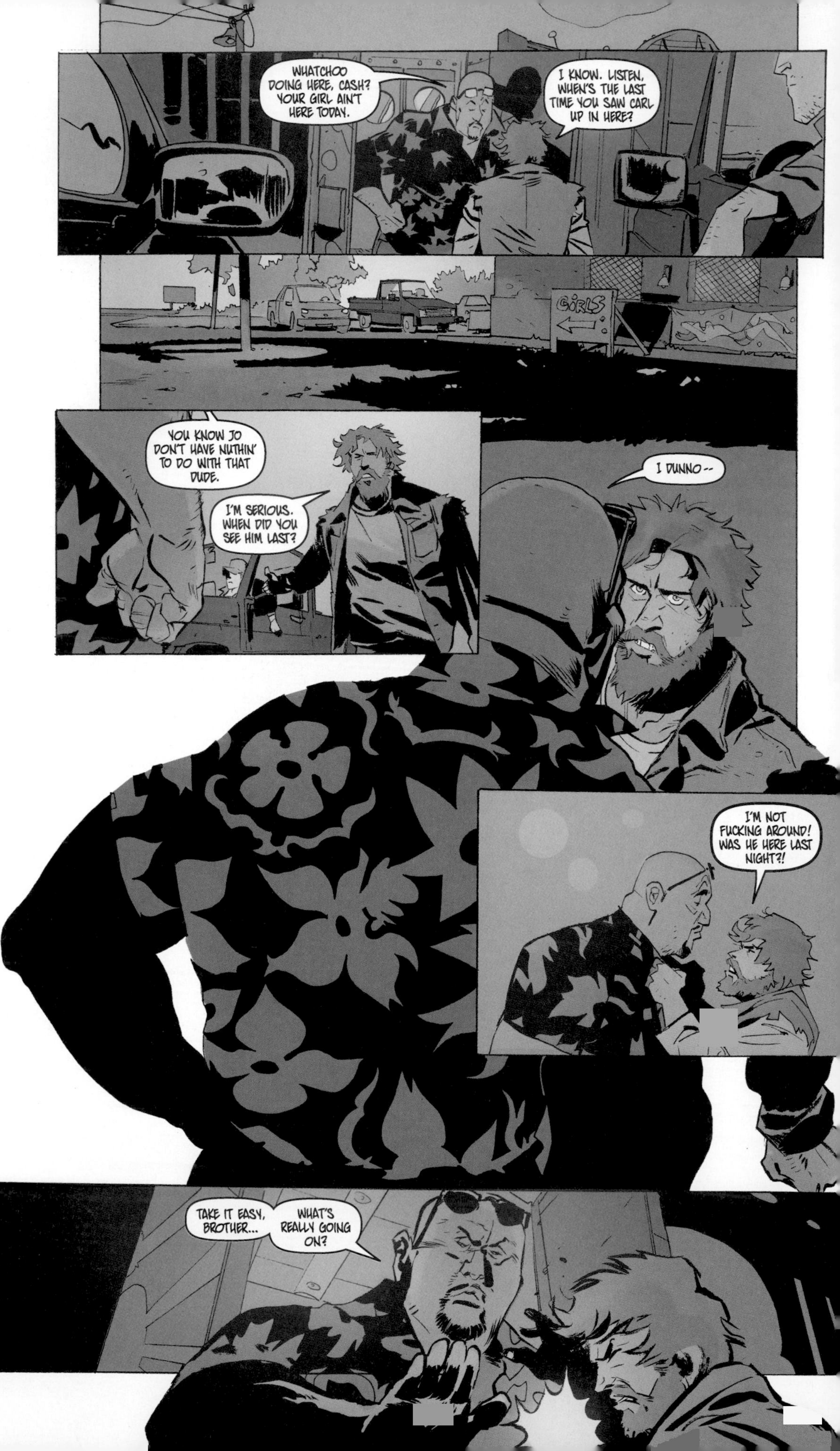
WHATCHOO DOING HERE, CASH? YOUR GIRL AIN'T HERE TODAY.
I KNOW. LISTEN, WHEN'S THE LAST TIME YOU SAW CARL UP IN HERE?
GIRLS
YOU KNOW JO DON'T HAVE NUTHIN' TO DO WITH THAT DUDE.
I'M SERIOUS. WHEN DID YOU SEE HIM LAST?
I DUNNO --
I'M NOT FUCKING AROUND! WAS HE HERE LAST NIGHT?!
TAKE IT EASY, BROTHER...
WHAT'S REALLY GOING ON?

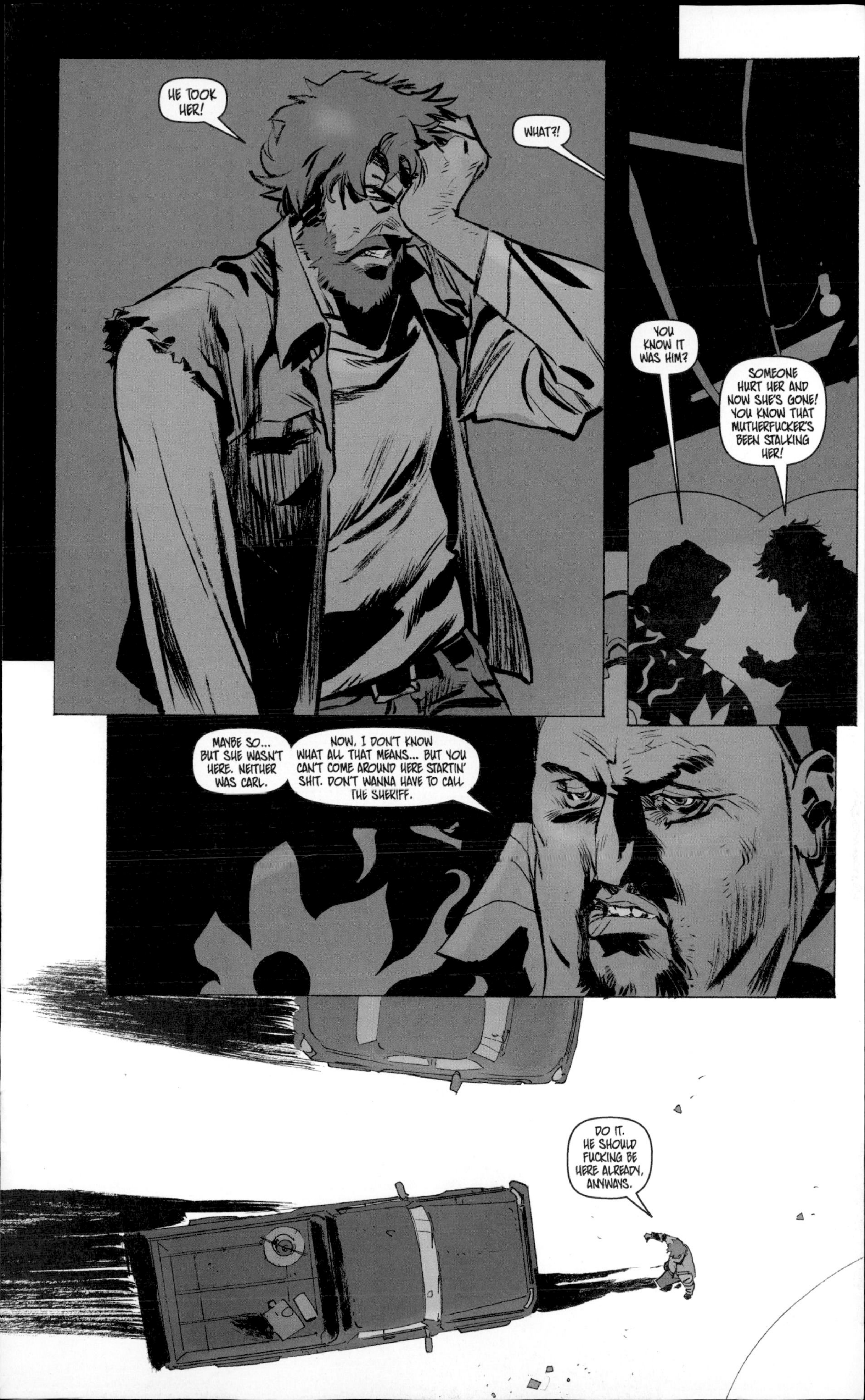
HE TOOK HER!
WHAT?!
YOU KNOW IT WAS HIM?
SOMEONE HURT HER AND NOW SHE'S GONE! YOU KNOW THAT MUTHERFUCKER'S BEEN STALKING HER!
MAYBE SO... BUT SHE WASN'T HERE. NEITHER WAS CARL.
NOW, I DON'T KNOW WHAT ALL THAT MEANS... BUT YOU CAN'T COME AROUND HERE STARTIN' SHIT. DON'T WANNA HAVE TO CALL THE SHERIFF.
DO IT. HE SHOULD FUCKING BE HERE ALREADY, ANYWAYS.

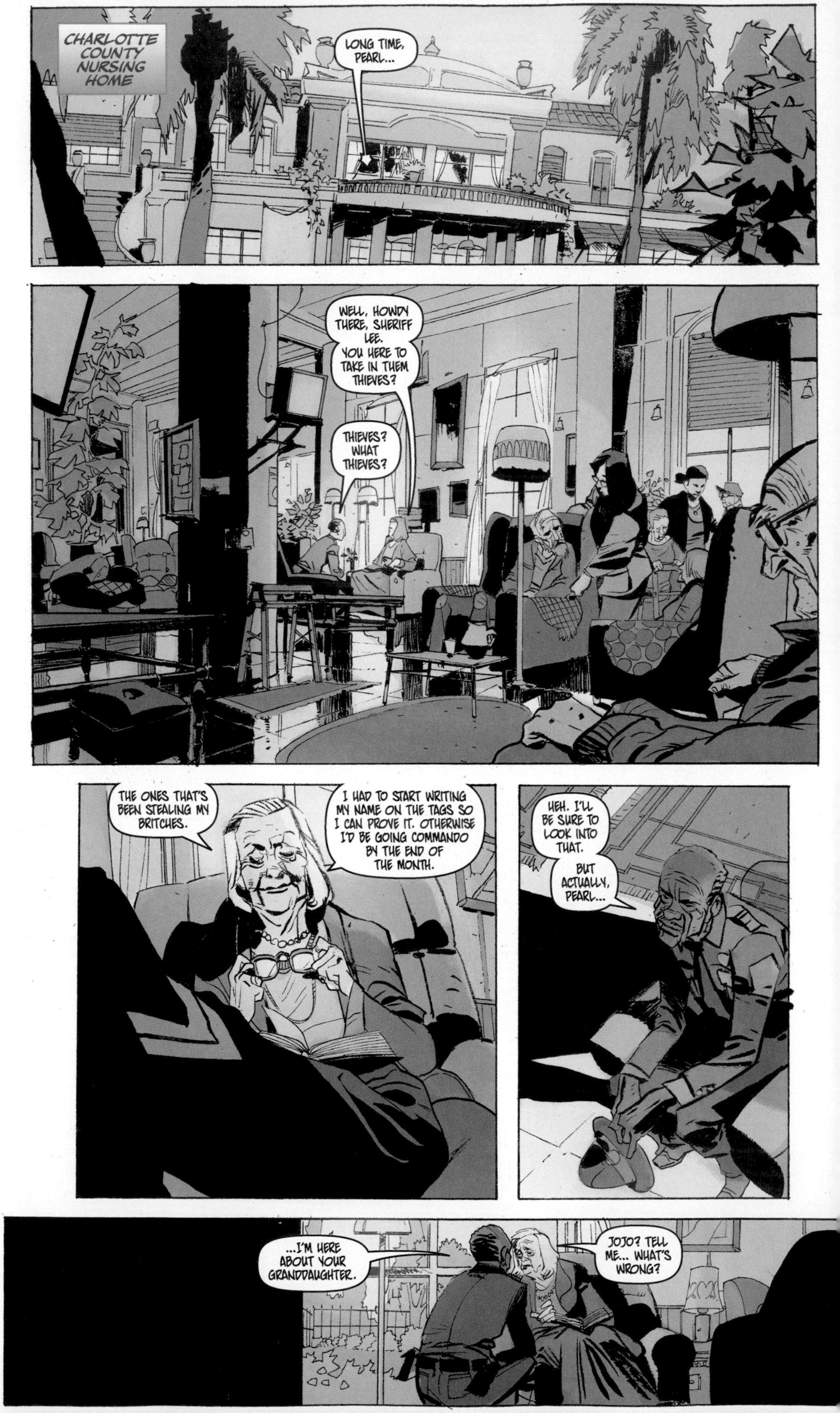
CHARLOTTE COUNTY NURSING HOME
LONG TIME, PEARL...
WELL, HOWDY THERE, SHERIFF LEE. YOU HERE TO TAKE IN THEM THIEVES?
THIEVES? WHAT THIEVES?
THE ONES THAT'S BEEN STEALING MY BRITCHES.
I HAD TO START WRITING MY NAME ON THE TAGS SO I CAN PROVE IT. OTHERWISE I'D BE GOING COMMANDO BY THE END OF THE MONTH.
HEH. I'LL BE SURE TO LOOK INTO THAT.
BUT ACTUALLY, PEARL...
...I'M HERE ABOUT YOUR GRANDDAUGHTER.
JOJO? TELL ME... WHAT'S WRONG?

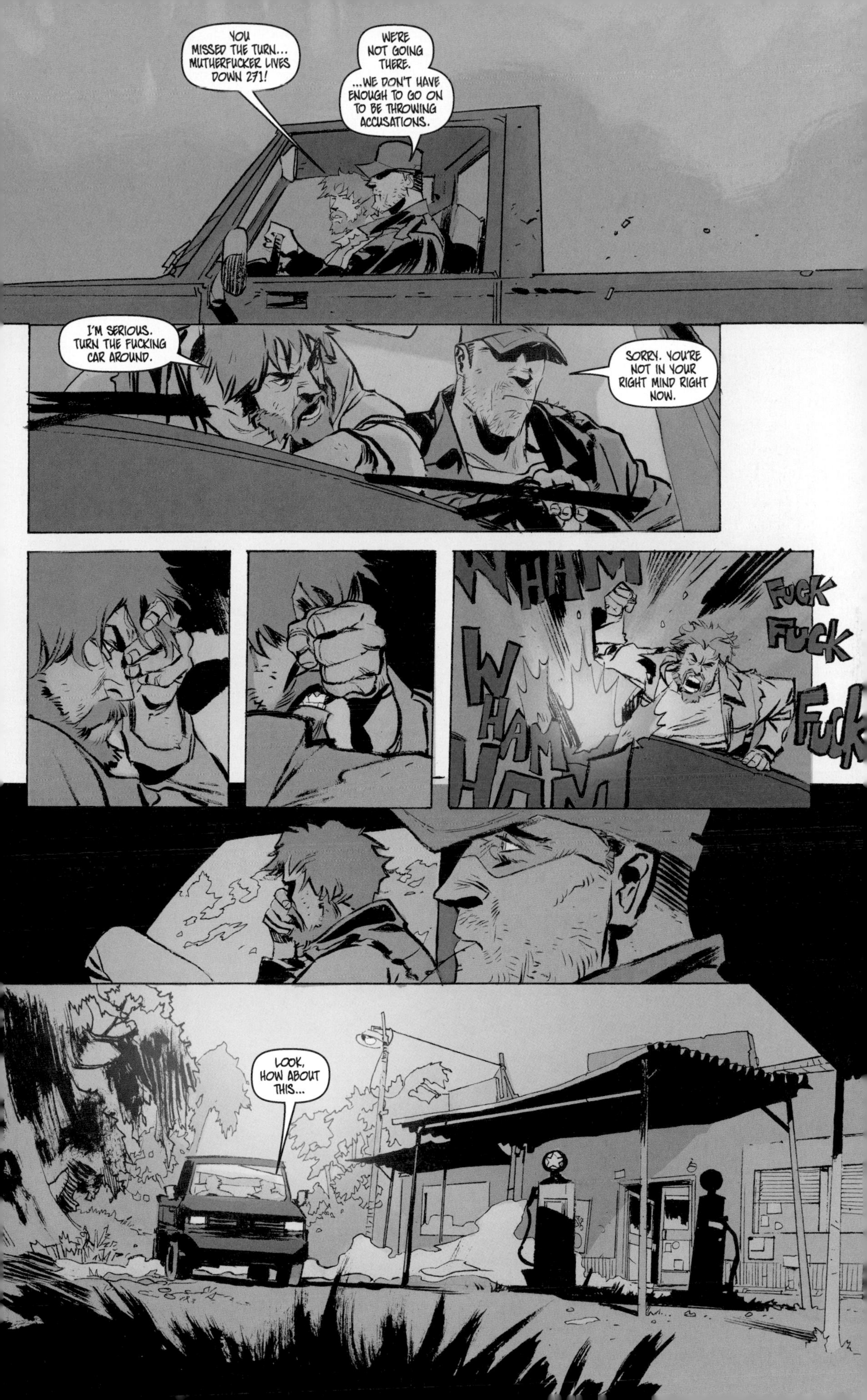

YOU MISSED THE TURN... MUTHERFUCKER LIVES DOWN 271!
WE'RE NOT GOING THERE. ...WE DON'T HAVE ENOUGH TO GO ON TO BE THROWING ACCUSATIONS.
I'M SERIOUS. TURN THE FUCKING CAR AROUND.
SORRY. YOU'RE NOT IN YOUR RIGHT MIND RIGHT NOW.
WHAM
WHAM
FUCK
FUCK
FUCK
LOOK, HOW ABOUT THIS...

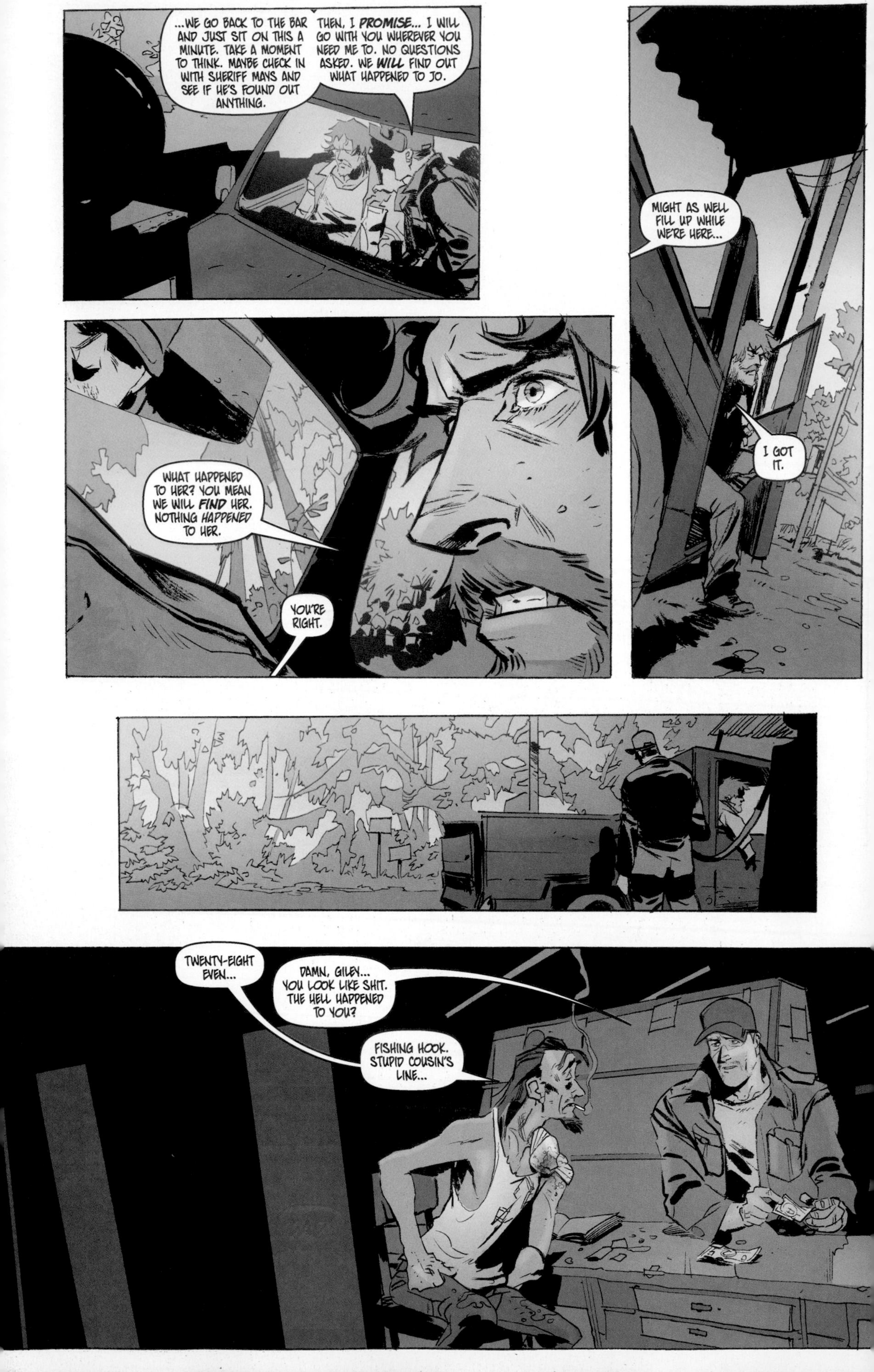
...WE GO BACK TO THE BAR AND JUST SIT ON THIS A MINUTE. TAKE A MOMENT TO THINK. MAYBE CHECK IN WITH SHERIFF MAYS AND SEE IF HE'S FOUND OUT ANYTHING.
THEN, I PROMISE... I WILL GO WITH YOU WHEREVER YOU NEED ME TO. NO QUESTIONS ASKED. WE WILL FIND OUT WHAT HAPPENED TO JO.
MIGHT AS WELL FILL UP WHILE WE'RE HERE...
WHAT HAPPENED TO HER? YOU MEAN WE WILL FIND HER. NOTHING HAPPENED TO HER.
YOU'RE RIGHT.
I GOT IT.
TWENTY-EIGHT EVEN...
DAMN, GILEY... YOU LOOK LIKE SHIT. THE HELL HAPPENED TO YOU?
FISHING HOOK. STUPID COUSIN'S LINE...

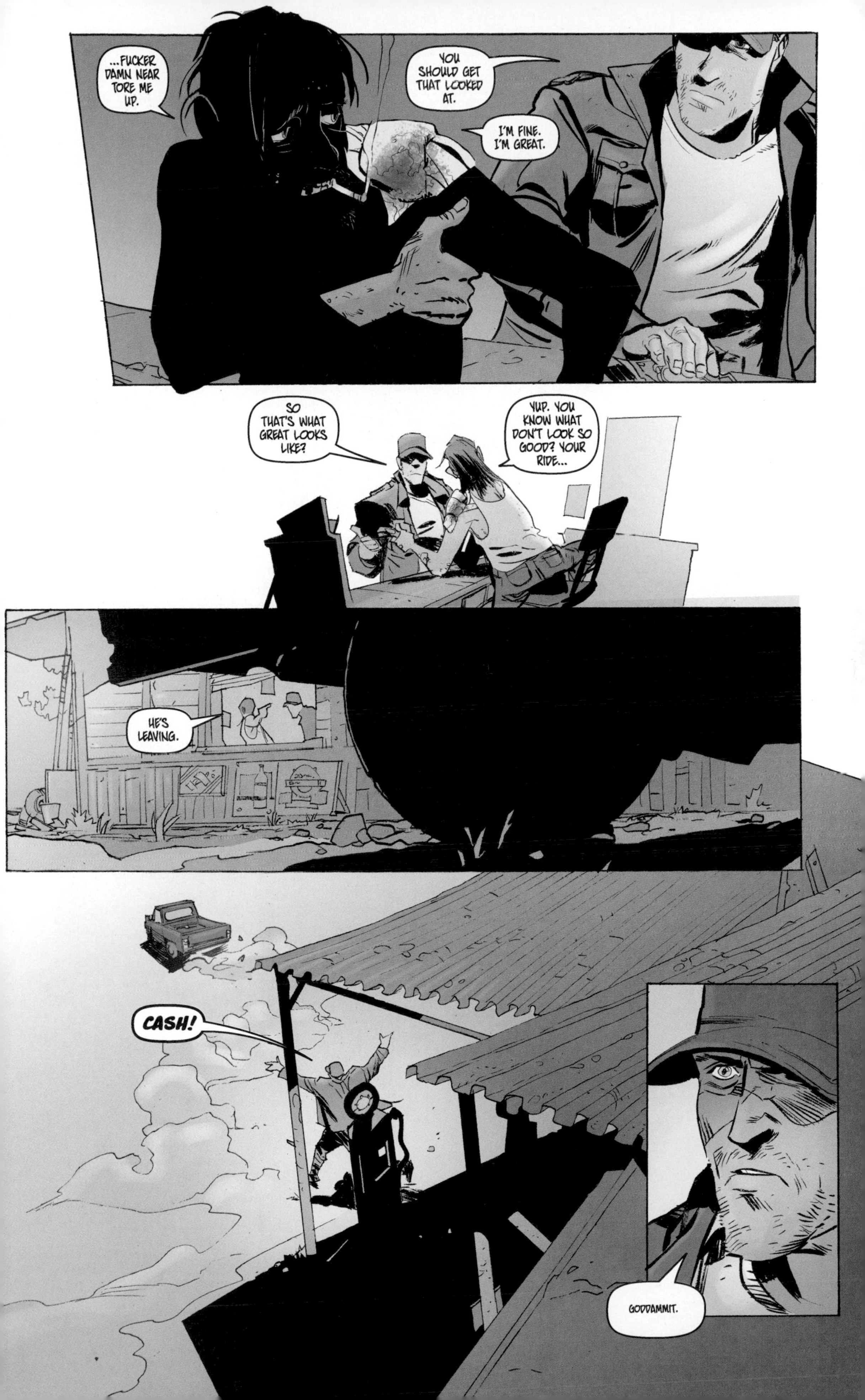
...FUCKER DAMN NEAR TORE ME UP.
YOU SHOULD GET THAT LOOKED AT.
I'M FINE. I'M GREAT.
SO THAT'S WHAT GREAT LOOKS LIKE?
YUP. YOU KNOW WHAT DON'T LOOK SO GOOD? YOUR RIDE...
HE'S LEAVING.
CASH!
GODDAMMIT.

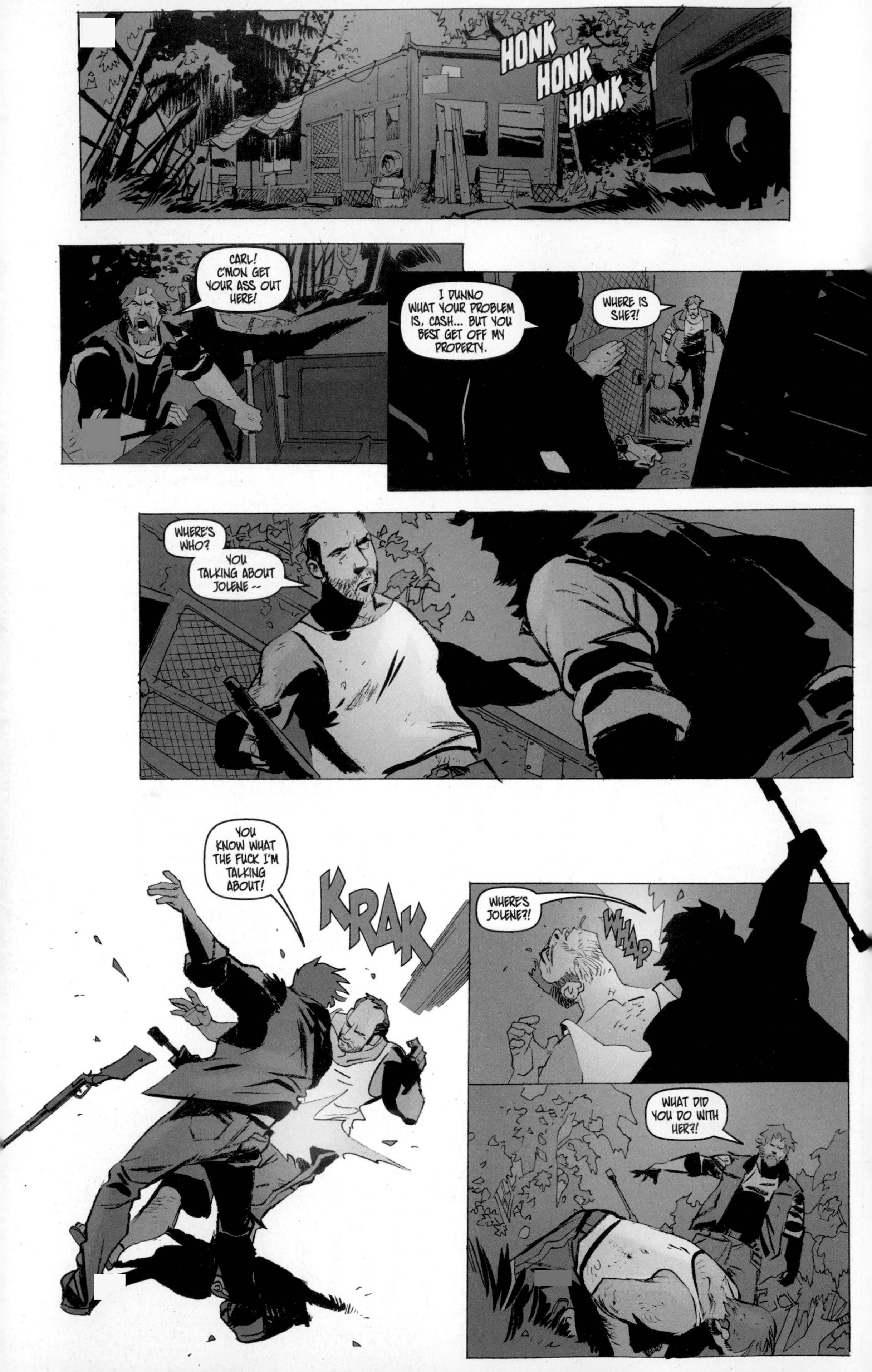
HONK HONK HONK
CARL! C'MON GET YOUR ASS OUT HERE!
I DUNNO WHAT YOUR PROBLEM IS, CASH... BUT YOU BEST GET OFF MY PROPERTY.
WHERE IS SHE?!
WHERE'S WHO?
YOU TALKING ABOUT JOLENE --
YOU KNOW WHAT THE FUCK I'M TALKING ABOUT!
KRAK
WHERE'S JOLENE?!
WHAP
WHAT DID YOU DO WITH HER?!

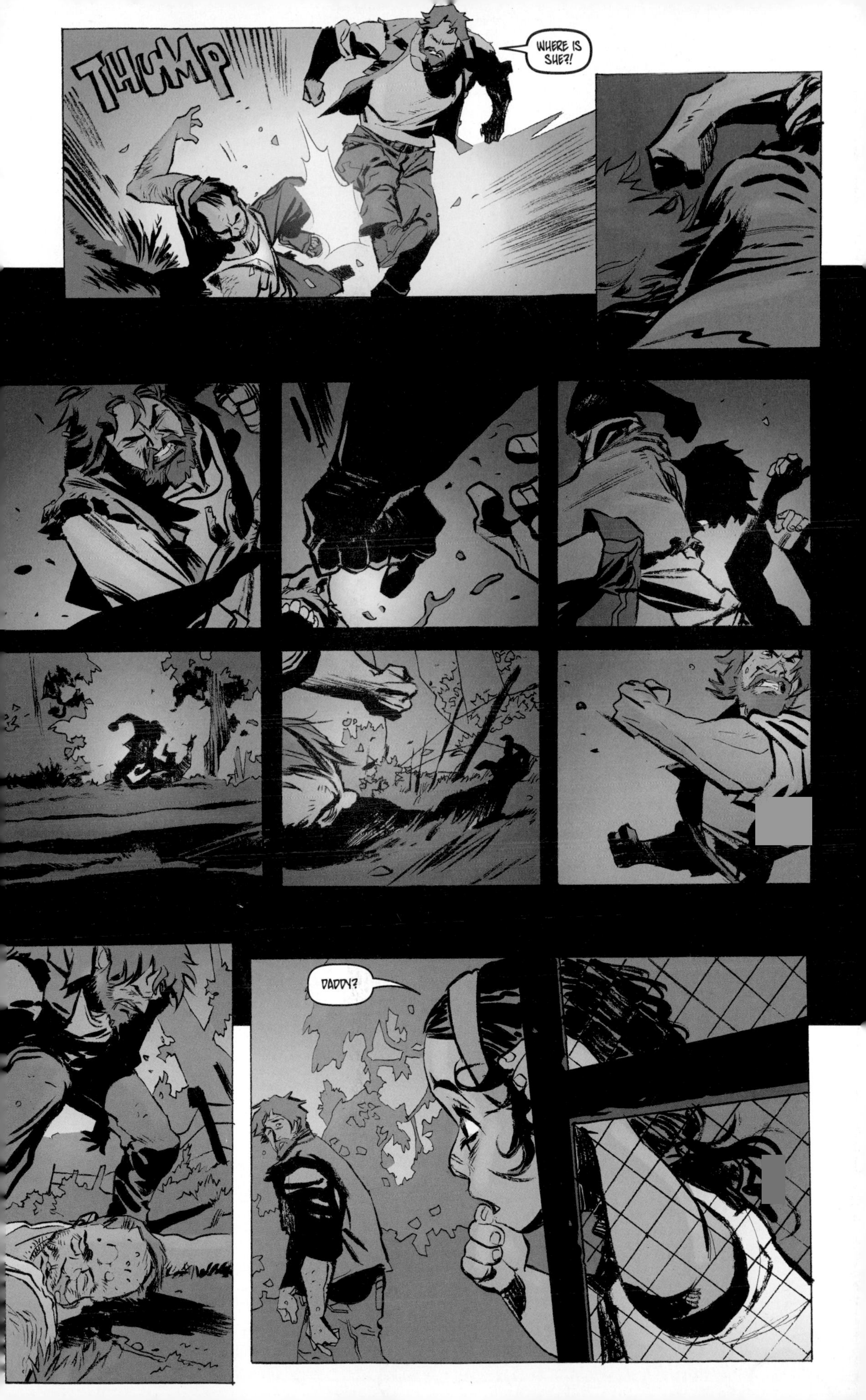
THUMP
WHERE IS SHE?!
DADDY?

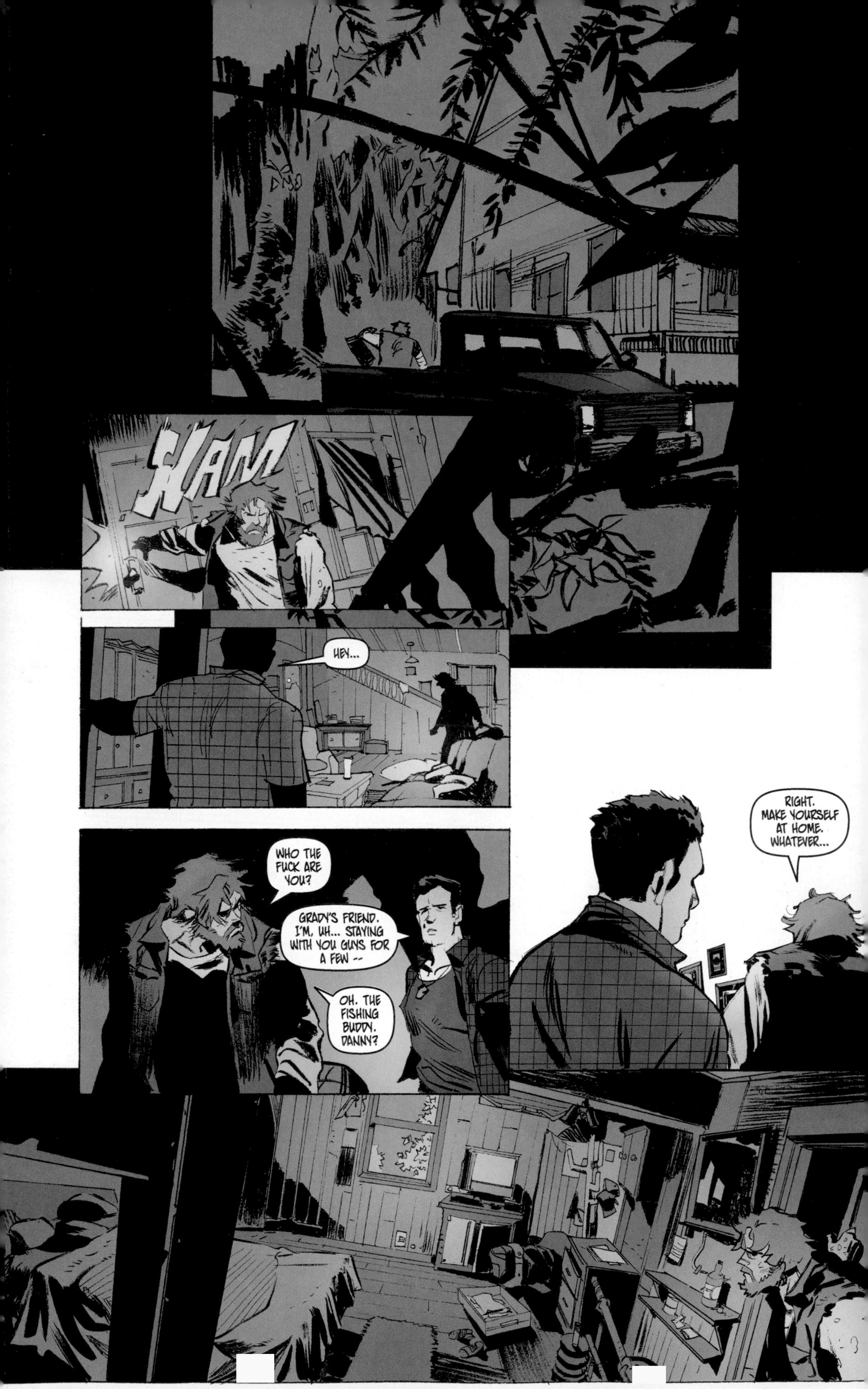
WHAM
HEY...
WHO THE FUCK ARE YOU?
GRADY'S FRIEND. I'M, UH... STAYING WITH YOU GUYS FOR A FEW --
OH. THE FISHING BUDDY. DANNY?
RIGHT. MAKE YOURSELF AT HOME. WHATEVER...

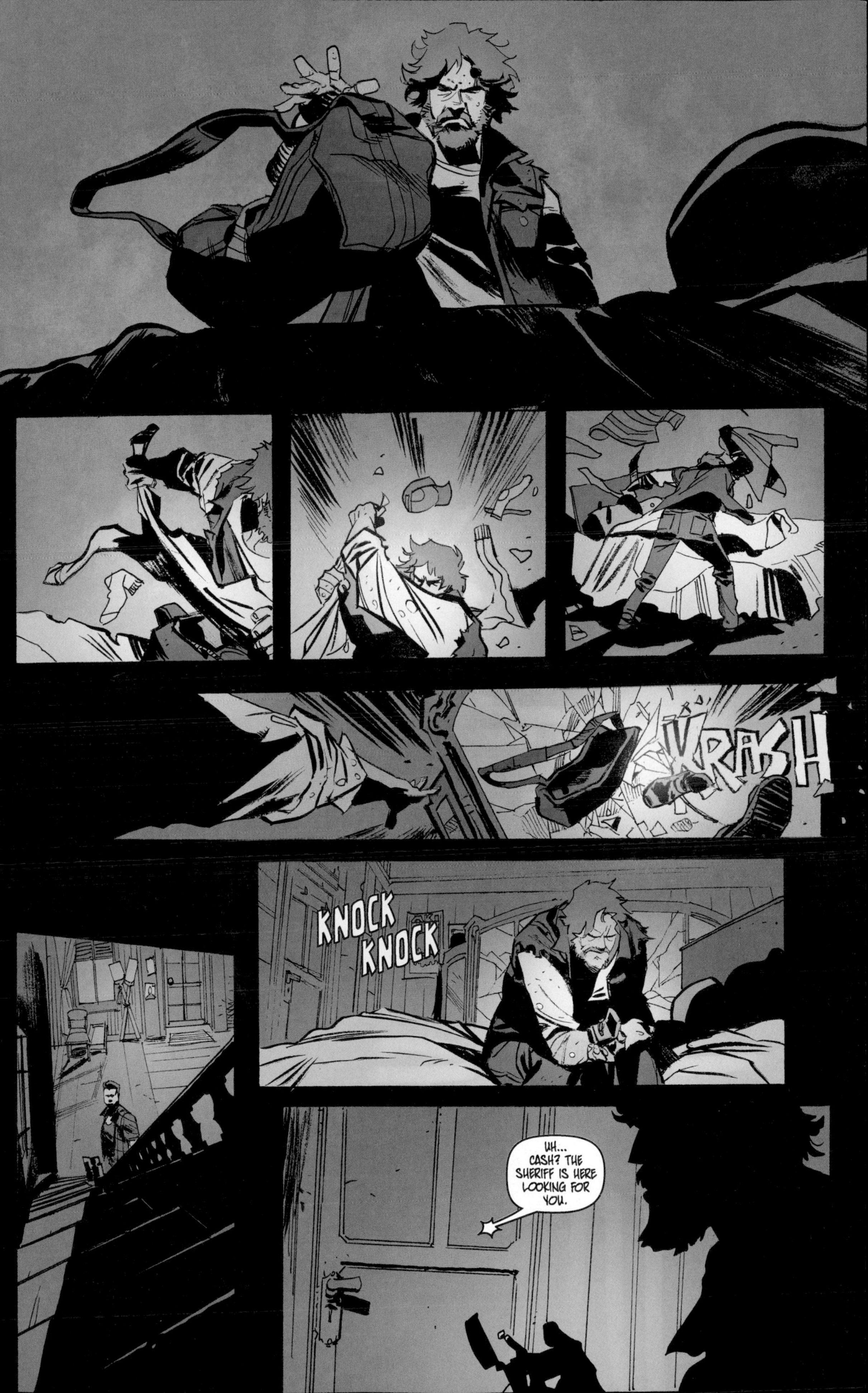
KRASH
KNOCK KNOCK
UH... CASH? THE SHERIFF IS HERE LOOKING FOR YOU.

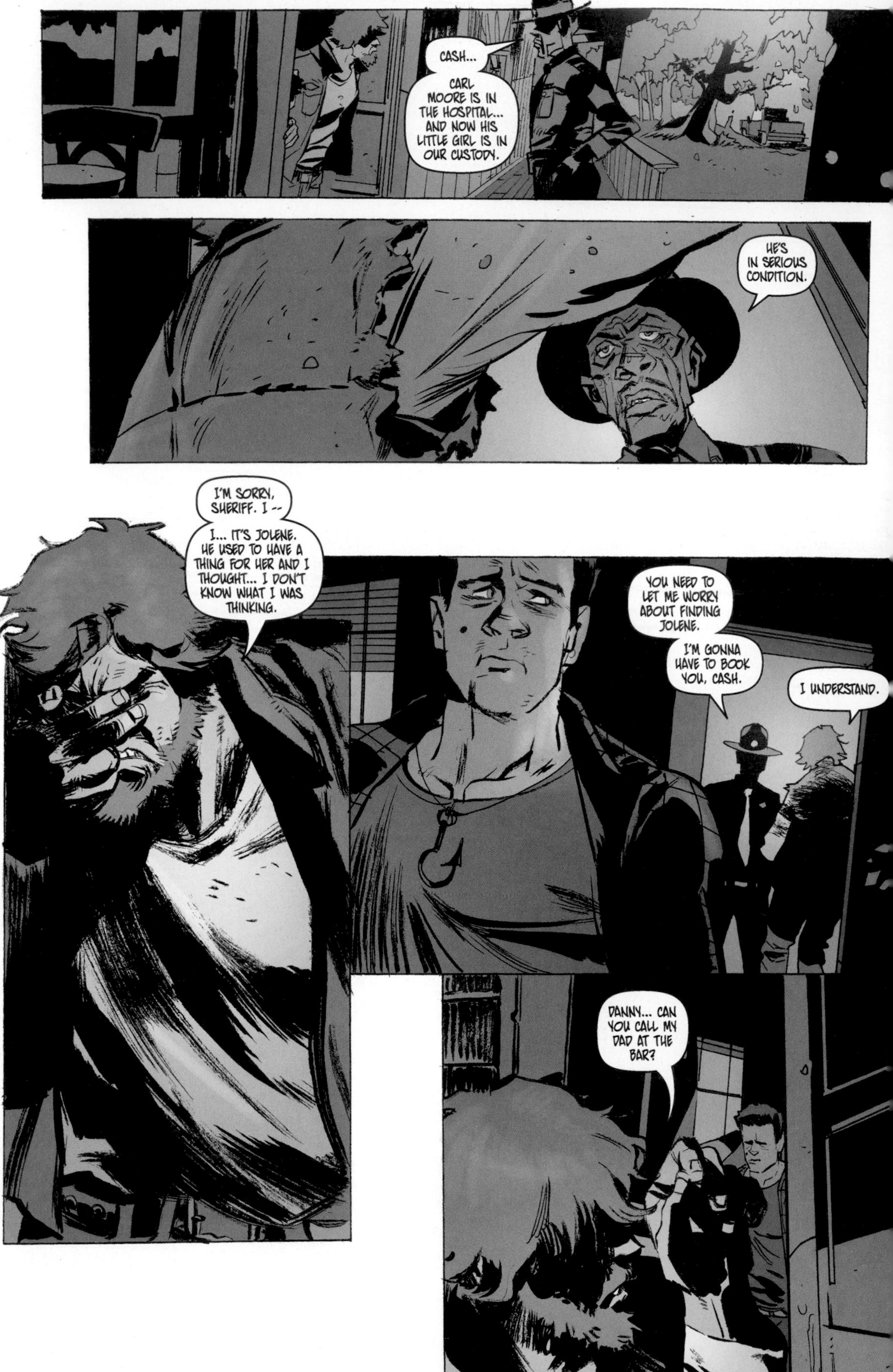
CASH...
CARL MOORE IS IN THE HOSPITAL... AND NOW HIS LITTLE GIRL IS IN OUR CUSTODY.
HE'S IN SERIOUS CONDITION.
I'M SORRY, SHERIFF. I --
I... IT'S JOLENE. HE USED TO HAVE A THING FOR HER AND I THOUGHT... I DON'T KNOW WHAT I WAS THINKING.
YOU NEED TO LET ME WORRY ABOUT FINDING JOLENE.
I'M GONNA HAVE TO BOOK YOU, CASH.
I UNDERSTAND.
DANNY... CAN YOU CALL MY DAD AT THE BAR?

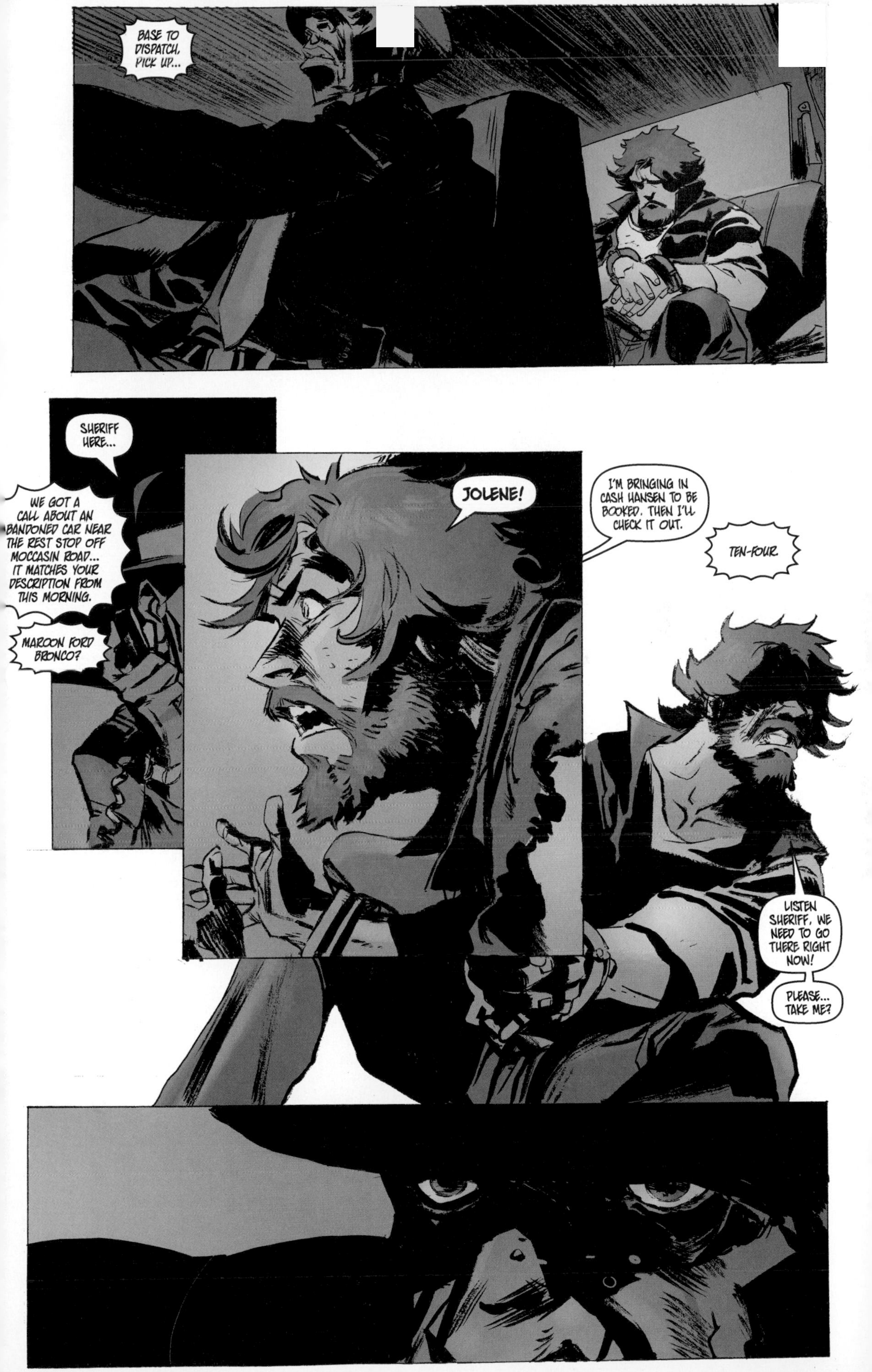

BASE TO DISPATCH, PICK UP...
SHERIFF HERE...
WE GOT A CALL ABOUT AN BANDONED CAR NEAR THE REST STOP OFF MOCCASIN ROAD... IT MATCHES YOUR DESCRIPTION FROM THIS MORNING.
MAROON FORD BRONCO?
JOLENE!
I'M BRINGING IN CASH HANSEN TO BE BOOKED. THEN I'LL CHECK IT OUT.
TEN-FOUR.
LISTEN SHERIFF, WE NEED TO GO THERE RIGHT NOW!
PLEASE... TAKE ME?

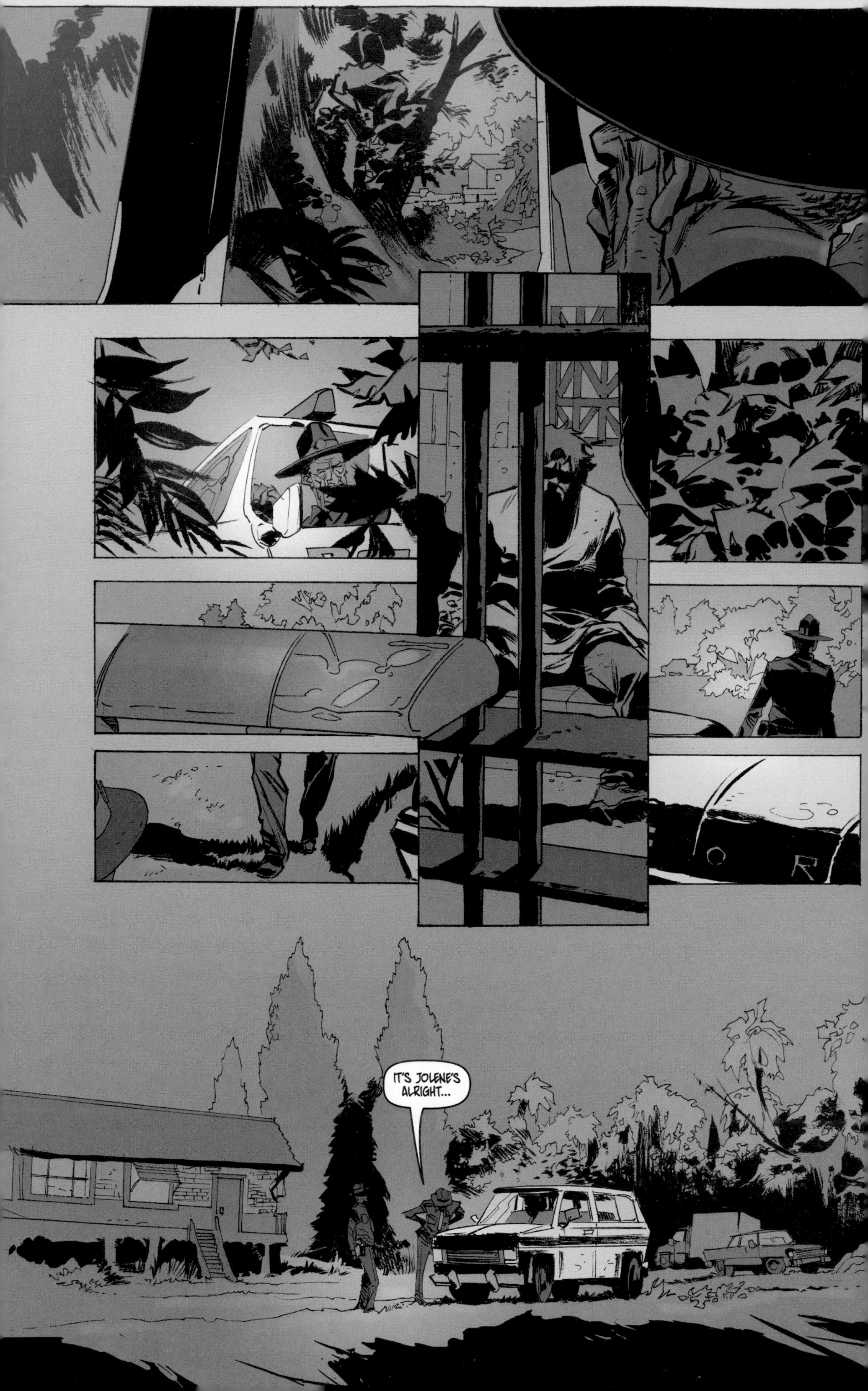
IT'S JOLENE'S ALRIGHT...

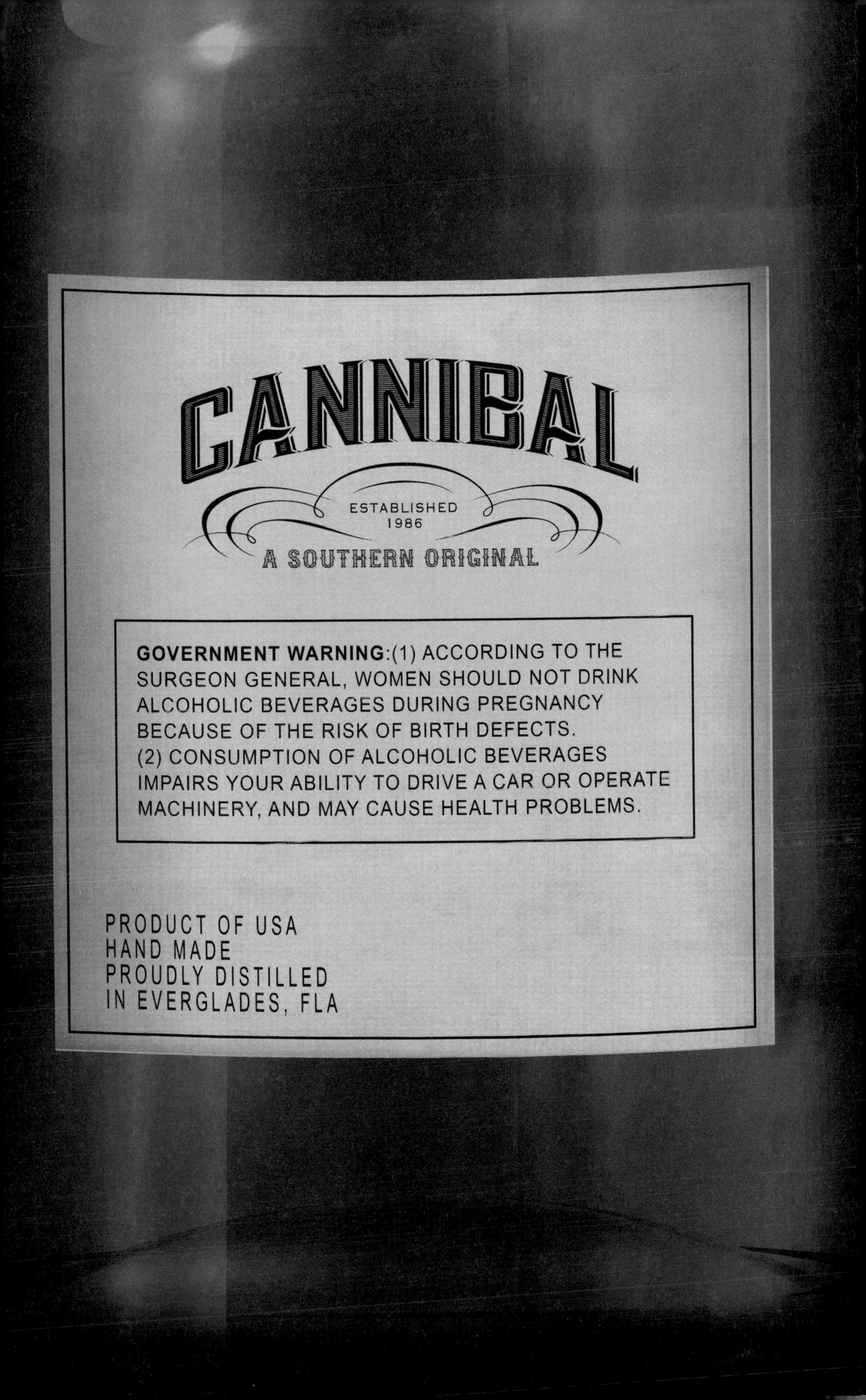
CANNIBAL
ESTABLISHED
1986
A SOUTHERN ORIGINAL
GOVERNMENT WARNING:(1) ACCORDING TO THE SURGEON GENERAL, WOMEN SHOULD NOT DRINK ALCOHOLIC BEVERAGES DURING PREGNANCY BECAUSE OF THE RISK OF BIRTH DEFECTS. (2) CONSUMPTION OF ALCOHOLIC BEVERAGES IMPAIRS YOUR ABILITY TO DRIVE A CAR OR OPERATE MACHINERY, AND MAY CAUSE HEALTH PROBLEMS.
PRODUCT OF USA
HAND MADE
PROUDLY DISTILLED
IN EVERGLADES, FLA

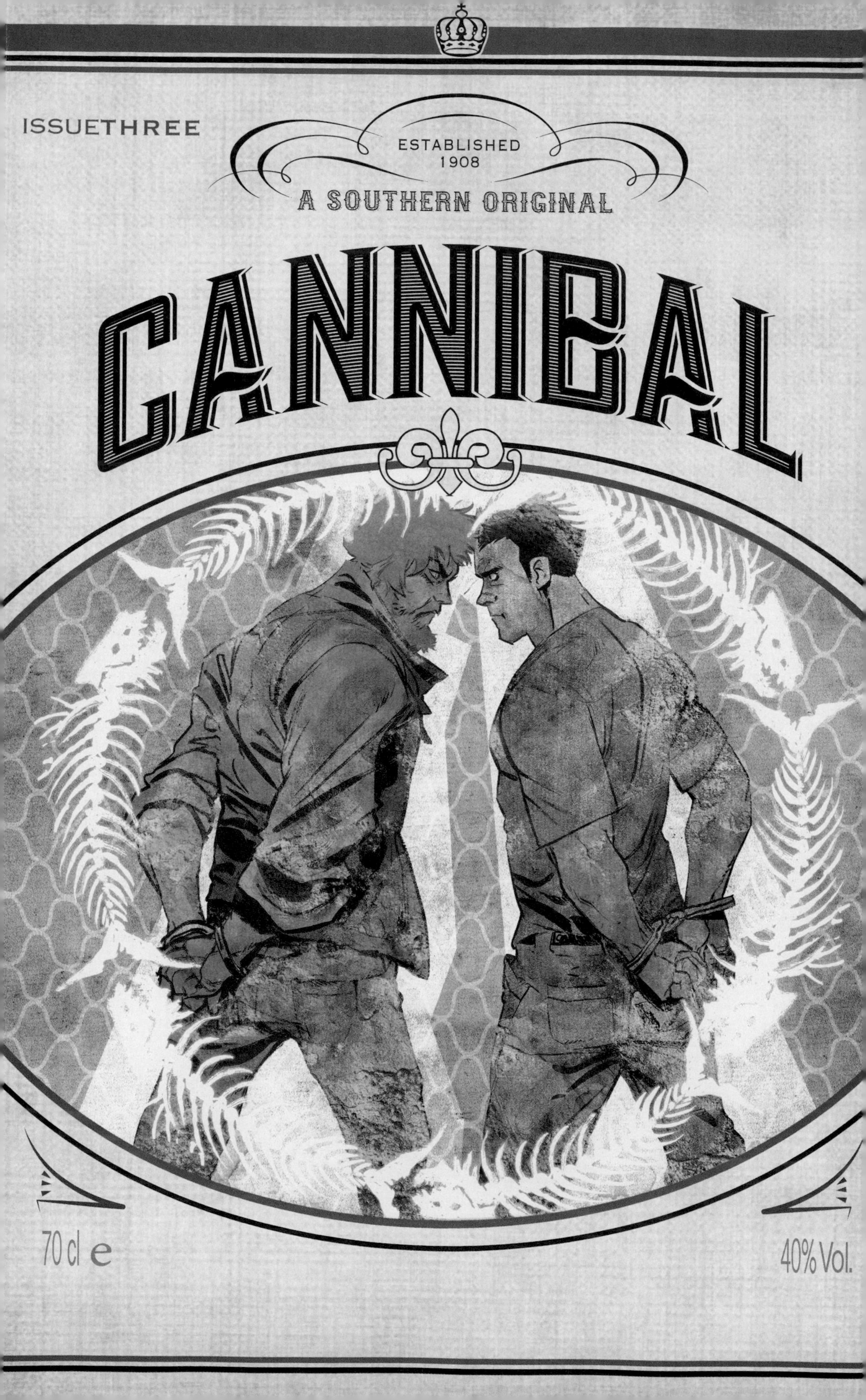
ISSUETHREE
ESTABLISHED
1908
A SOUTHERN ORIGINAL
CANNIBAL
70 cl e
40% Vol.

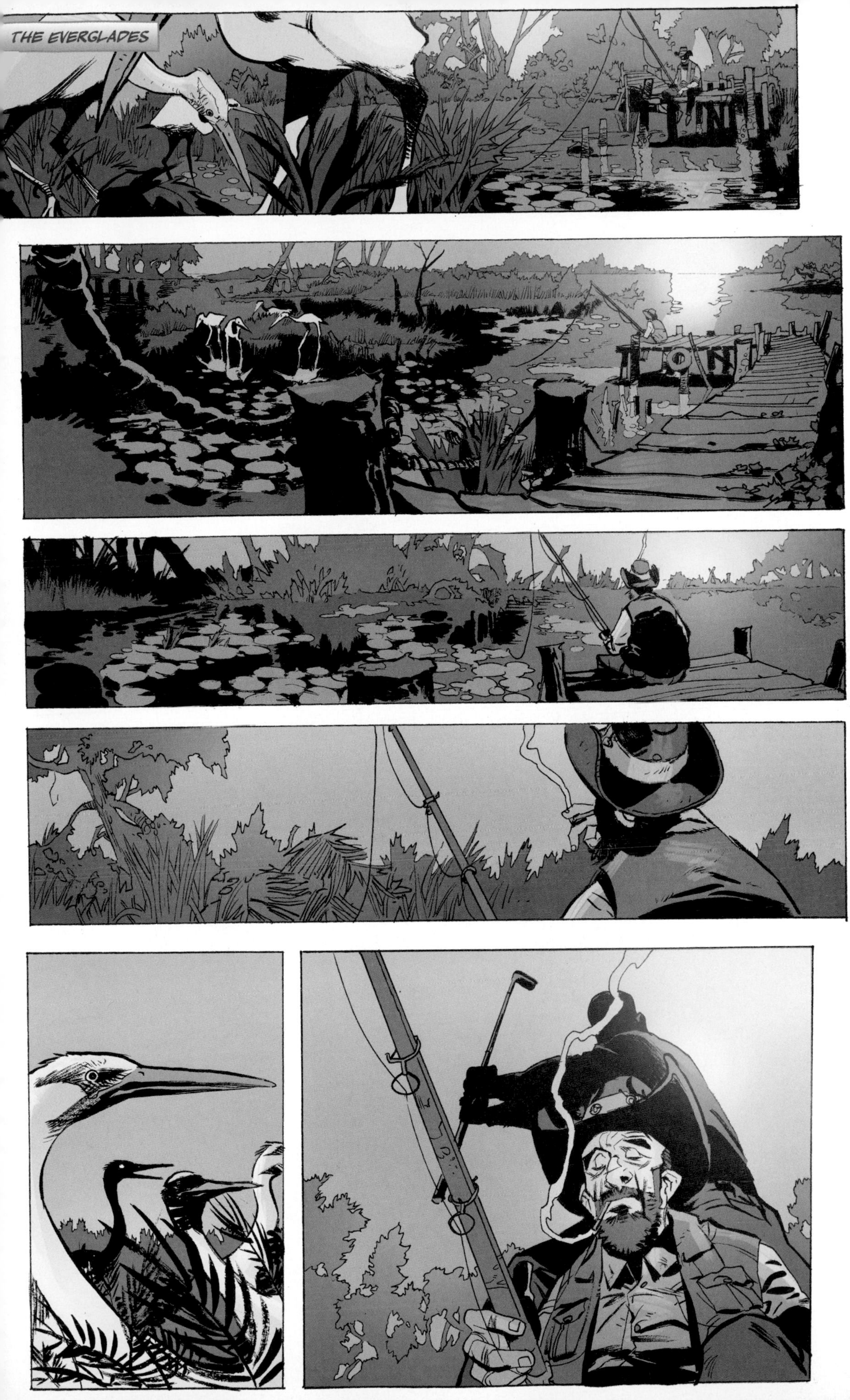
THE EVERGLADES

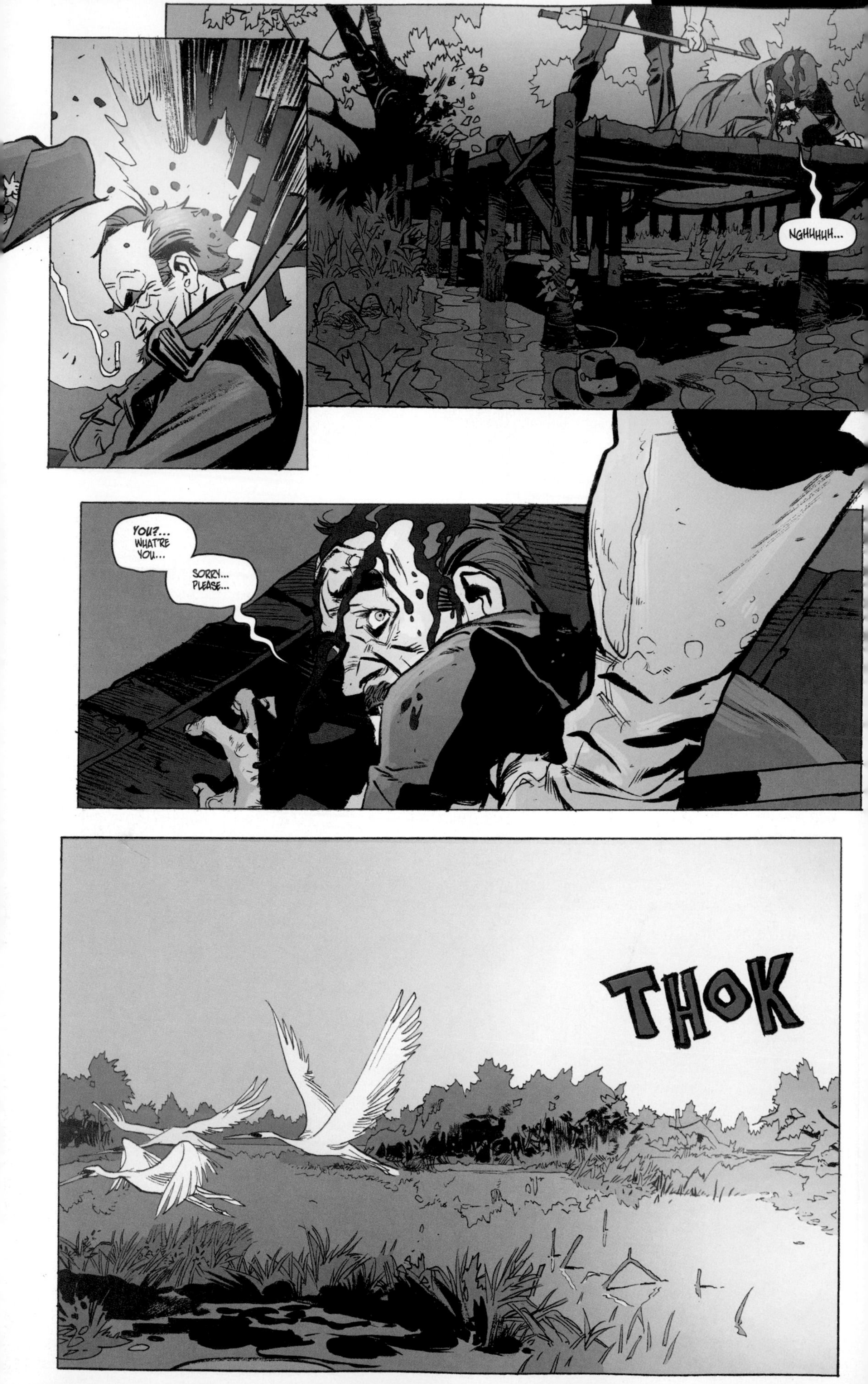
NGHHHHH...
YOU?... WHAT'RE YOU...
SORRY... PLEASE...
THOK

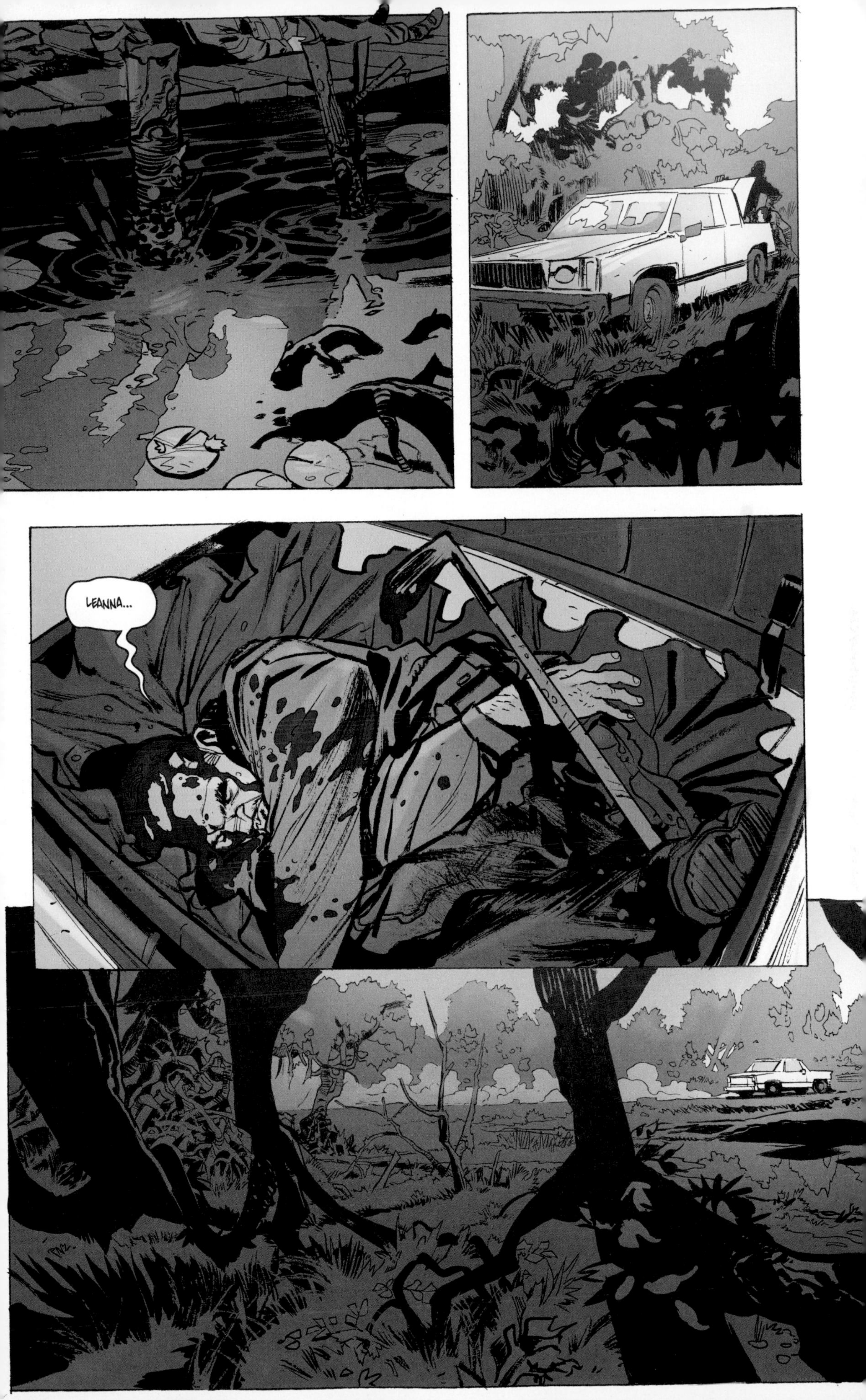
LEANNA...

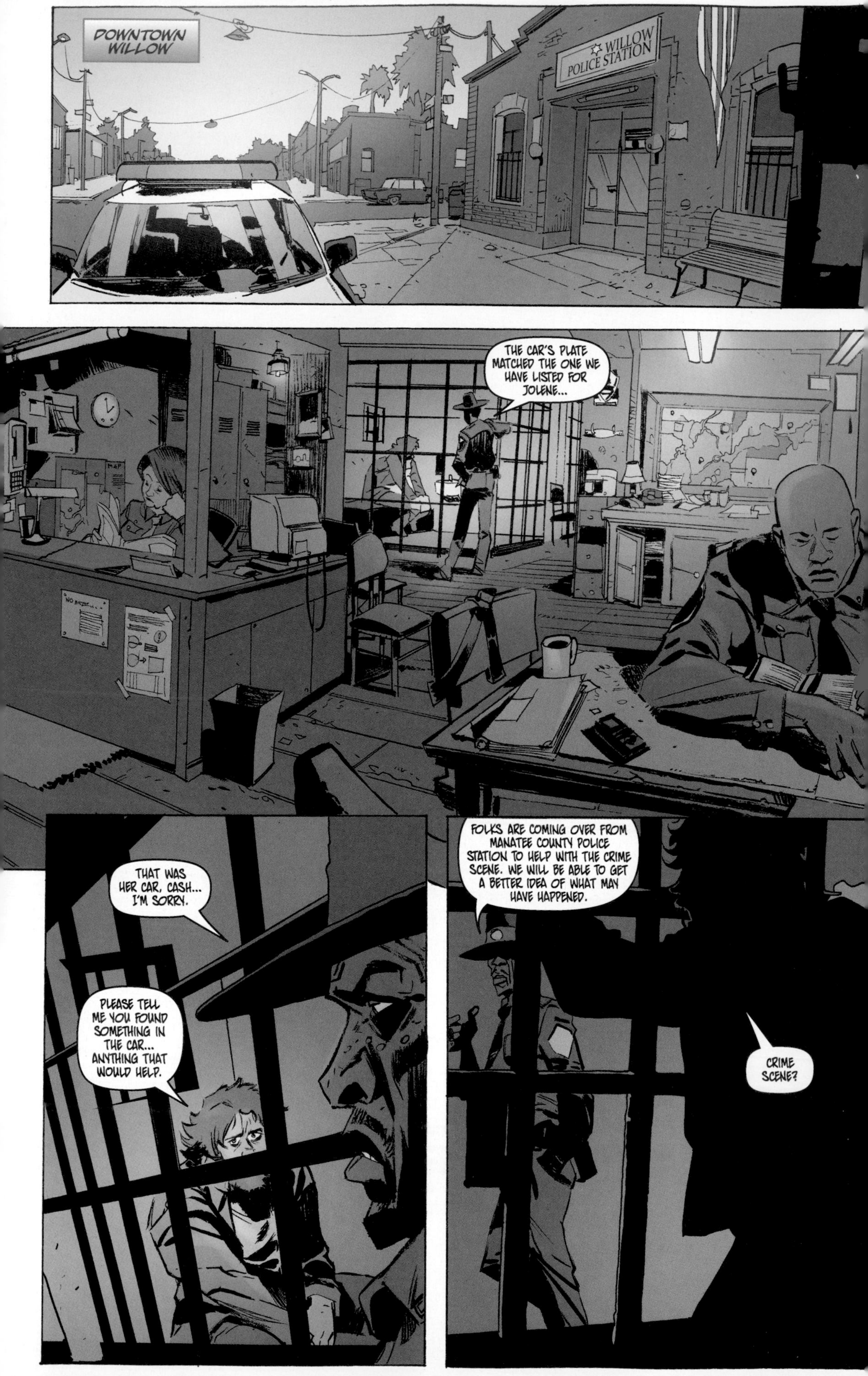
DOWNTOWN WILLOW
WILLOW POLICE STATION
THE CAR'S PLATE MATCHED THE ONE WE HAVE LISTED FOR JOLENE...
THAT WAS HER CAR, CASH... I'M SORRY.
PLEASE TELL ME YOU FOUND SOMETHING IN THE CAR... ANYTHING THAT WOULD HELP.
FOLKS ARE COMING OVER FROM MANATEE COUNTY POLICE STATION TO HELP WITH THE CRIME SCENE. WE WILL BE ABLE TO GET A BETTER IDEA OF WHAT MAY HAVE HAPPENED.
CRIME SCENE?

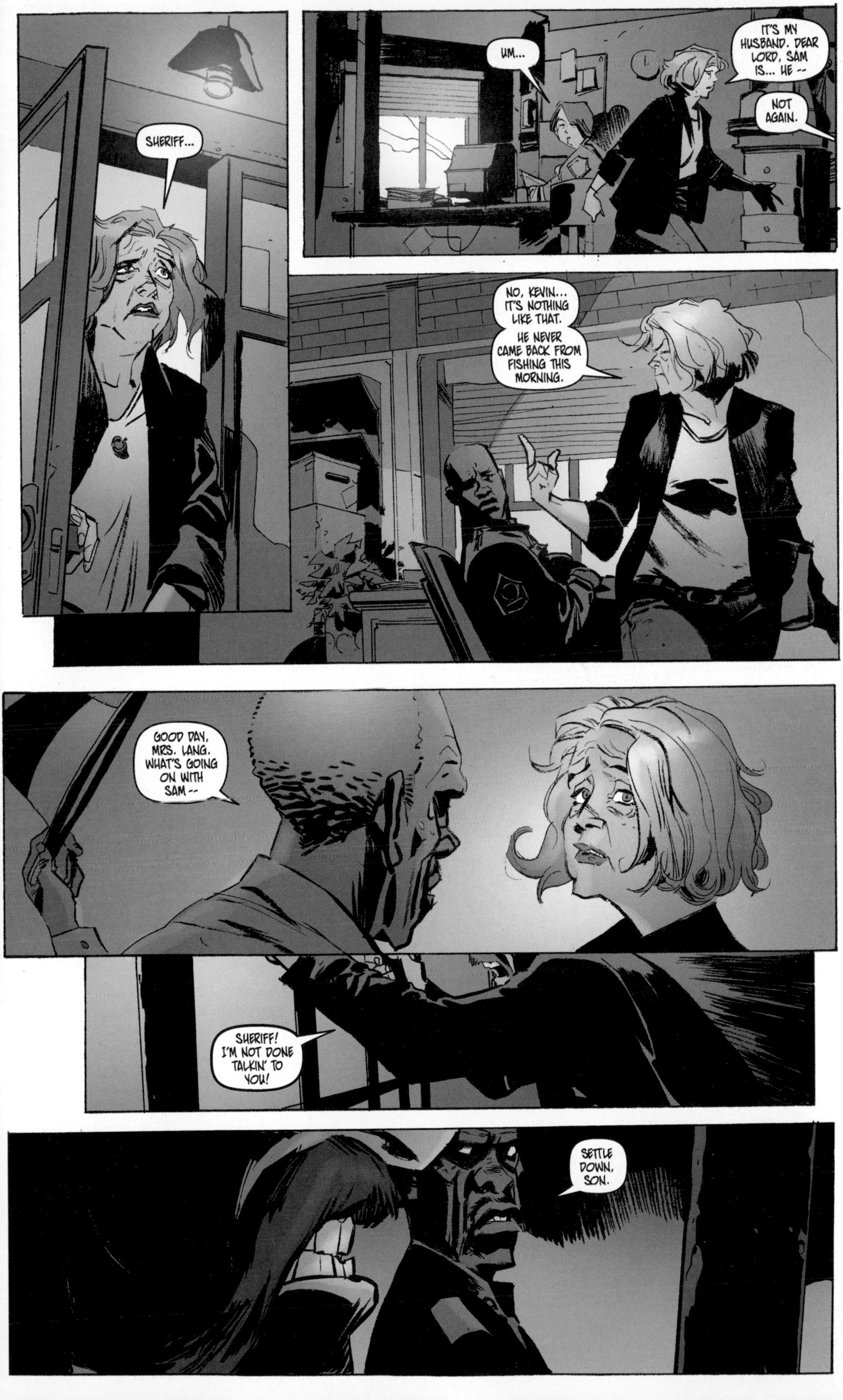
SHERIFF...
UM...
IT'S MY HUSBAND. DEAR LORD, SAM IS... HE --
NOT AGAIN.
NO, KEVIN... IT'S NOTHING LIKE THAT.
HE NEVER CAME BACK FROM FISHING THIS MORNING.
GOOD DAY, MRS. LANG. WHAT'S GOING ON WITH SAM --
SHERIFF! I'M NOT DONE TALKIN' TO YOU!
SETTLE DOWN, SON.

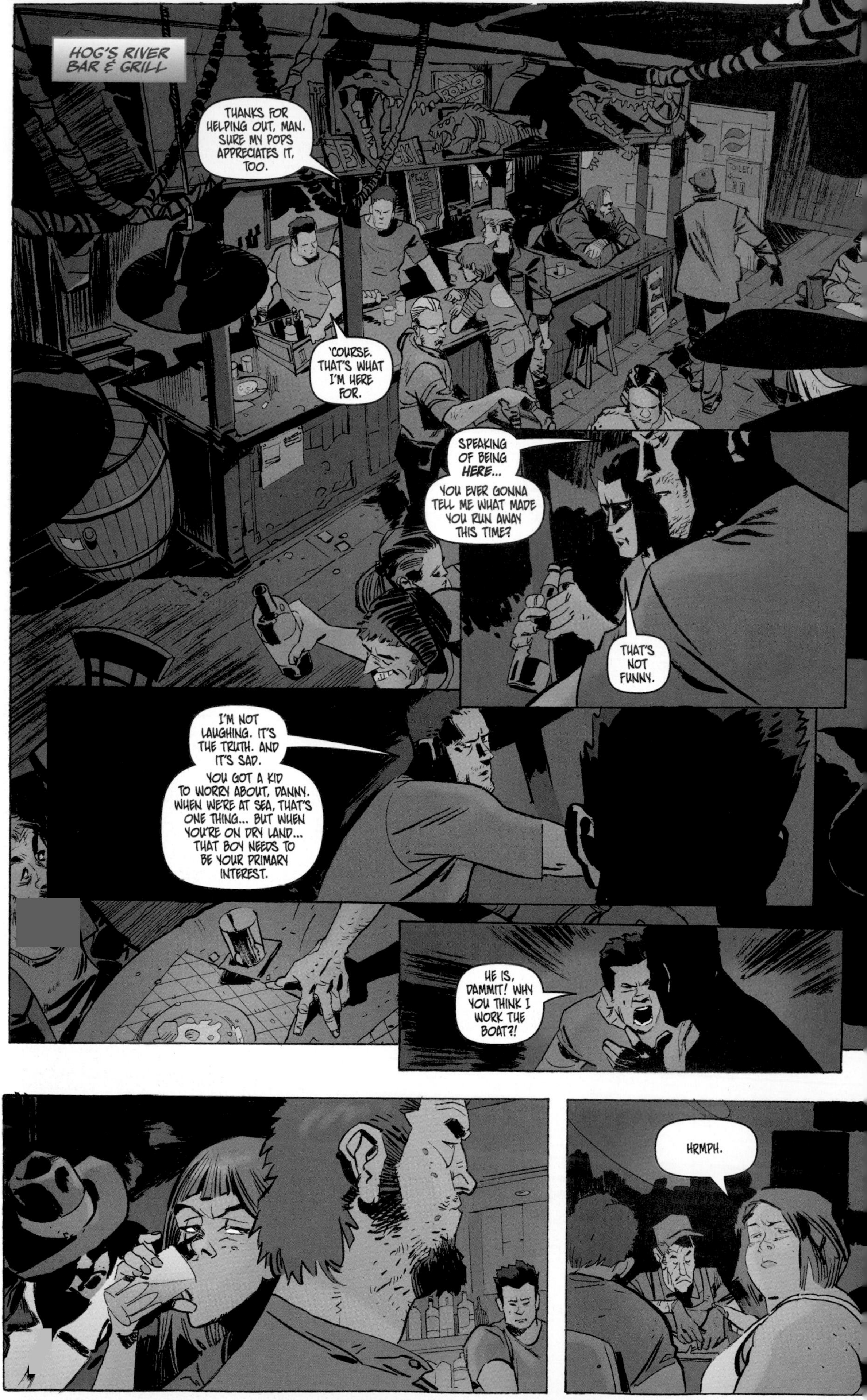
HOG'S RIVER BAR & GRILL
THANKS FOR HELPING OUT, MAN. SURE MY POPS APPRECIATES IT, TOO.
'COURSE. THAT'S WHAT I'M HERE FOR.
SPEAKING OF BEING HERE...
YOU EVER GONNA TELL ME WHAT MADE YOU RUN AWAY THIS TIME?
THAT'S NOT FUNNY.
I'M NOT LAUGHING. IT'S THE TRUTH. AND IT'S SAD.
YOU GOT A KID TO WORRY ABOUT, DANNY. WHEN WE'RE AT SEA, THAT'S ONE THING... BUT WHEN YOU'RE ON DRY LAND... THAT BOY NEEDS TO BE YOUR PRIMARY INTEREST.
HE IS, DAMMIT! WHY YOU THINK I WORK THE BOAT?!
HRMPH.

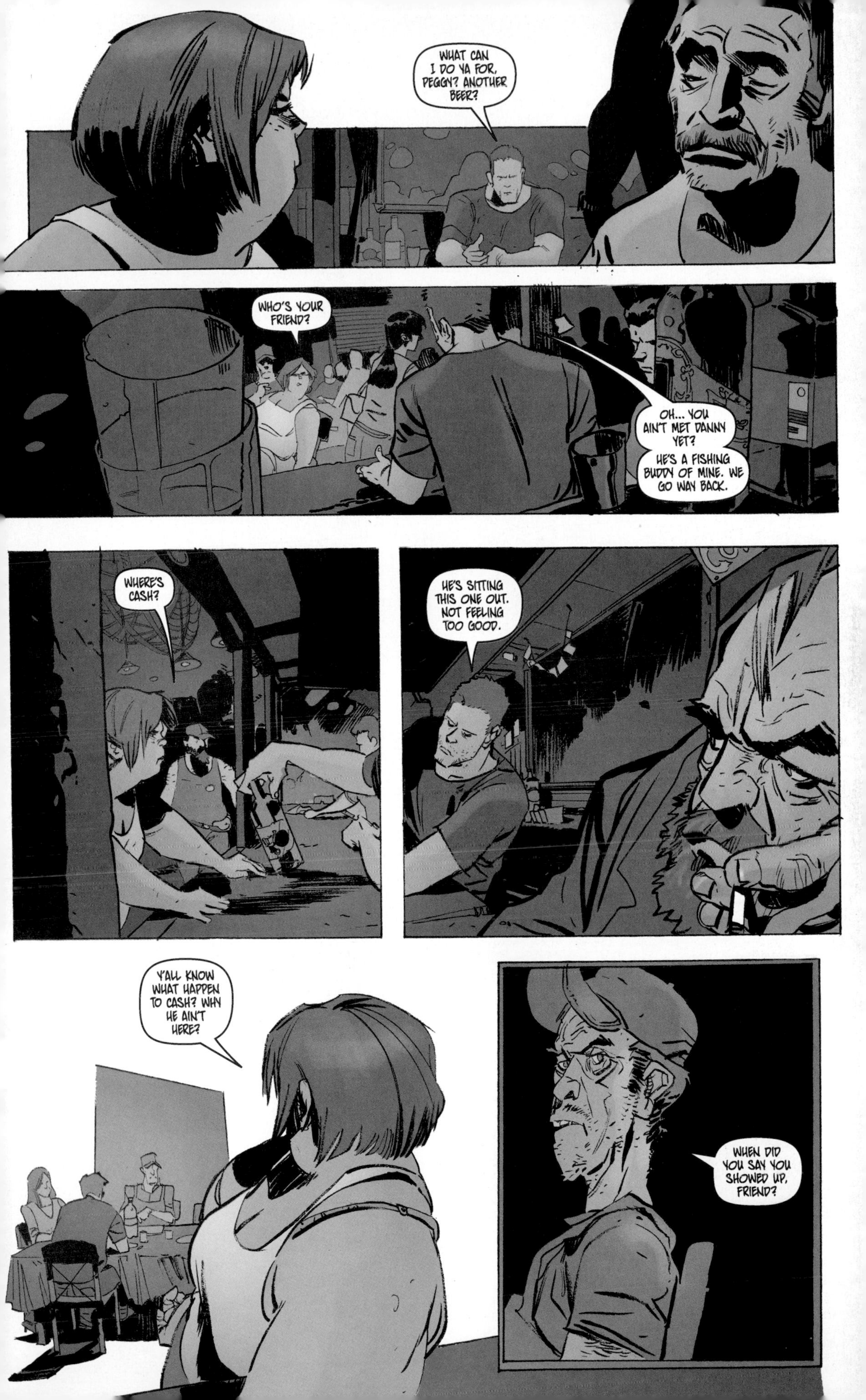
WHAT CAN I DO YA FOR, PEGGY? ANOTHER BEER?
WHO'S YOUR FRIEND?
OH... YOU AIN'T MET DANNY YET?
HE'S A FISHING BUDDY OF MINE. WE GO WAY BACK.
WHERE'S CASH?
HE'S SITTING THIS ONE OUT. NOT FEELING TOO GOOD.
Y'ALL KNOW WHAT HAPPEN TO CASH? WHY HE AIN'T HERE?
WHEN DID YOU SAY YOU SHOWED UP, FRIEND?

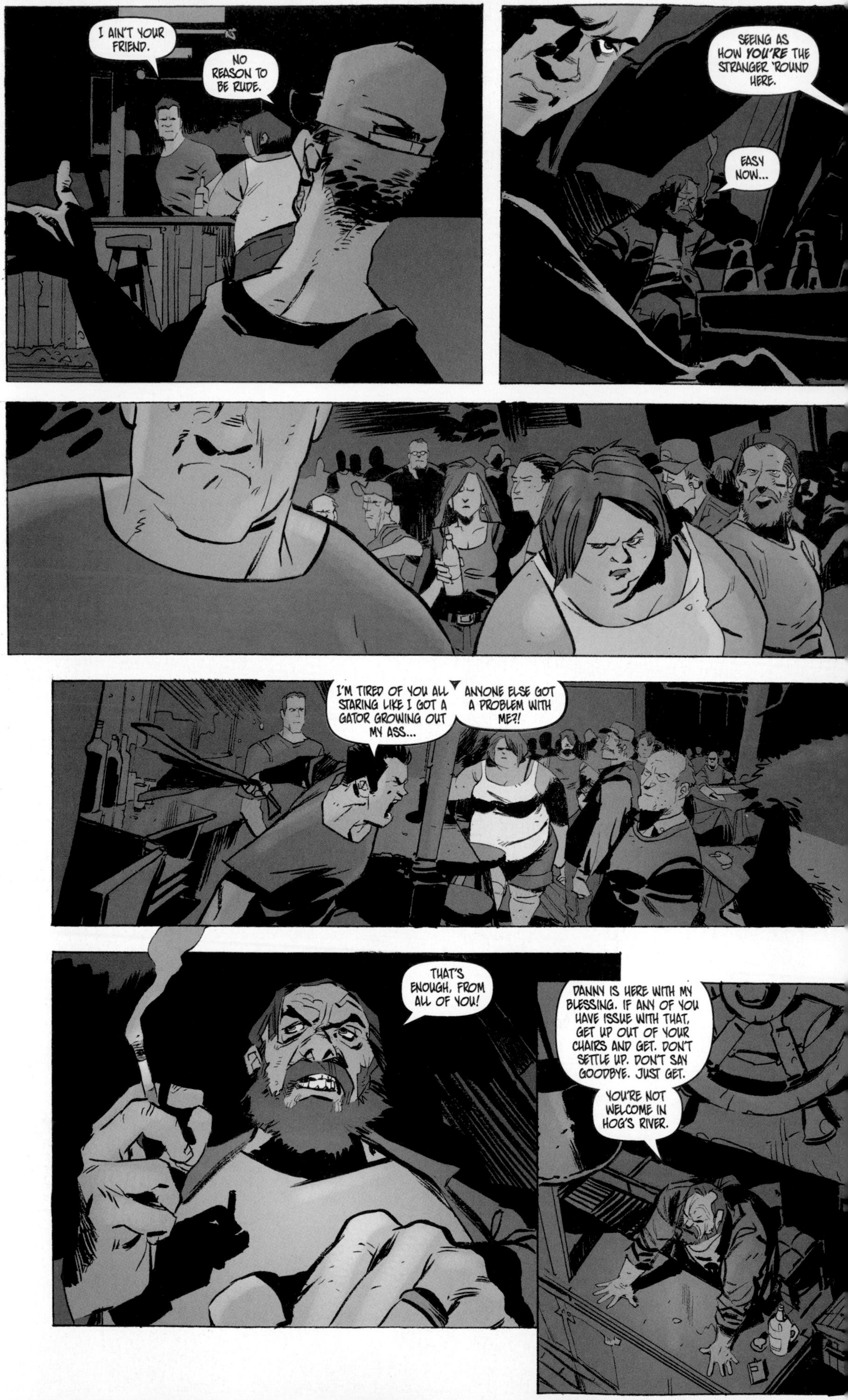
I AIN'T YOUR FRIEND.
NO REASON TO BE RUDE.
SEEING AS HOW *YOU'RE* THE STRANGER 'ROUND HERE.
EASY NOW...
I'M TIRED OF YOU ALL STARING LIKE I GOT A GATOR GROWING OUT MY ASS...
ANYONE ELSE GOT A PROBLEM WITH ME?!
THAT'S ENOUGH, FROM ALL OF YOU!
DANNY IS HERE WITH MY BLESSING. IF ANY OF YOU HAVE ISSUE WITH THAT, GET UP OUT OF YOUR CHAIRS AND GET. DON'T SETTLE UP. DON'T SAY GOODBYE. JUST GET.
YOU'RE NOT WELCOME IN HOG'S RIVER.

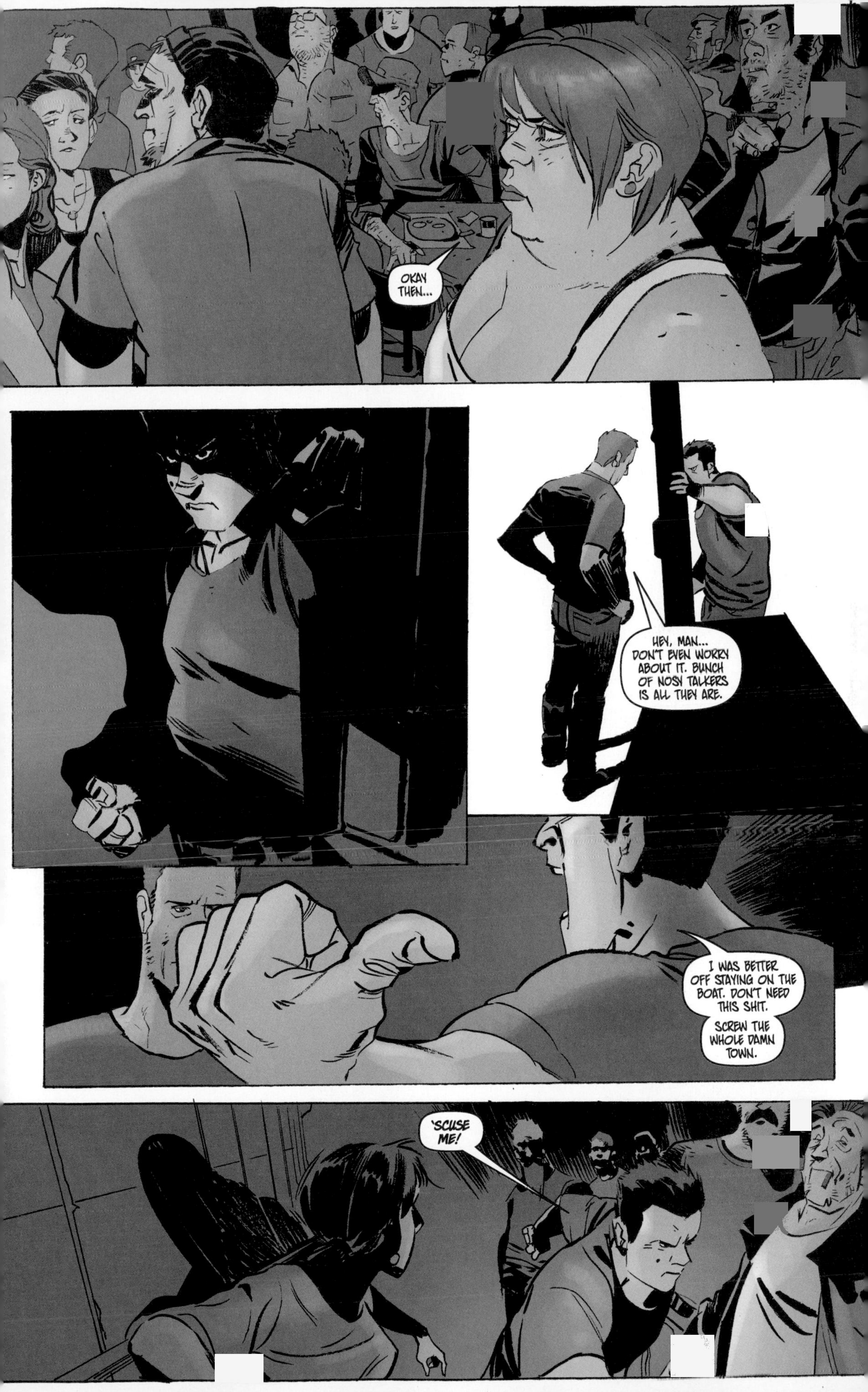
OKAY THEN...
HEY, MAN... DON'T EVEN WORRY ABOUT IT. BUNCH OF NOSY TALKERS IS ALL THEY ARE.
I WAS BETTER OFF STAYING ON THE BOAT. DON'T NEED THIS SHIT.
SCREW THE WHOLE DAMN TOWN.
'SCUSE ME!

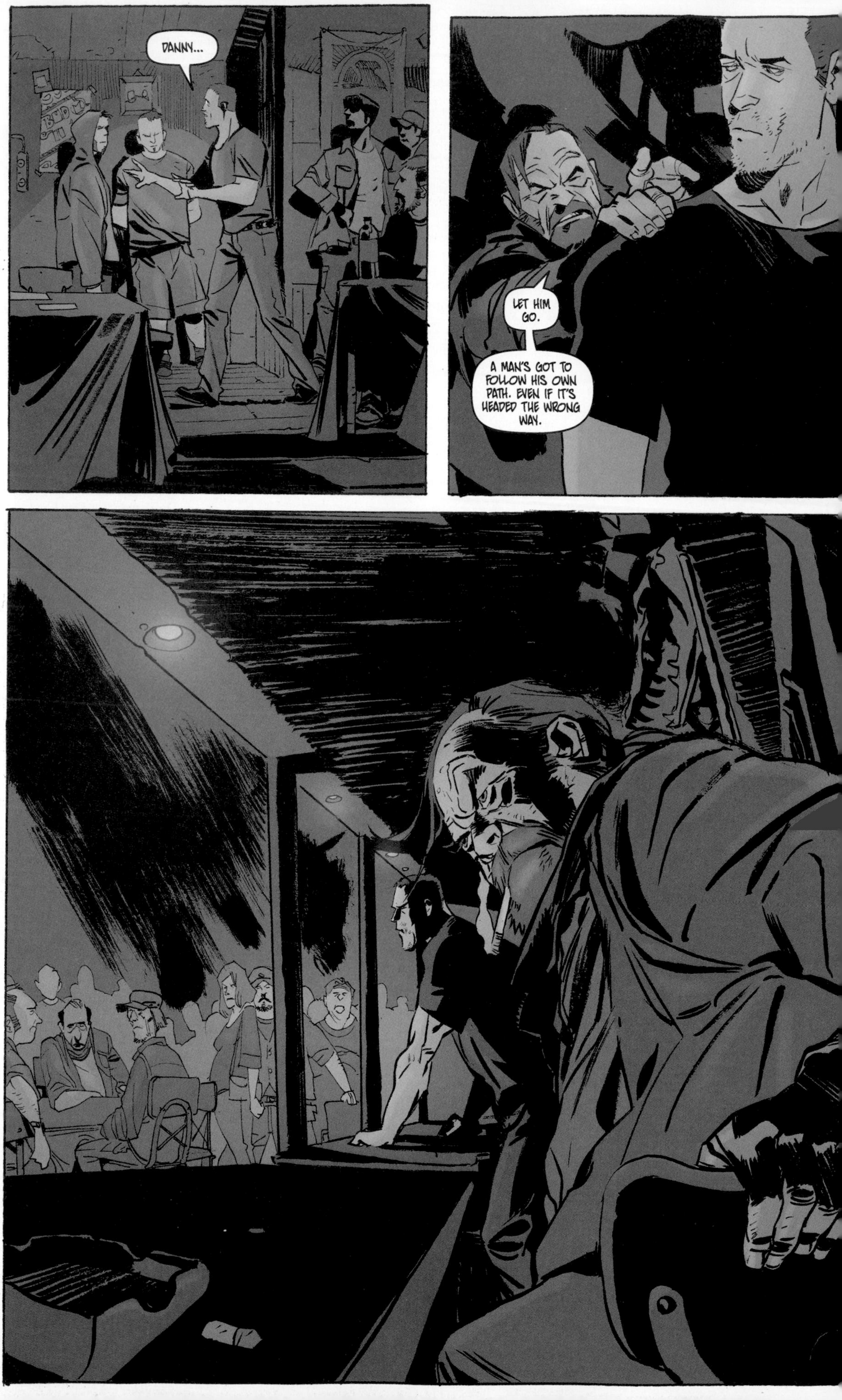
DANNY...
LET HIM GO.
A MAN'S GOT TO FOLLOW HIS OWN PATH. EVEN IF IT'S HEADED THE WRONG WAY.

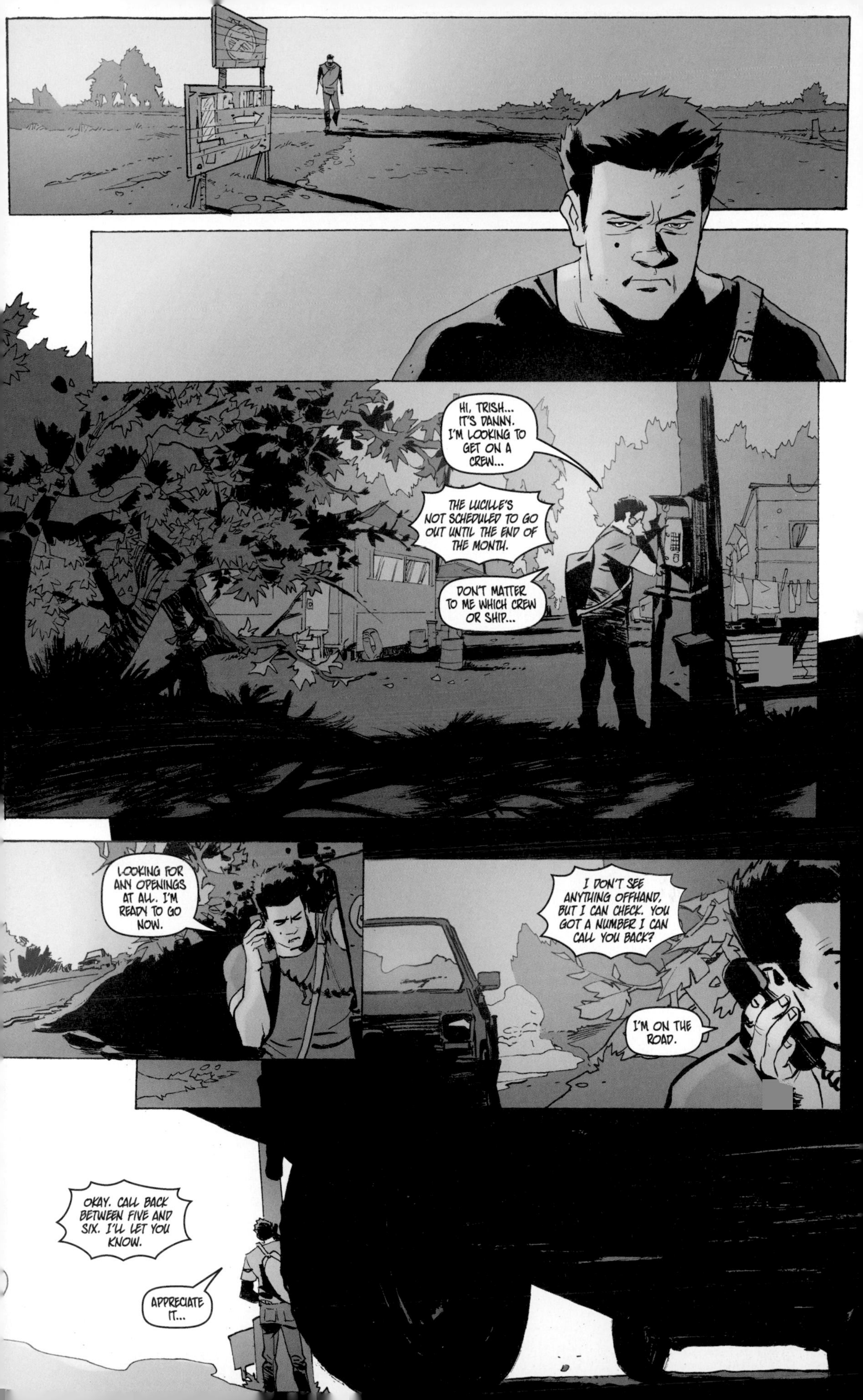
HI, TRISH... IT'S DANNY. I'M LOOKING TO GET ON A CREW...
THE LUCILLE'S NOT SCHEDULED TO GO OUT UNTIL THE END OF THE MONTH.
DON'T MATTER TO ME WHICH CREW OR SHIP...
LOOKING FOR ANY OPENINGS AT ALL. I'M READY TO GO NOW.
I DON'T SEE ANYTHING OFFHAND, BUT I CAN CHECK. YOU GOT A NUMBER I CAN CALL YOU BACK?
I'M ON THE ROAD.
OKAY. CALL BACK BETWEEN FIVE AND SIX. I'LL LET YOU KNOW.
APPRECIATE IT...

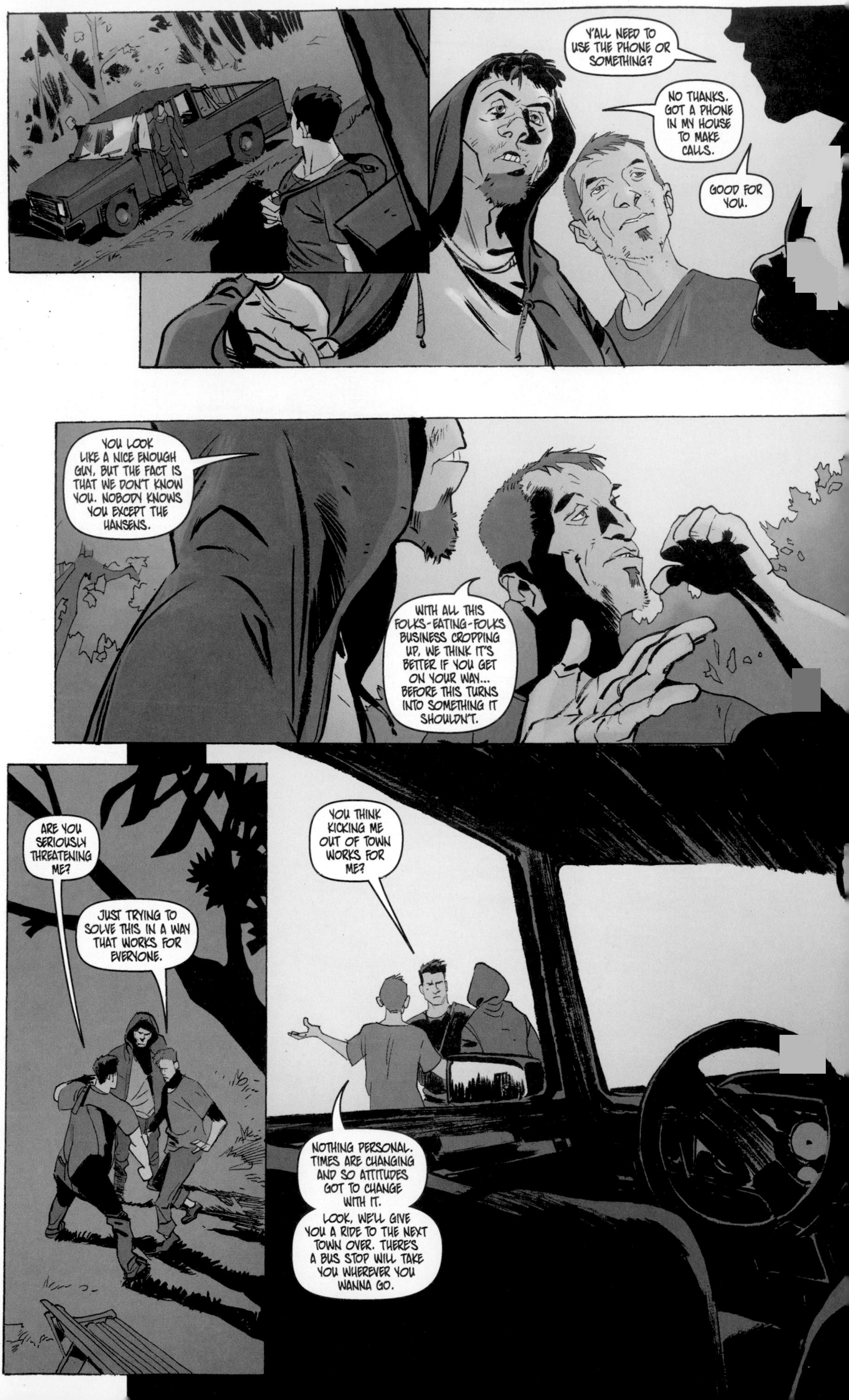
Y'ALL NEED TO USE THE PHONE OR SOMETHING?
NO THANKS. GOT A PHONE IN MY HOUSE TO MAKE CALLS.
GOOD FOR YOU.
YOU LOOK LIKE A NICE ENOUGH GUY, BUT THE FACT IS THAT WE DON'T KNOW YOU. NOBODY KNOWS YOU EXCEPT THE HANSENS.
WITH ALL THIS FOLKS-EATING-FOLKS BUSINESS CROPPING UP, WE THINK IT'S BETTER IF YOU GET ON YOUR WAY... BEFORE THIS TURNS INTO SOMETHING IT SHOULDN'T.
ARE YOU SERIOUSLY THREATENING ME?
JUST TRYING TO SOLVE THIS IN A WAY THAT WORKS FOR EVERYONE.
YOU THINK KICKING ME OUT OF TOWN WORKS FOR ME?
NOTHING PERSONAL. TIMES ARE CHANGING AND SO ATTITUDES GOT TO CHANGE WITH IT.
LOOK, WE'LL GIVE YOU A RIDE TO THE NEXT TOWN OVER. THERE'S A BUS STOP WILL TAKE YOU WHEREVER YOU WANNA GO.

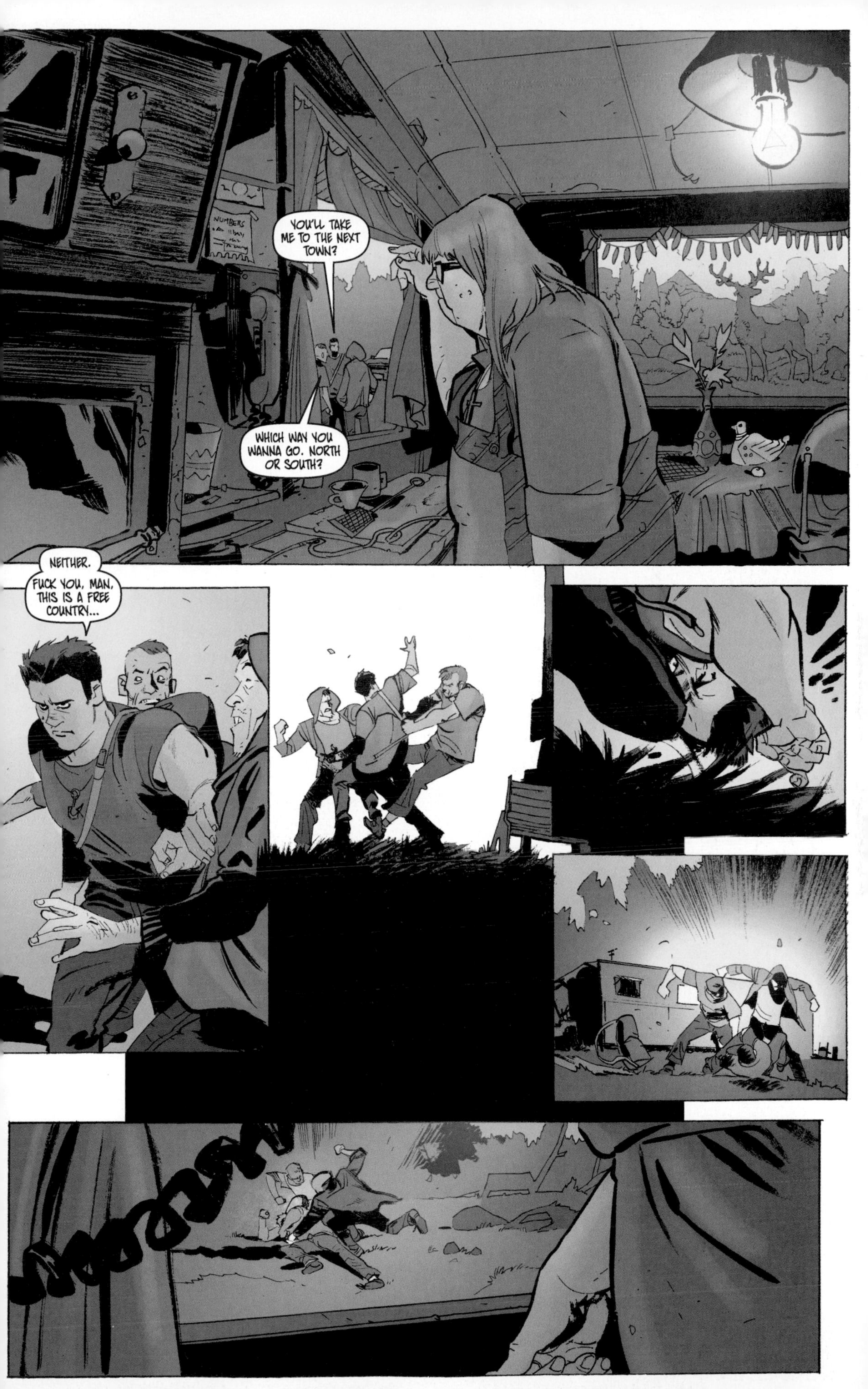
YOU'LL TAKE ME TO THE NEXT TOWN?
WHICH WAY YOU WANNA GO. NORTH OR SOUTH?
NEITHER. FUCK YOU, MAN. THIS IS A FREE COUNTRY...

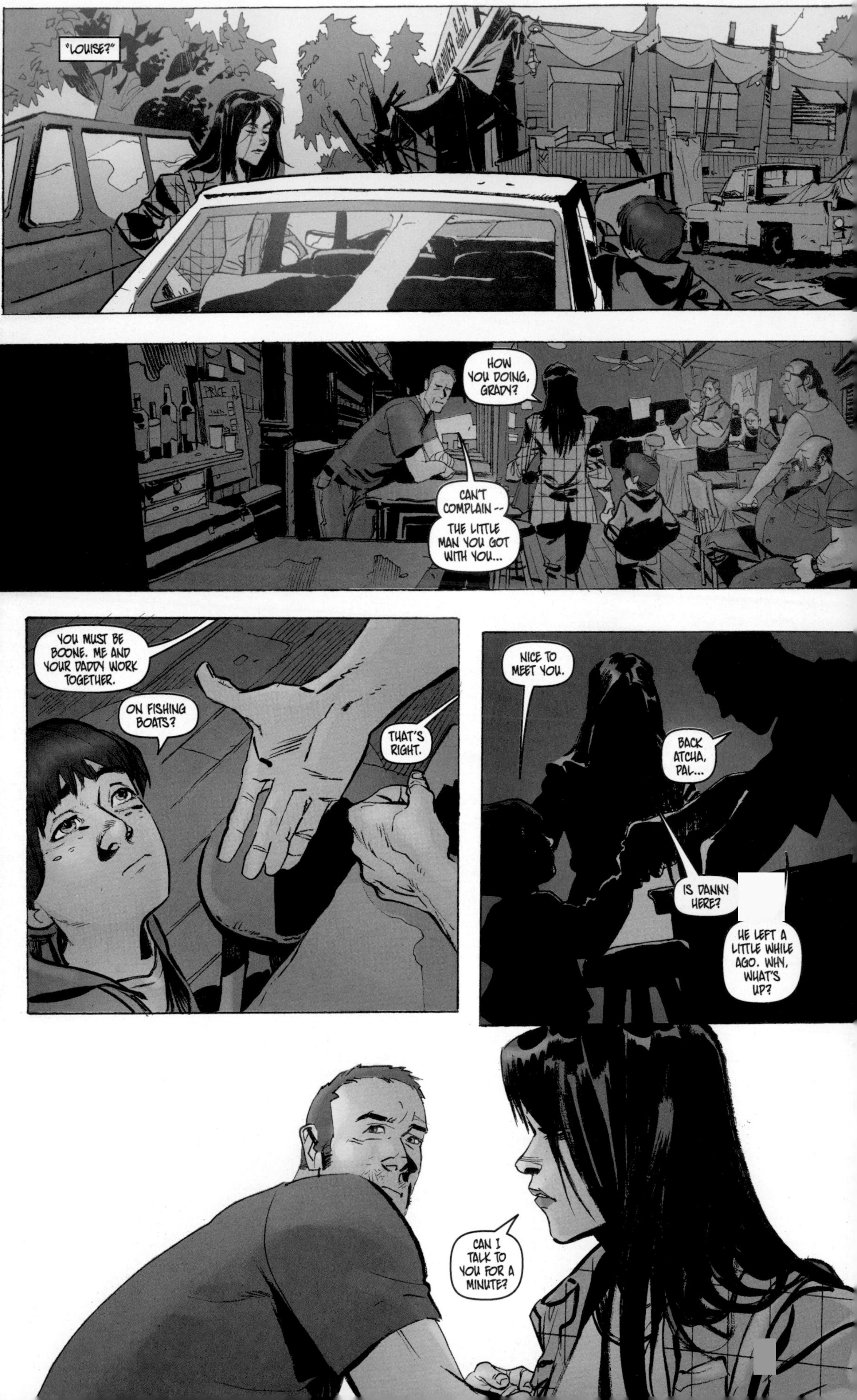
"LOUISE?"
HOW YOU DOING, GRADY?
CAN'T COMPLAIN -- THE LITTLE MAN YOU GOT WITH YOU...
YOU MUST BE BOONE. ME AND YOUR DADDY WORK TOGETHER.
ON FISHING BOATS?
THAT'S RIGHT.
NICE TO MEET YOU.
BACK ATCHA, PAL...
IS DANNY HERE?
HE LEFT A LITTLE WHILE AGO. WHY, WHAT'S UP?
CAN I TALK TO YOU FOR A MINUTE?

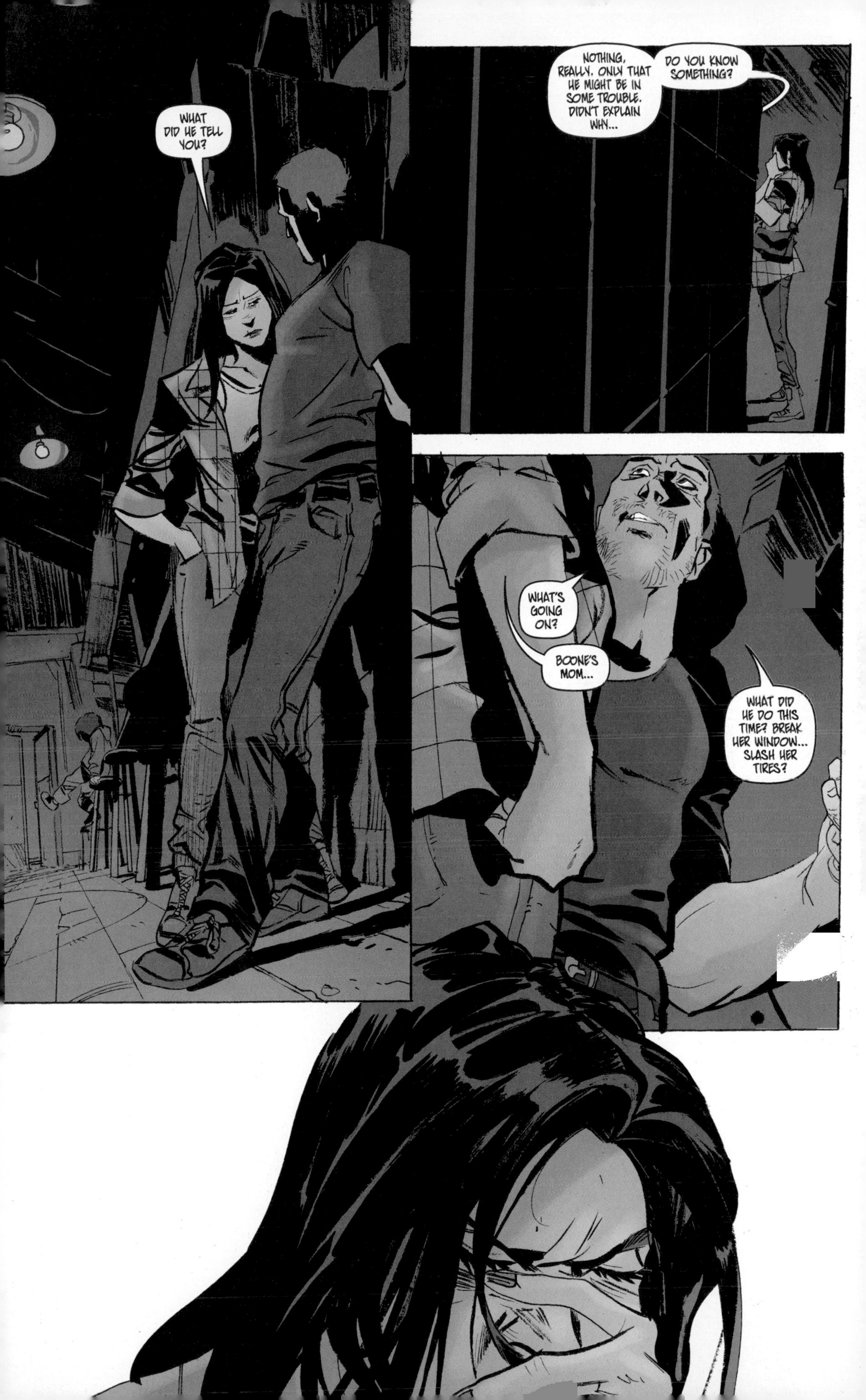
WHAT DID HE TELL YOU?
NOTHING, REALLY. ONLY THAT HE MIGHT BE IN SOME TROUBLE. DIDN'T EXPLAIN WHY...
DO YOU KNOW SOMETHING?
WHAT'S GOING ON?
BOONE'S MOM...
WHAT DID HE DO THIS TIME? BREAK HER WINDOW... SLASH HER TIRES?

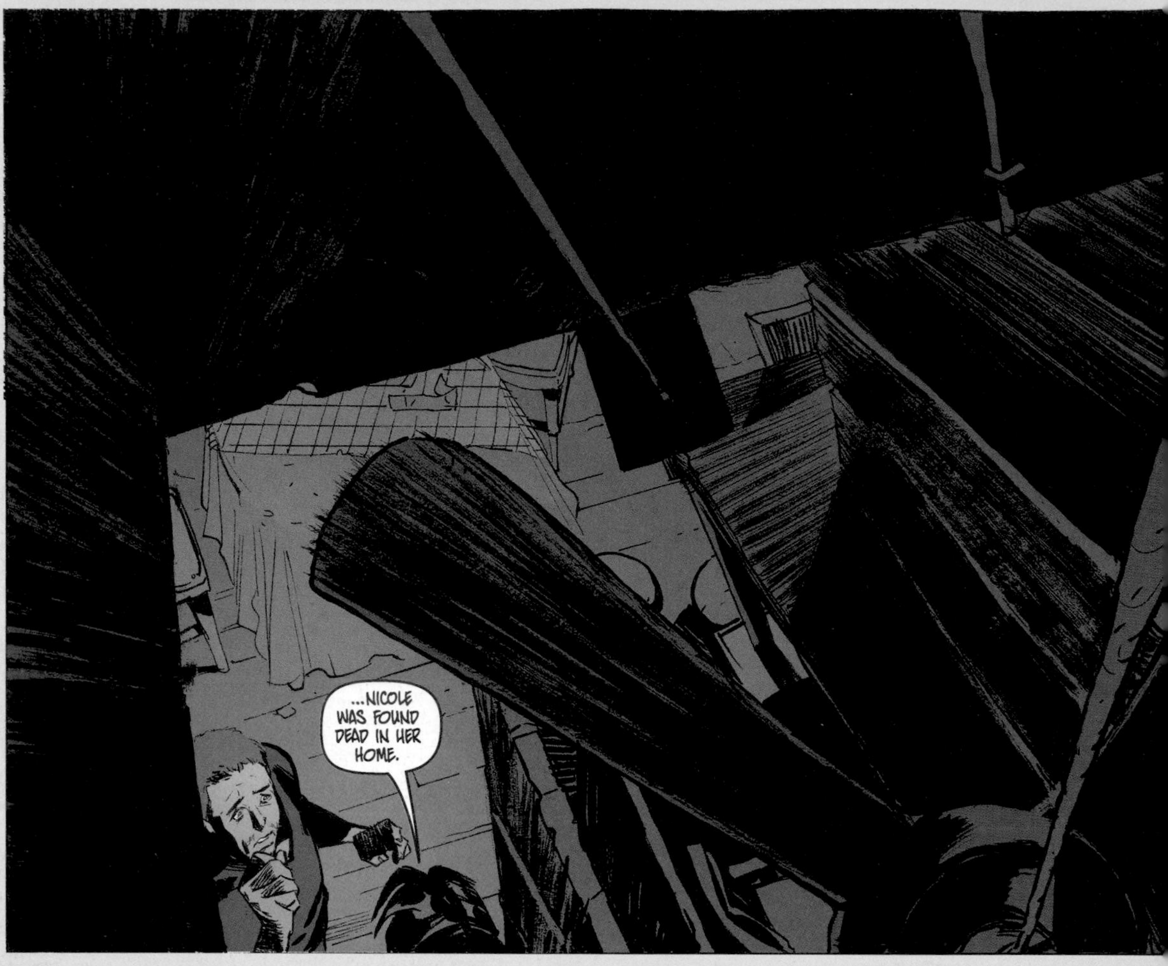
...NICOLE WAS FOUND DEAD IN HER HOME.

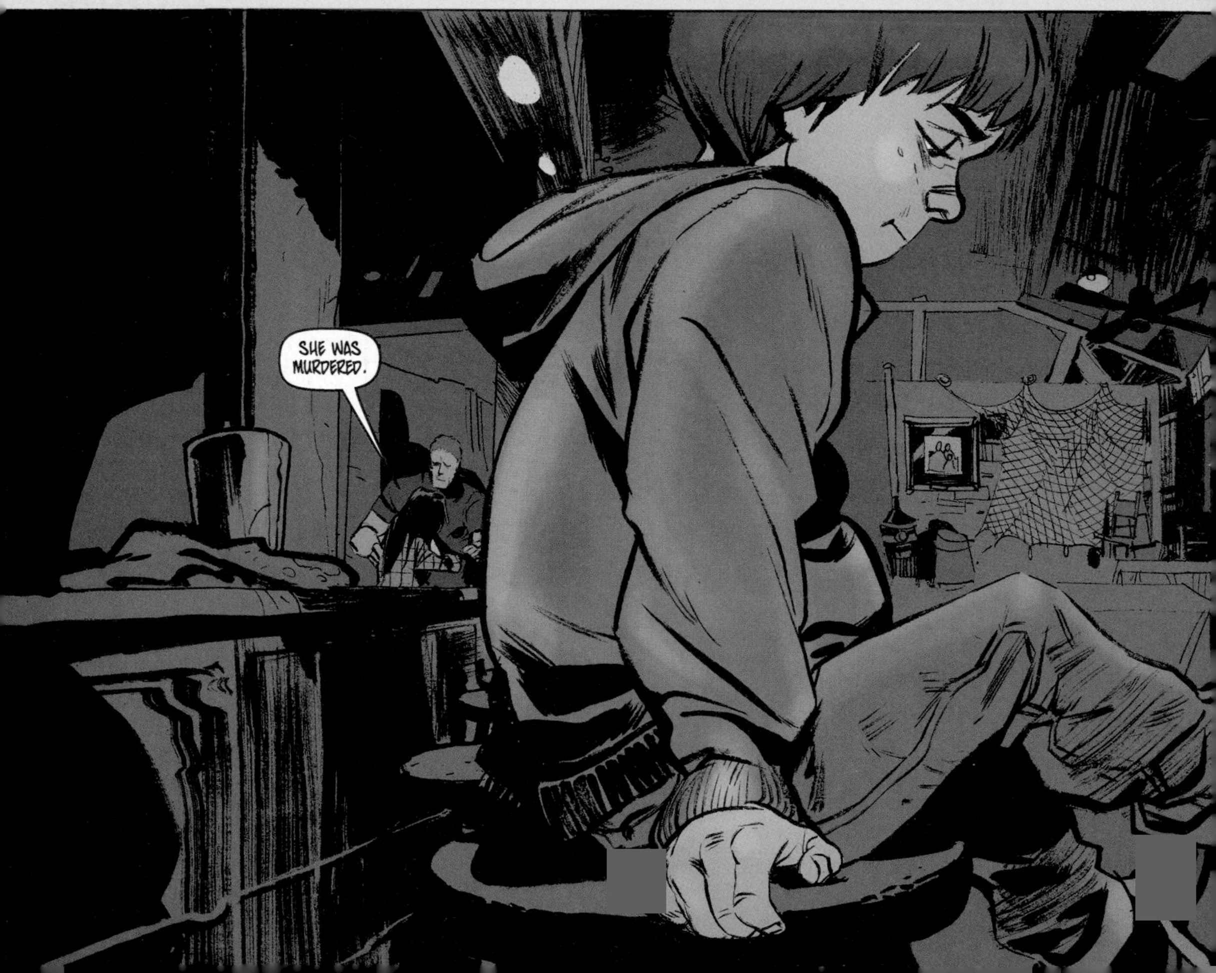
SHE WAS MURDERED.

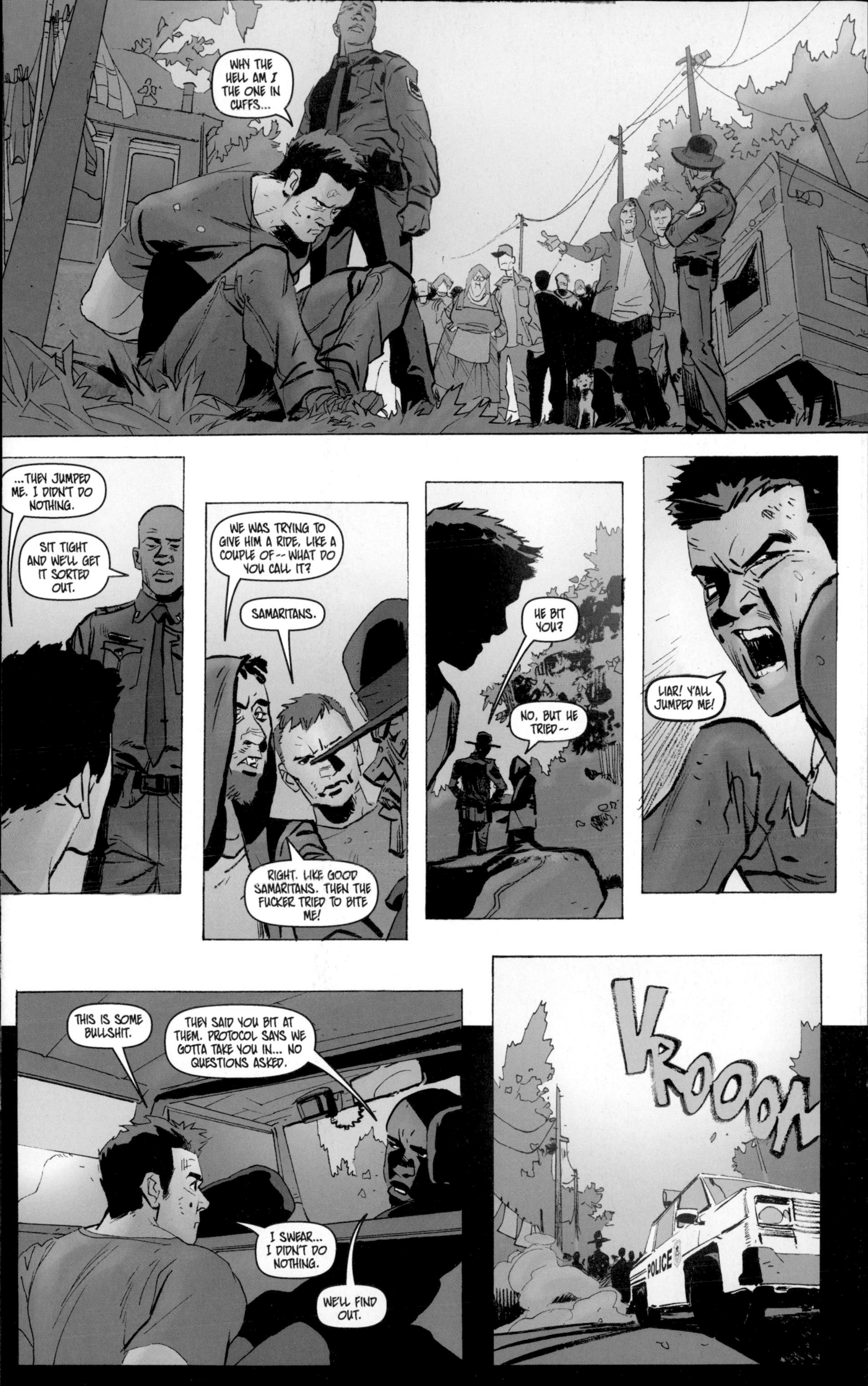

WHY THE HELL AM I THE ONE IN CUFFS...
...THEY JUMPED ME. I DIDN'T DO NOTHING.
SIT TIGHT AND WE'LL GET IT SORTED OUT.
WE WAS TRYING TO GIVE HIM A RIDE, LIKE A COUPLE OF-- WHAT DO YOU CALL IT?
SAMARITANS.
RIGHT. LIKE GOOD SAMARITANS. THEN THE FUCKER TRIED TO BITE ME!
HE BIT YOU?
NO, BUT HE TRIED--
LIAR! Y'ALL JUMPED ME!
THIS IS SOME BULLSHIT.
THEY SAID YOU BIT AT THEM. PROTOCOL SAYS WE GOTTA TAKE YOU IN... NO QUESTIONS ASKED.
I SWEAR... I DIDN'T DO NOTHING.
WE'LL FIND OUT.
VROOOM
POLICE

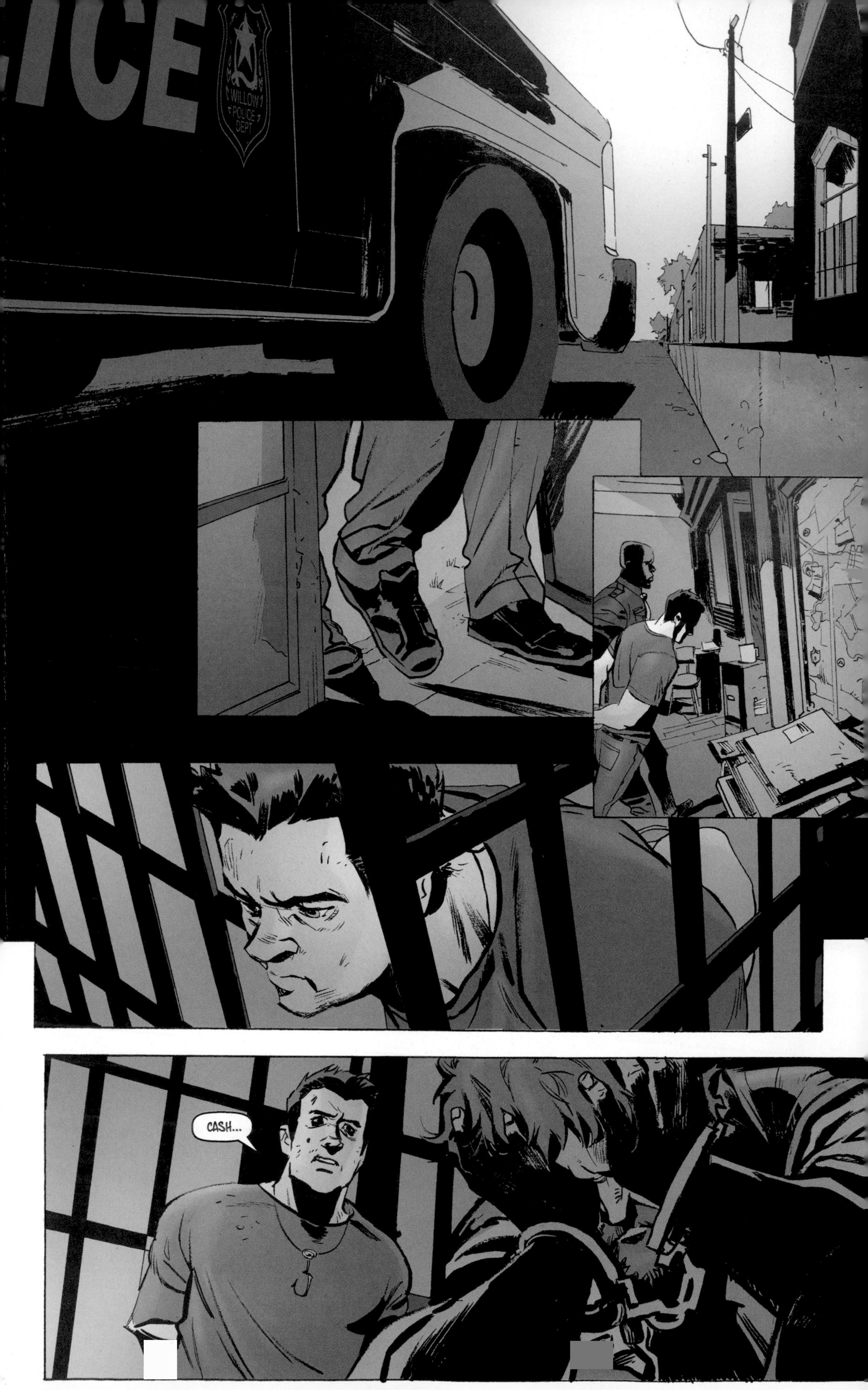
WILLOW POLICE DEPT
CASH...

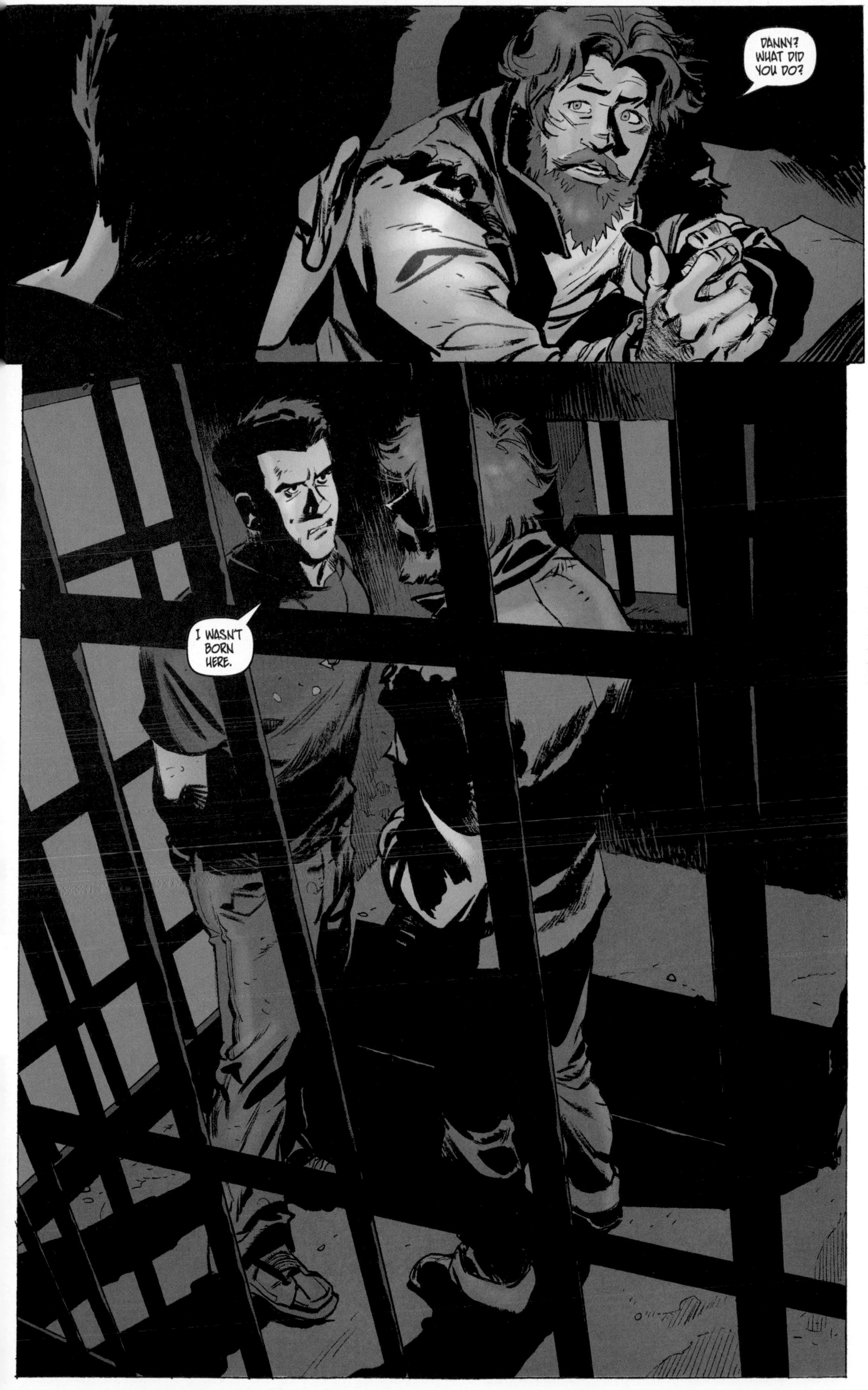
DANNY? WHAT DID YOU DO?
I WASN'T BORN HERE.

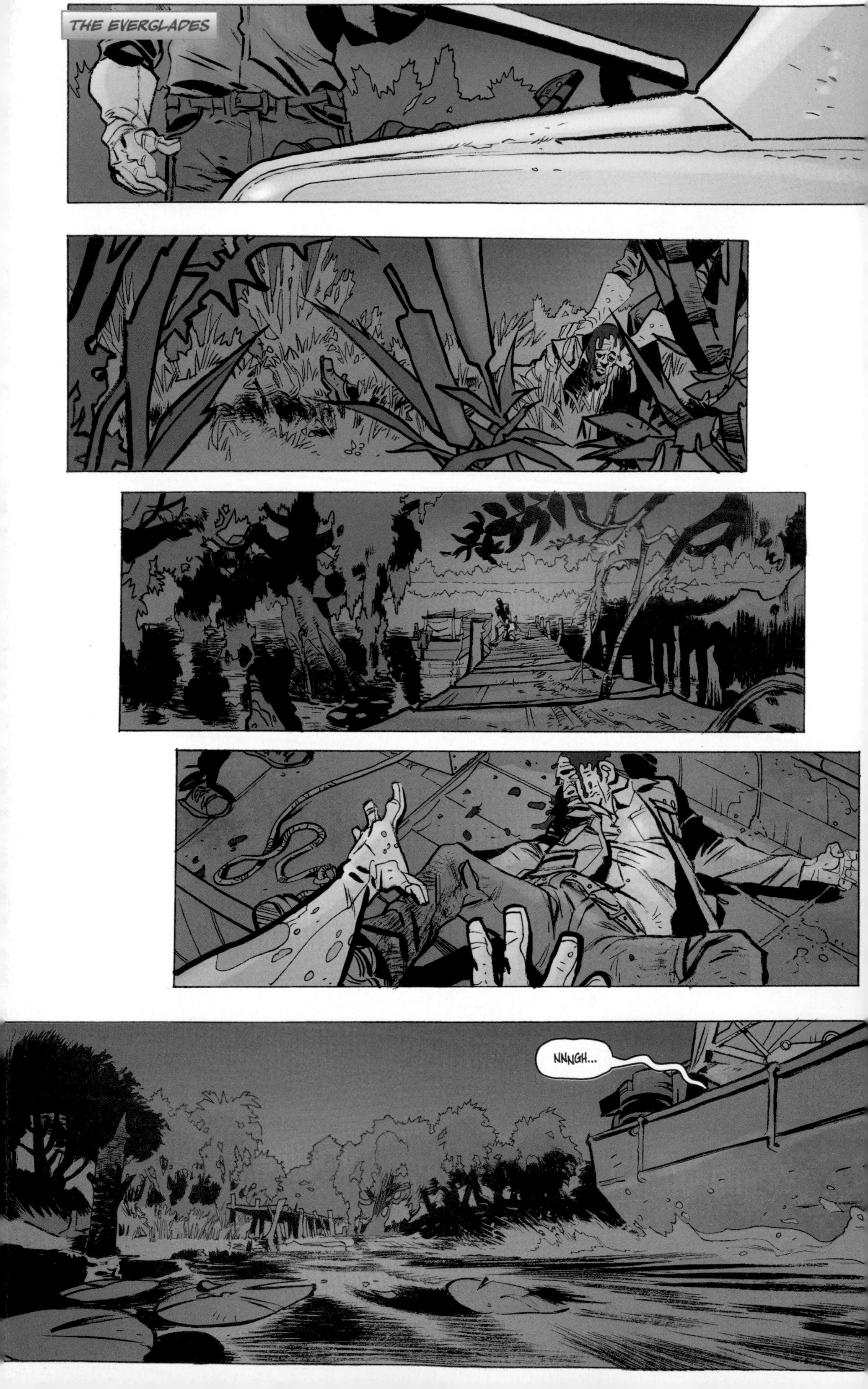
THE EVERGLADES
NNNGH...

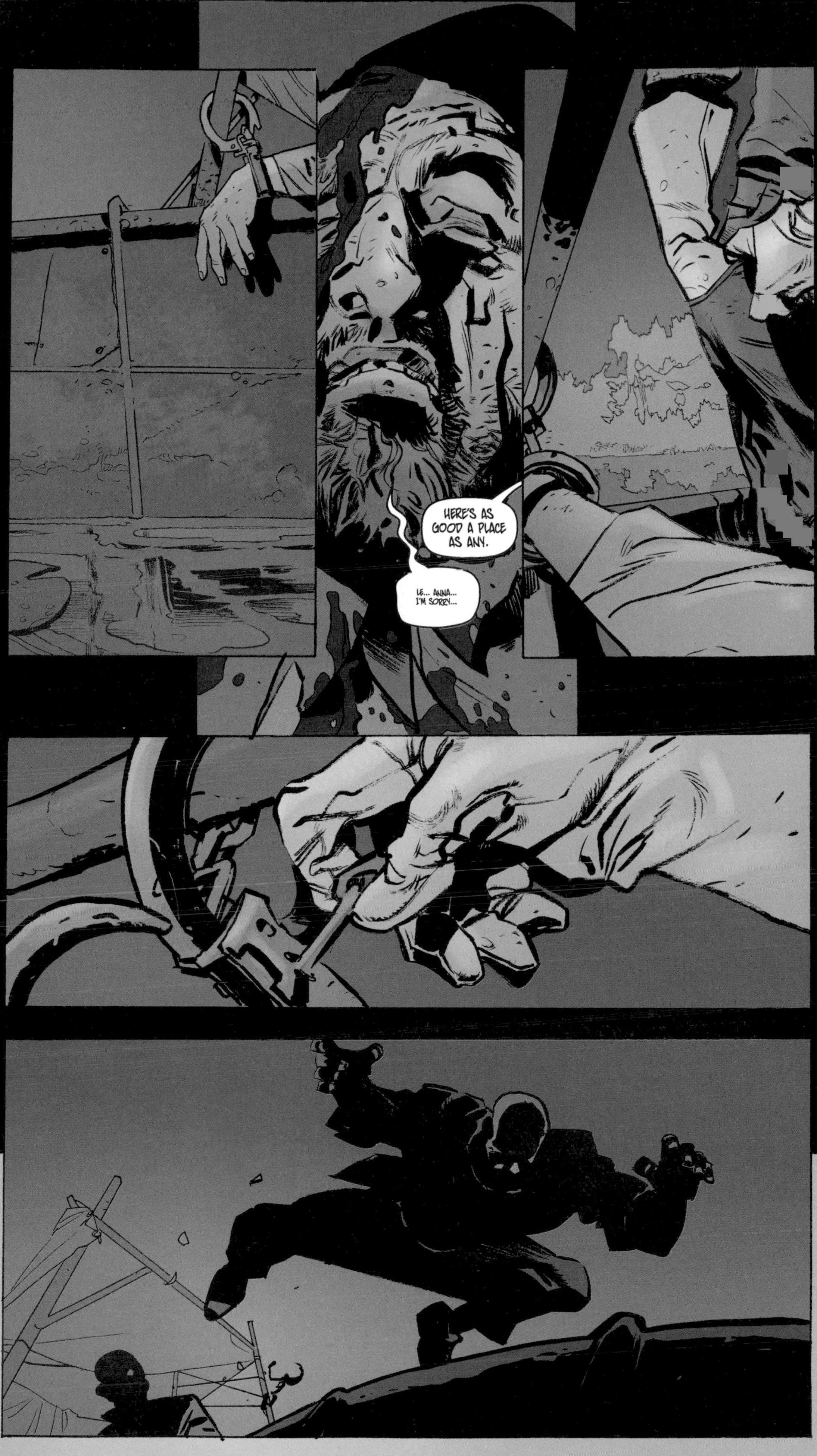
HERE'S AS GOOD A PLACE AS ANY.
LE... ANNA... I'M SORRY...

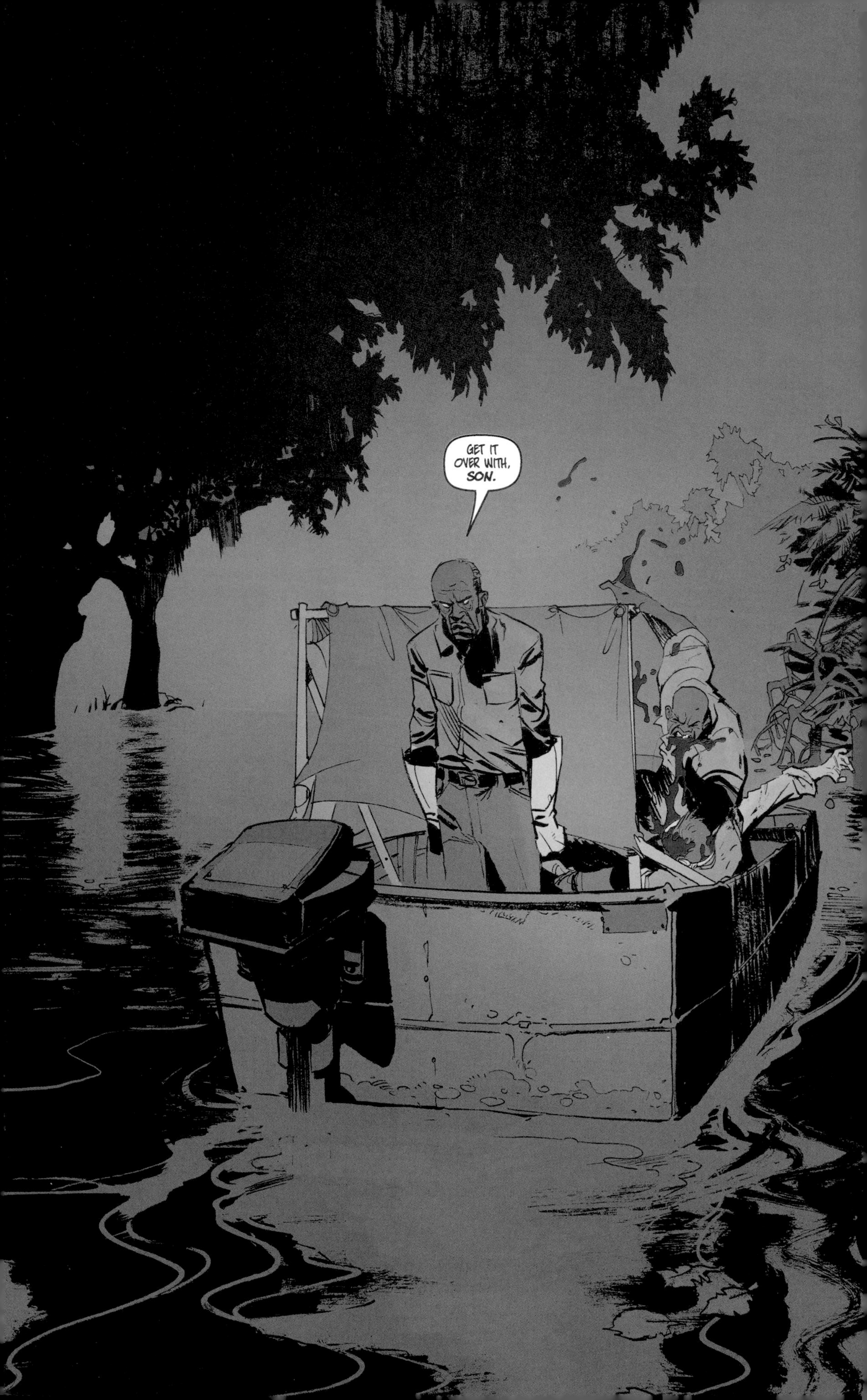
GET IT OVER WITH, SON.

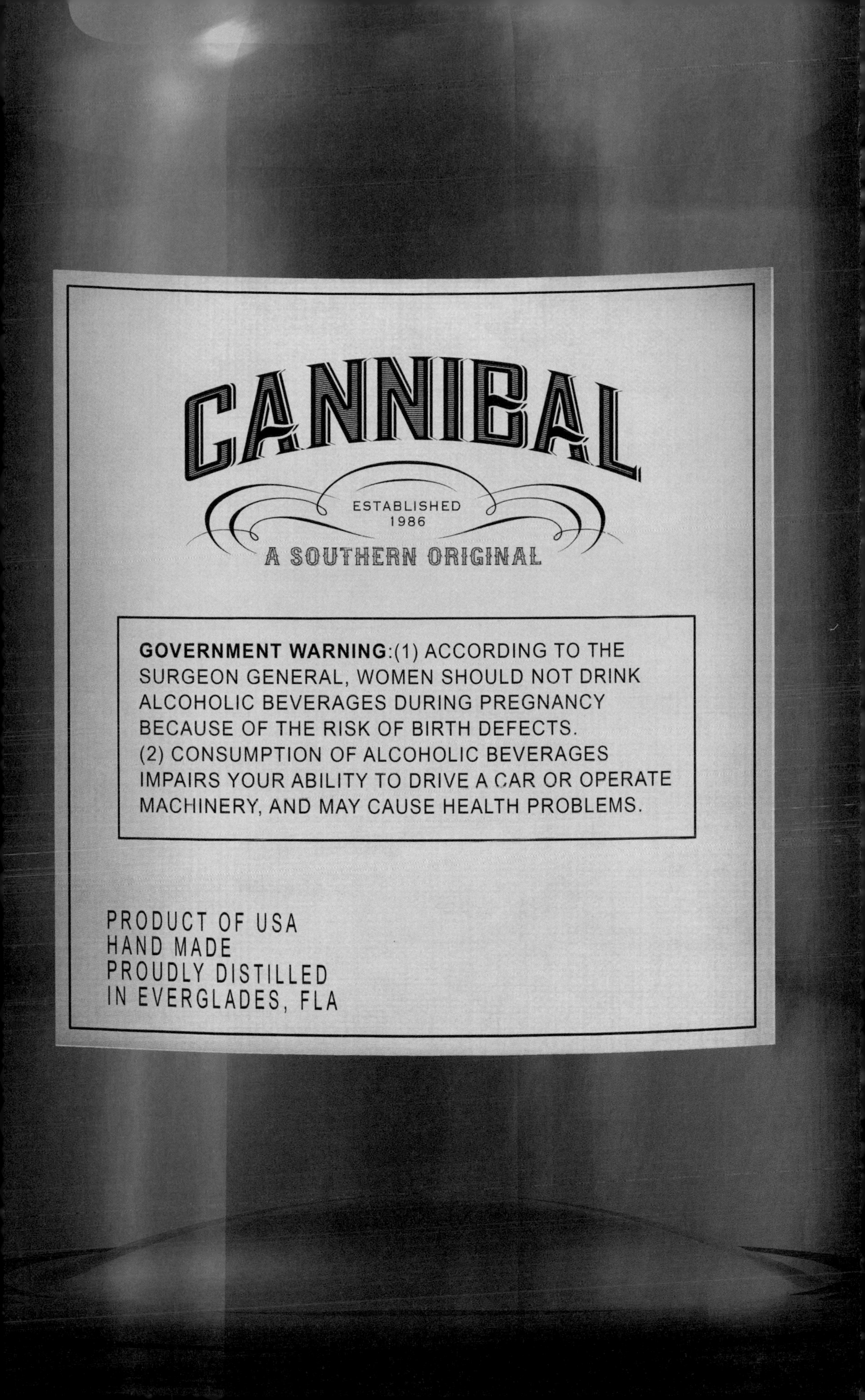
CANNIBAL
ESTABLISHED
1986
A SOUTHERN ORIGINAL
GOVERNMENT WARNING:(1) ACCORDING TO THE SURGEON GENERAL, WOMEN SHOULD NOT DRINK ALCOHOLIC BEVERAGES DURING PREGNANCY BECAUSE OF THE RISK OF BIRTH DEFECTS. (2) CONSUMPTION OF ALCOHOLIC BEVERAGES IMPAIRS YOUR ABILITY TO DRIVE A CAR OR OPERATE MACHINERY, AND MAY CAUSE HEALTH PROBLEMS.
PRODUCT OF USA
HAND MADE
PROUDLY DISTILLED
IN EVERGLADES, FLA

ISSUEFOUR

ESTABLISHED
1986

A SOUTHERN ORIGINAL

CANNIBAL

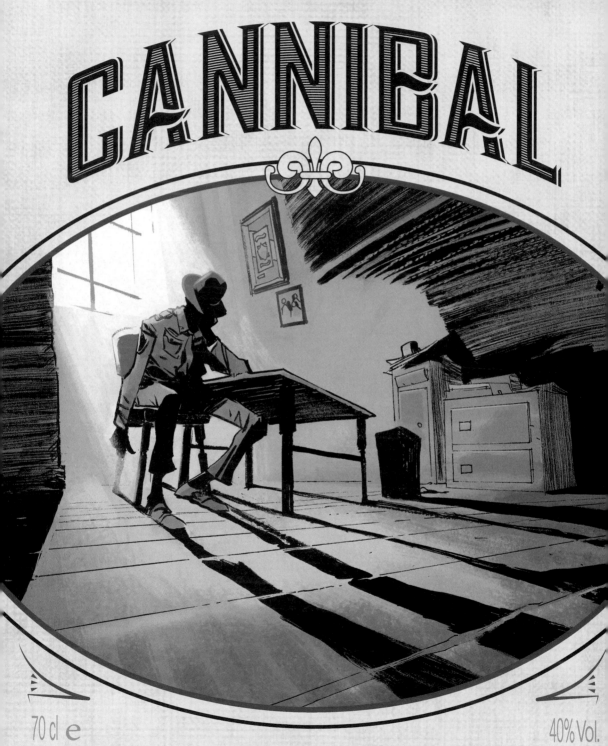

70 cl e

40% Vol.

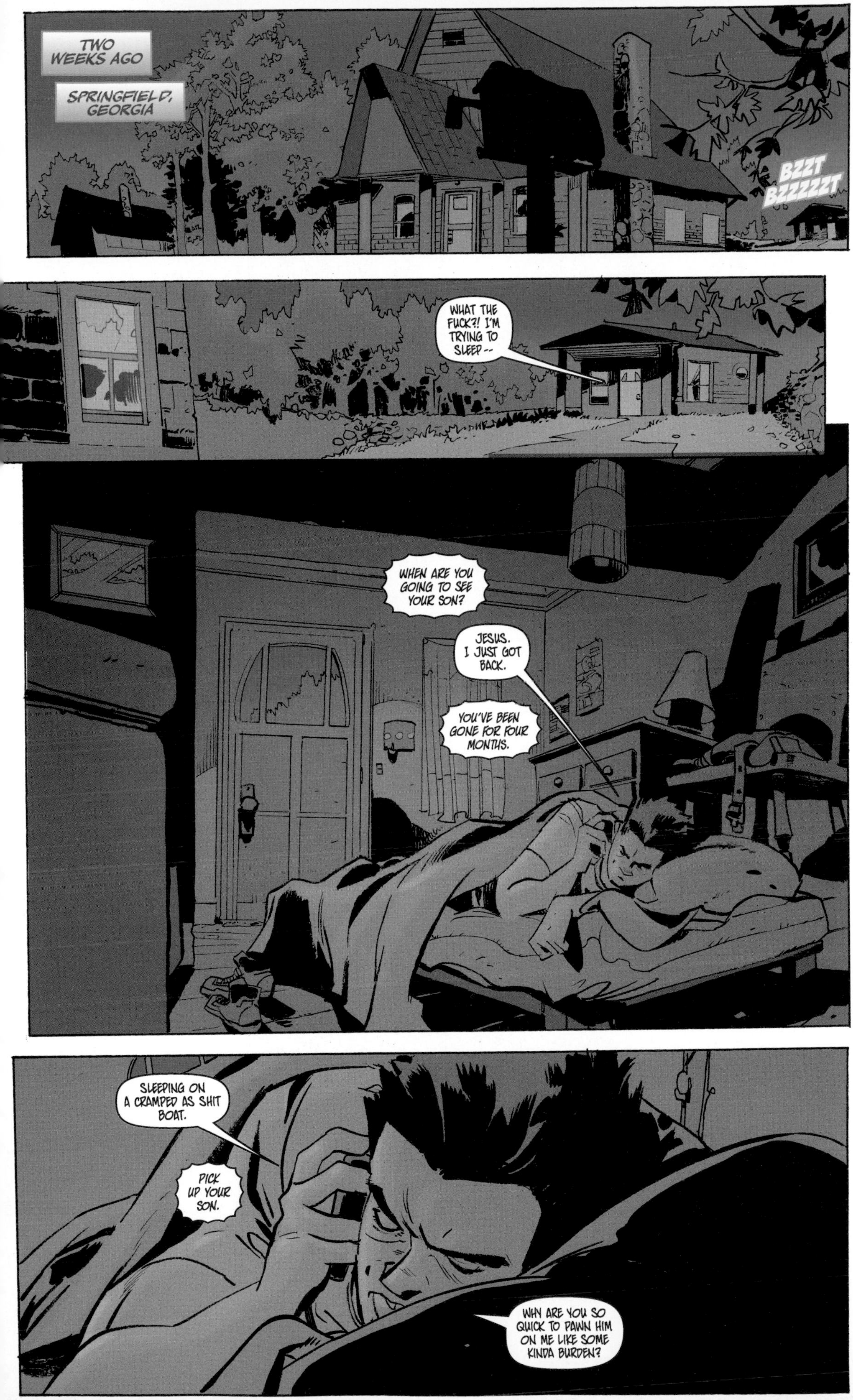
TWO WEEKS AGO
SPRINGFIELD, GEORGIA
BZZT BZZZZZT
WHAT THE FUCK?! I'M TRYING TO SLEEP --
WHEN ARE YOU GOING TO SEE YOUR SON?
JESUS. I JUST GOT BACK.
YOU'VE BEEN GONE FOR FOUR MONTHS.
SLEEPING ON A CRAMPED AS SHIT BOAT.
PICK UP YOUR SON.
WHY ARE YOU SO QUICK TO PAWN HIM ON ME LIKE SOME KINDA BURDEN?

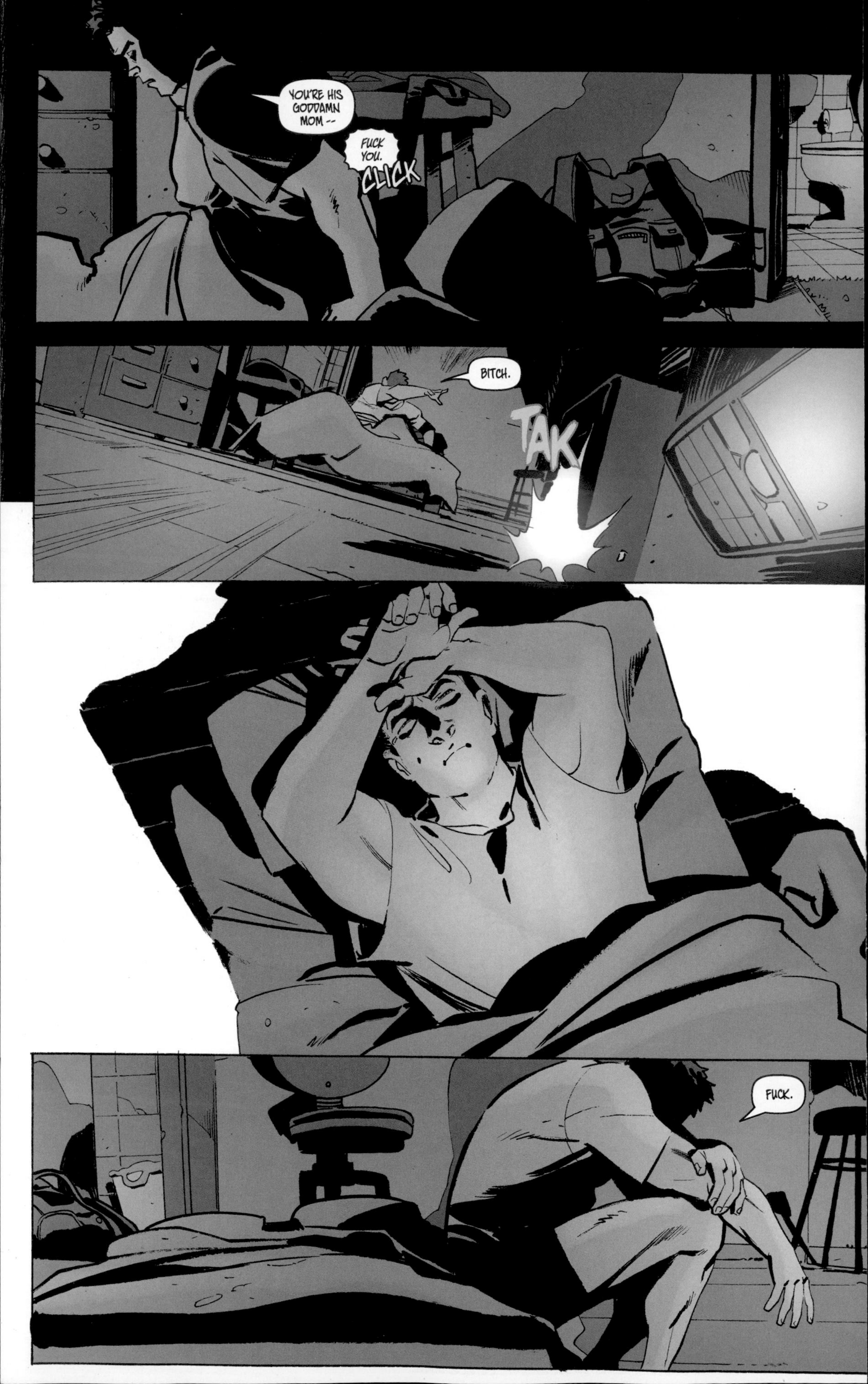
YOU'RE HIS GODDAMN MOM --
FUCK YOU.
CLICK
BITCH.
TAK
FUCK.

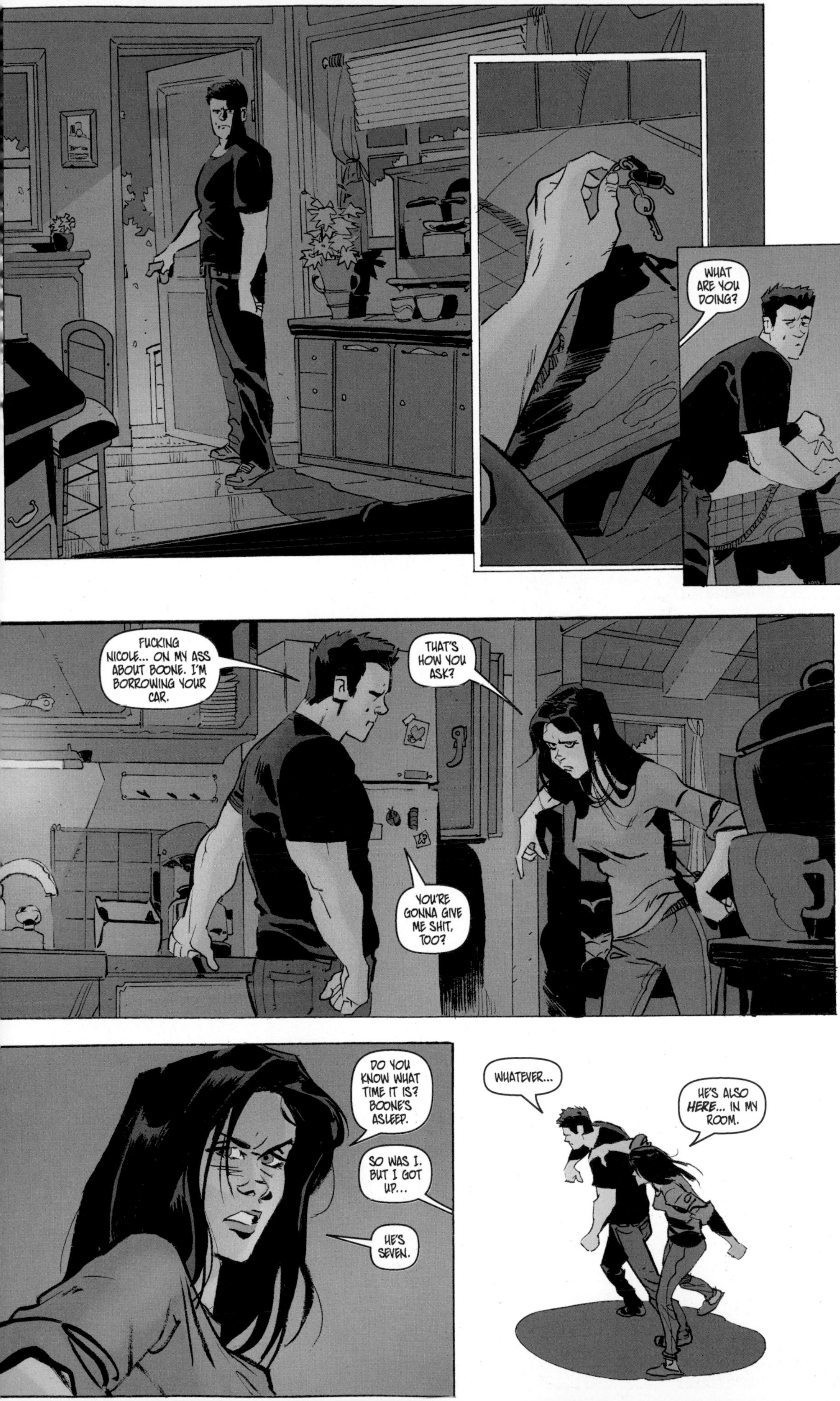
WHAT ARE YOU DOING?
FUCKING NICOLE... ON MY ASS ABOUT BOONE. I'M BORROWING YOUR CAR.
THAT'S HOW YOU ASK?
YOU'RE GONNA GIVE ME SHIT, TOO?
DO YOU KNOW WHAT TIME IT IS? BOONE'S ASLEEP.
SO WAS I. BUT I GOT UP...
HE'S SEVEN.
WHATEVER...
HE'S ALSO HERE... IN MY ROOM.

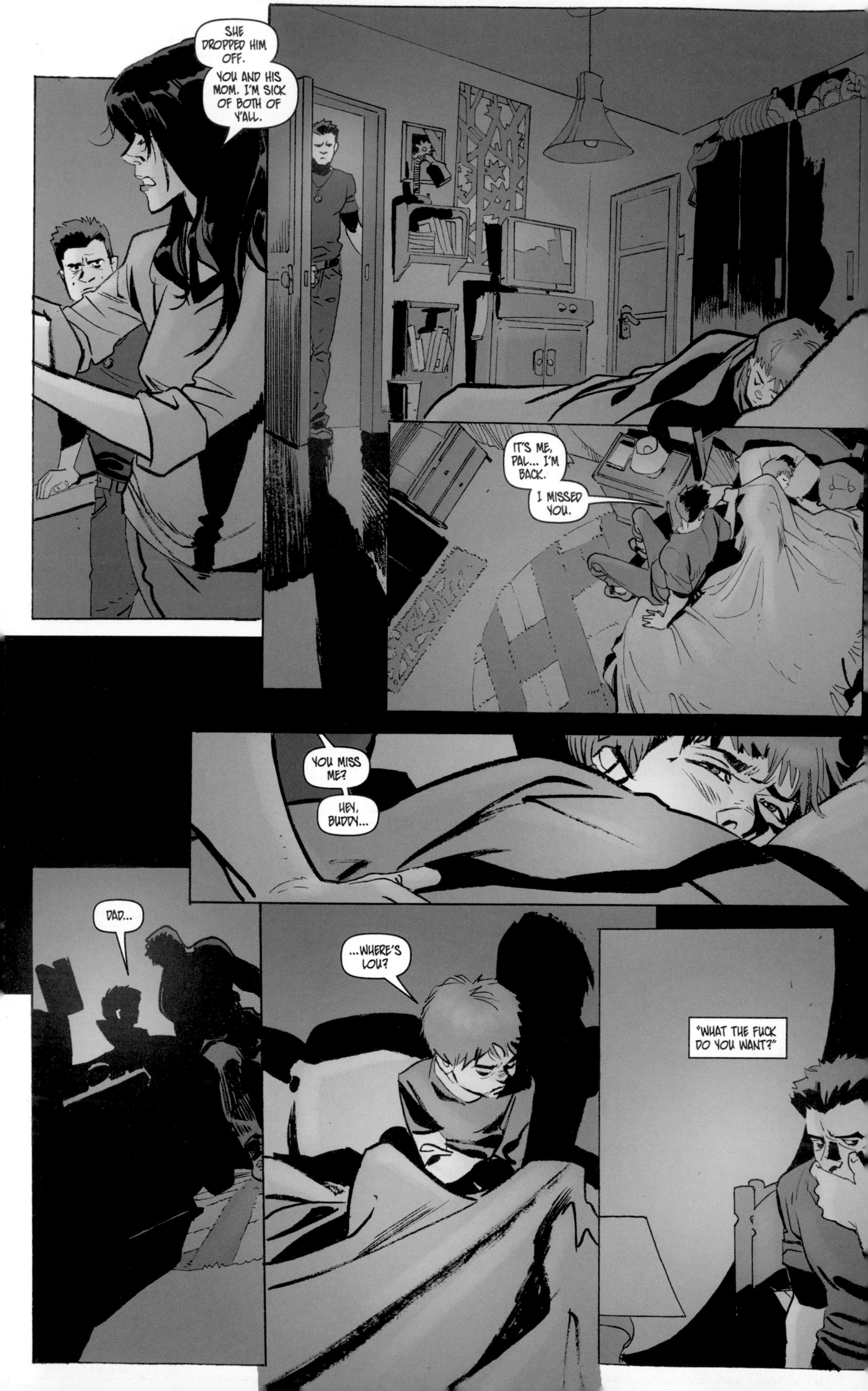
SHE DROPPED HIM OFF.
YOU AND HIS MOM. I'M SICK OF BOTH OF Y'ALL.
IT'S ME, PAL... I'M BACK.
I MISSED YOU.
YOU MISS ME?
HEY, BUDDY...
DAD...
...WHERE'S LOU?
"WHAT THE FUCK DO YOU WANT?"

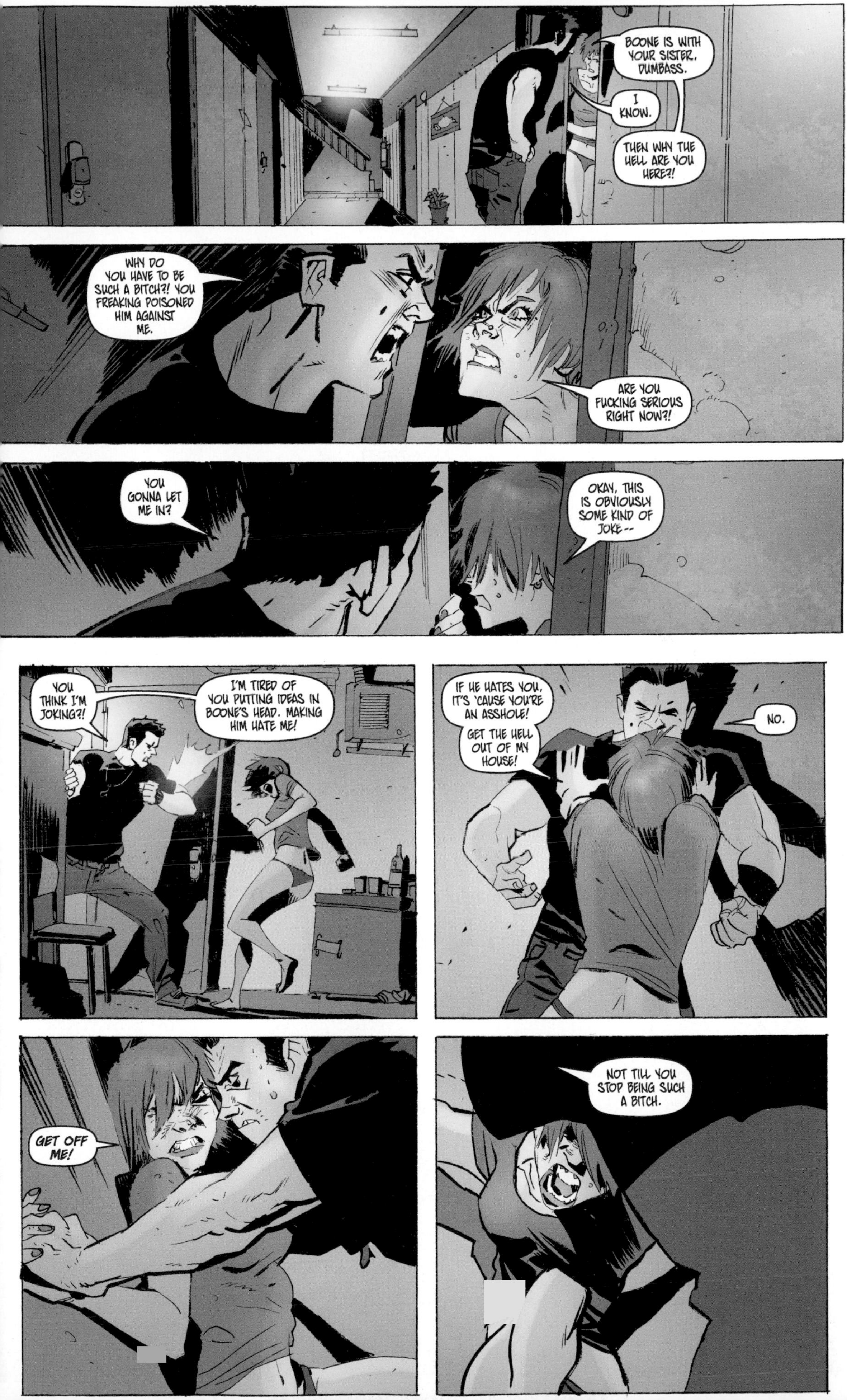
BOONE IS WITH YOUR SISTER, DUMBASS.
I KNOW.
THEN WHY THE HELL ARE YOU HERE?!
WHY DO YOU HAVE TO BE SUCH A BITCH?! YOU FREAKING POISONED HIM AGAINST ME.
ARE YOU FUCKING SERIOUS RIGHT NOW?!
YOU GONNA LET ME IN?
OKAY, THIS IS OBVIOUSLY SOME KIND OF JOKE--
YOU THINK I'M JOKING?!
I'M TIRED OF YOU PUTTING IDEAS IN BOONE'S HEAD. MAKING HIM HATE ME!
IF HE HATES YOU, IT'S 'CAUSE YOU'RE AN ASSHOLE!
GET THE HELL OUT OF MY HOUSE!
NO.
GET OFF ME!
NOT TILL YOU STOP BEING SUCH A BITCH.

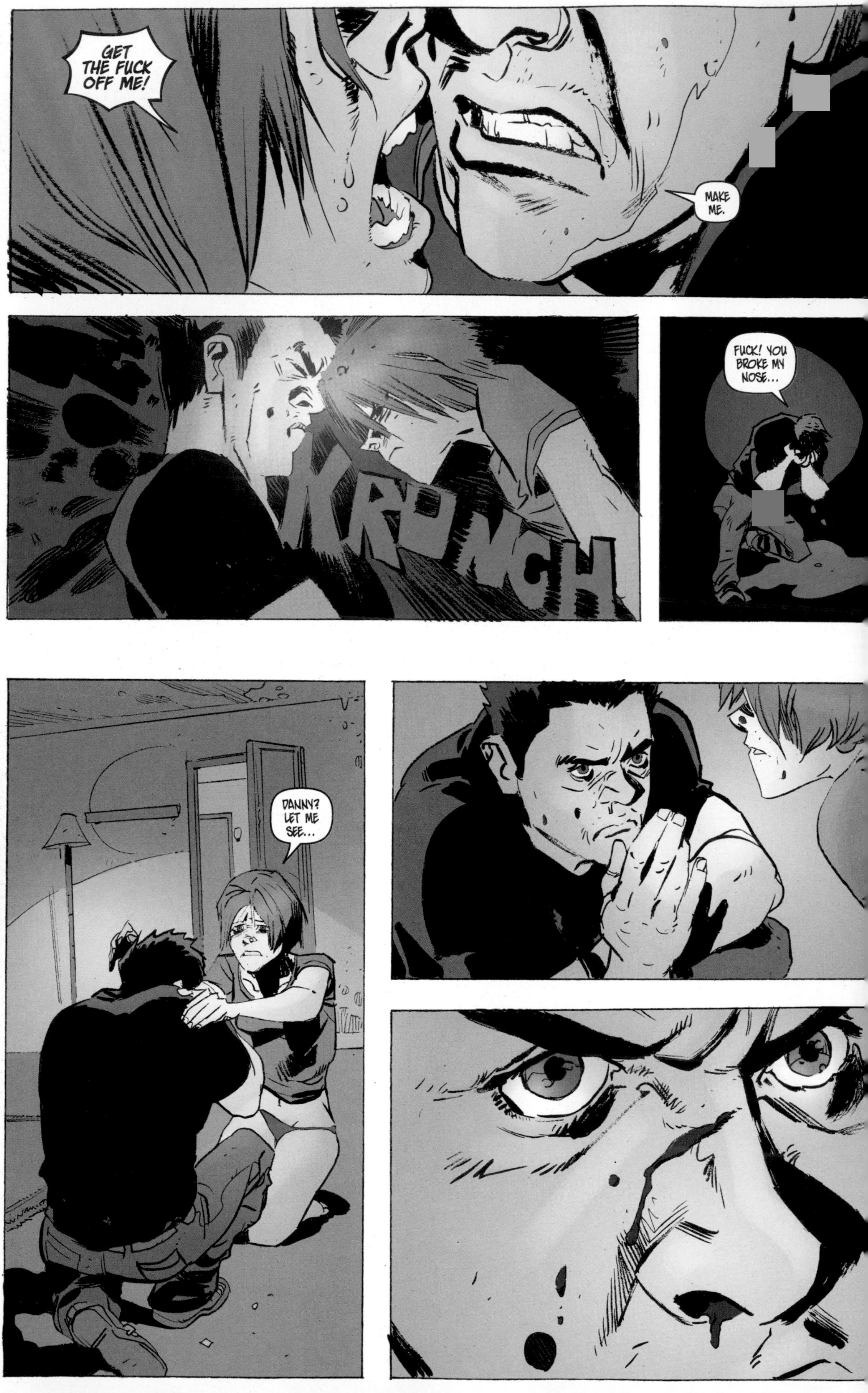
GET THE FUCK OFF ME!
MAKE ME.
KRUNCH
FUCK! YOU BROKE MY NOSE...
DANNY? LET ME SEE...

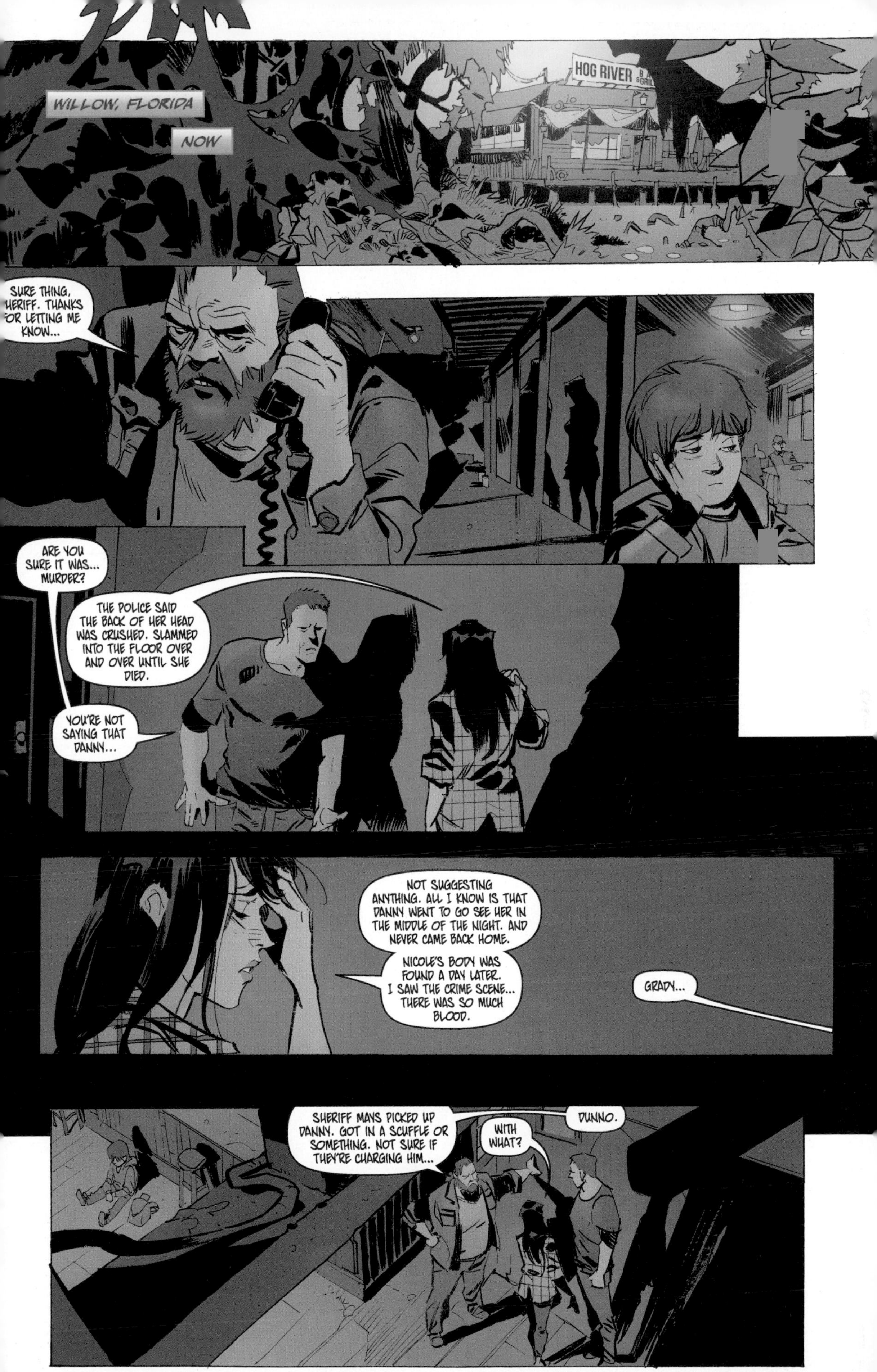

HOG RIVER
WILLOW, FLORIDA
NOW
SURE THING, SHERIFF. THANKS FOR LETTING ME KNOW...
ARE YOU SURE IT WAS... MURDER?
THE POLICE SAID THE BACK OF HER HEAD WAS CRUSHED. SLAMMED INTO THE FLOOR OVER AND OVER UNTIL SHE DIED.
YOU'RE NOT SAYING THAT DANNY...
NOT SUGGESTING ANYTHING. ALL I KNOW IS THAT DANNY WENT TO GO SEE HER IN THE MIDDLE OF THE NIGHT. AND NEVER CAME BACK HOME.
NICOLE'S BODY WAS FOUND A DAY LATER. I SAW THE CRIME SCENE... THERE WAS SO MUCH BLOOD.
GRADY...
SHERIFF MAYS PICKED UP DANNY. GOT IN A SCUFFLE OR SOMETHING. NOT SURE IF THEY'RE CHARGING HIM...
WITH WHAT?
DUNNO.

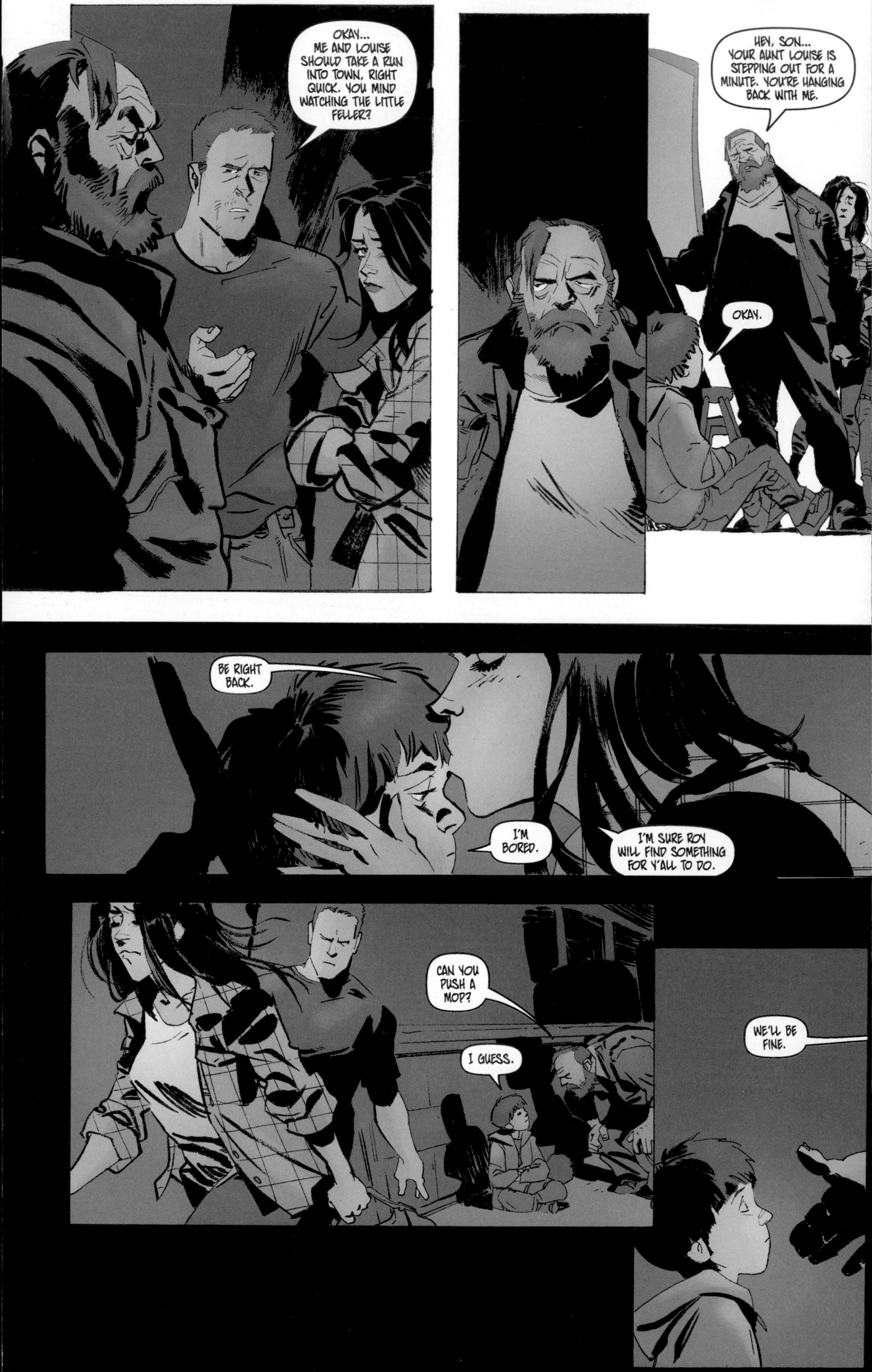
OKAY... ME AND LOUISE SHOULD TAKE A RUN INTO TOWN, RIGHT QUICK. YOU MIND WATCHING THE LITTLE FELLER?
HEY, SON... YOUR AUNT LOUISE IS STEPPING OUT FOR A MINUTE. YOU'RE HANGING BACK WITH ME.
OKAY.
BE RIGHT BACK.
I'M BORED.
I'M SURE ROY WILL FIND SOMETHING FOR Y'ALL TO DO.
CAN YOU PUSH A MOP?
I GUESS.
WE'LL BE FINE.

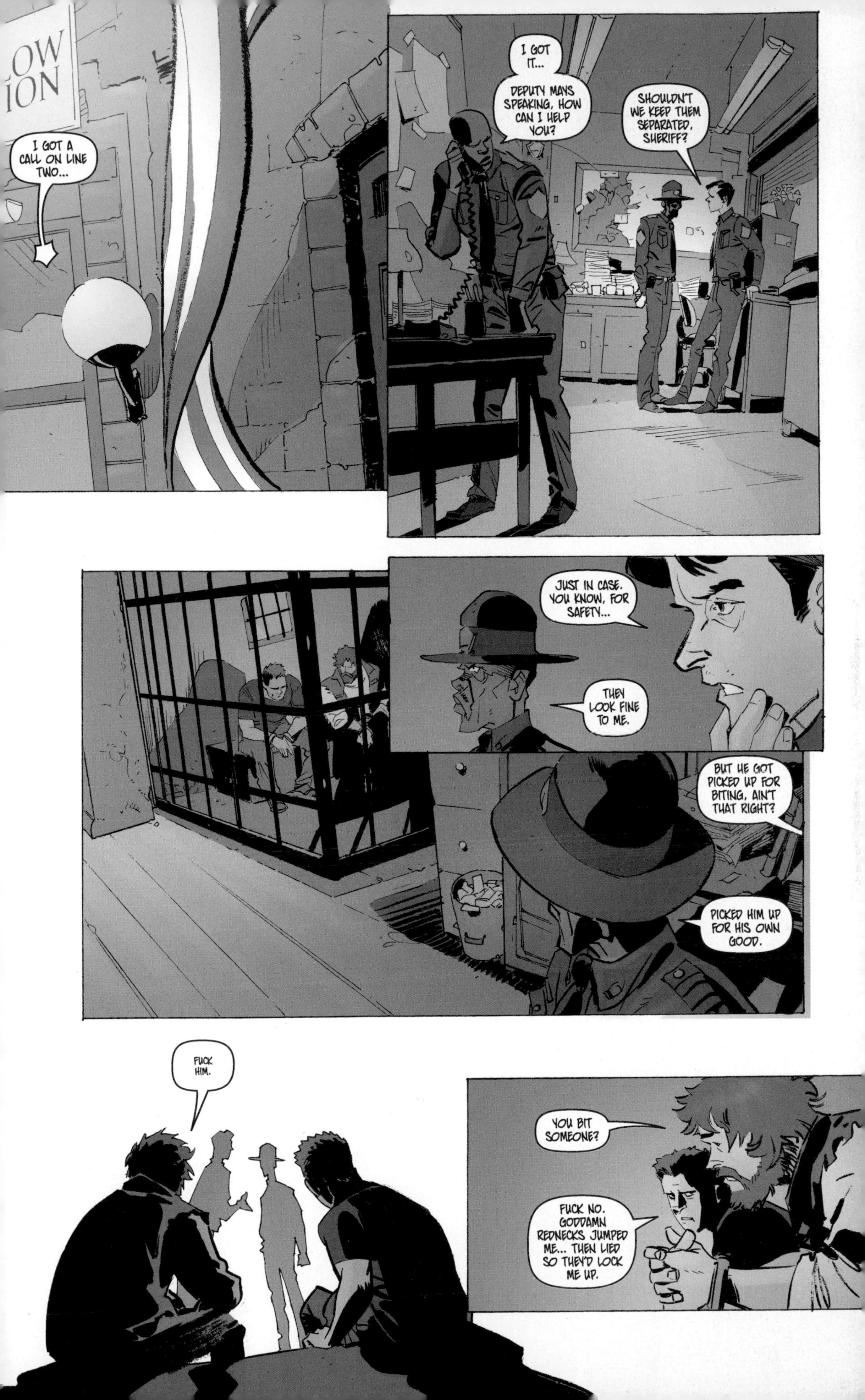

OW
ION
I GOT A CALL ON LINE TWO...
I GOT IT...
DEPUTY MAYS SPEAKING, HOW CAN I HELP YOU?
SHOULDN'T WE KEEP THEM SEPARATED, SHERIFF?
JUST IN CASE. YOU KNOW, FOR SAFETY...
THEY LOOK FINE TO ME.
BUT HE GOT PICKED UP FOR BITING, AIN'T THAT RIGHT?
PICKED HIM UP FOR HIS OWN GOOD.
FUCK HIM.
YOU BIT SOMEONE?
FUCK NO. GODDAMN REDNECKS JUMPED ME... THEN LIED SO THEY'D LOCK ME UP.

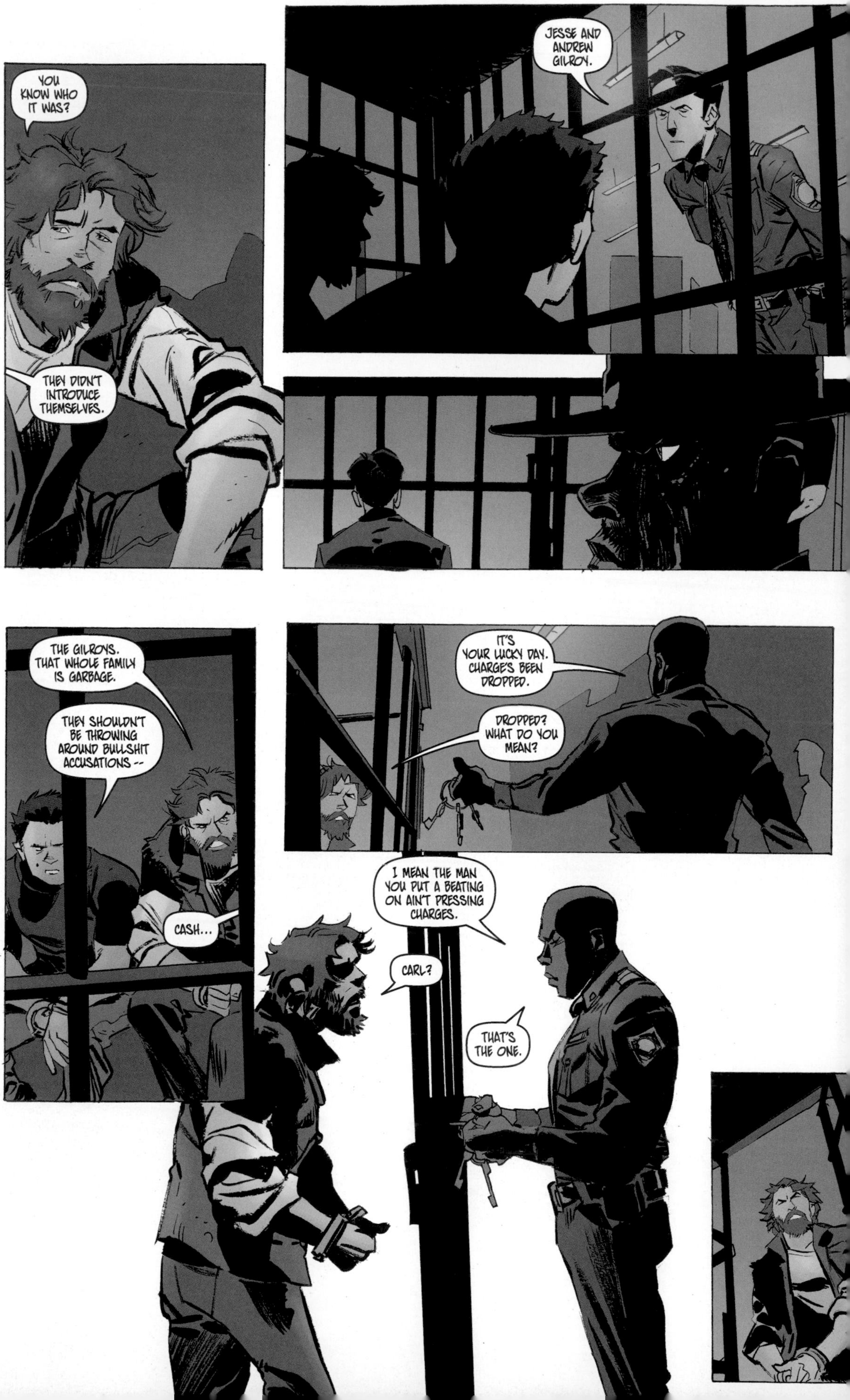
YOU KNOW WHO IT WAS?
JESSE AND ANDREW GILROY.
THEY DIDN'T INTRODUCE THEMSELVES.
THE GILROYS. THAT WHOLE FAMILY IS GARBAGE.
THEY SHOULDN'T BE THROWING AROUND BULLSHIT ACCUSATIONS --
CASH...
IT'S YOUR LUCKY DAY. CHARGE'S BEEN DROPPED.
DROPPED? WHAT DO YOU MEAN?
I MEAN THE MAN YOU PUT A BEATING ON AIN'T PRESSING CHARGES.
CARL?
THAT'S THE ONE.

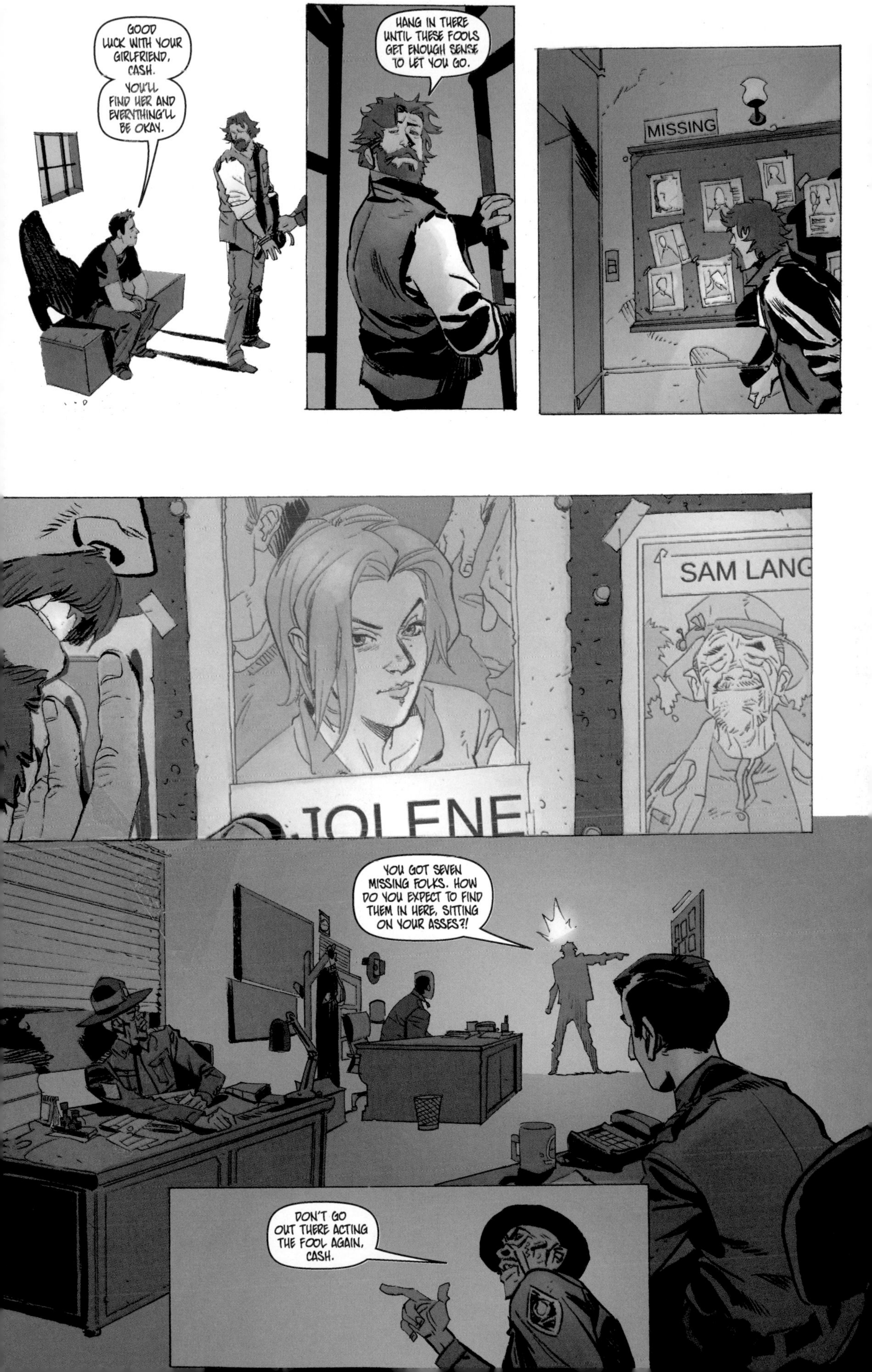
GOOD LUCK WITH YOUR GIRLFRIEND, CASH.
YOU'LL FIND HER AND EVERYTHING'LL BE OKAY.
HANG IN THERE UNTIL THESE FOOLS GET ENOUGH SENSE TO LET YOU GO.
MISSING
SAM LANG
JOLENE
YOU GOT SEVEN MISSING FOLKS. HOW DO YOU EXPECT TO FIND THEM IN HERE, SITTING ON YOUR ASSES?!
DON'T GO OUT THERE ACTING THE FOOL AGAIN, CASH.

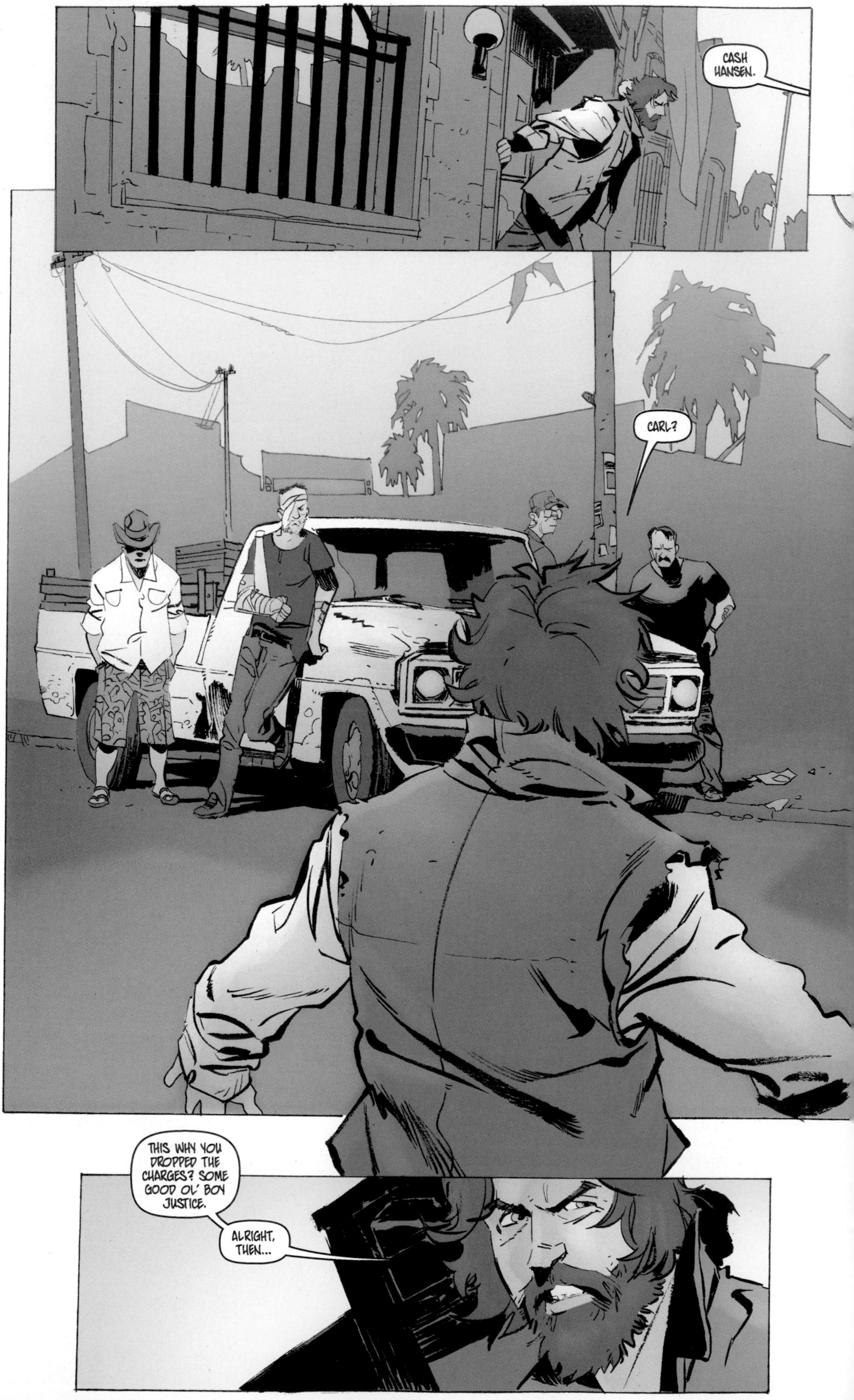
CASH HANSEN.
CARL?
THIS WHY YOU DROPPED THE CHARGES? SOME GOOD OL' BOY JUSTICE.
ALRIGHT, THEN...

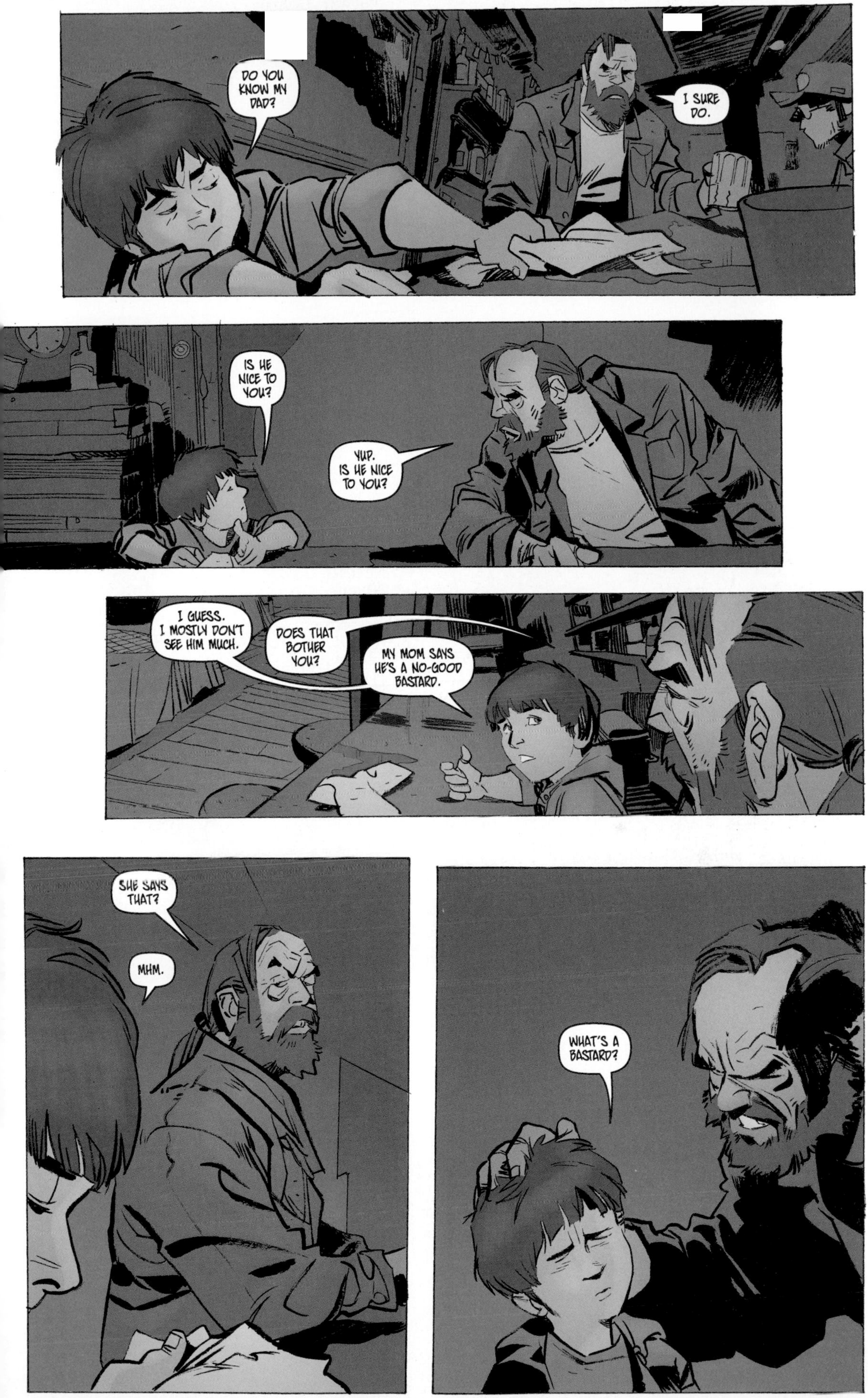
DO YOU KNOW MY DAD?
I SURE DO.
IS HE NICE TO YOU?
YUP. IS HE NICE TO YOU?
I GUESS. I MOSTLY DON'T SEE HIM MUCH.
DOES THAT BOTHER YOU?
MY MOM SAYS HE'S A NO-GOOD BASTARD.
SHE SAYS THAT?
MHM.
WHAT'S A BASTARD?

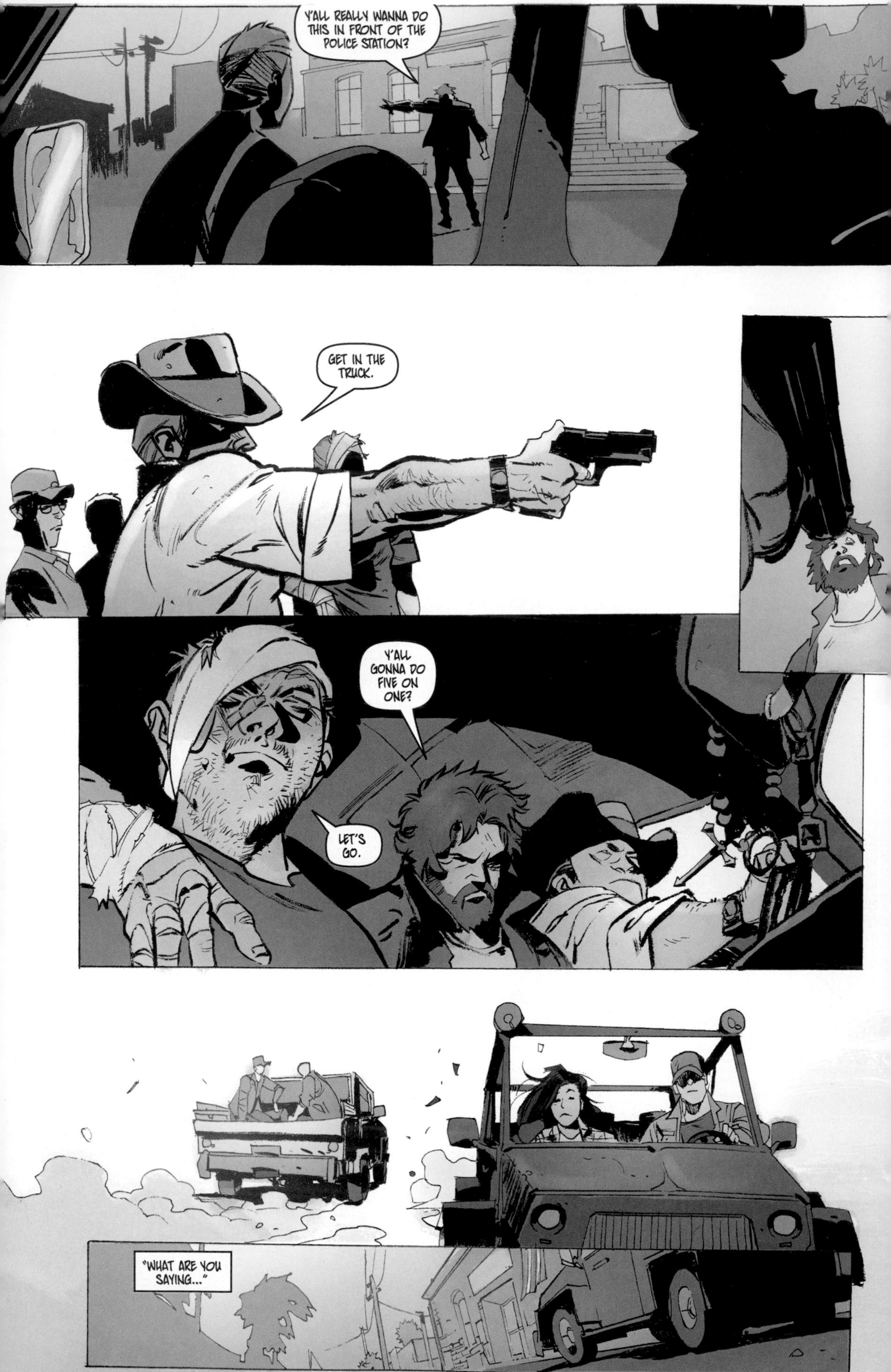
Y'ALL REALLY WANNA DO THIS IN FRONT OF THE POLICE STATION?
GET IN THE TRUCK.
Y'ALL GONNA DO FIVE ON ONE?
LET'S GO.
"WHAT ARE YOU SAYING..."

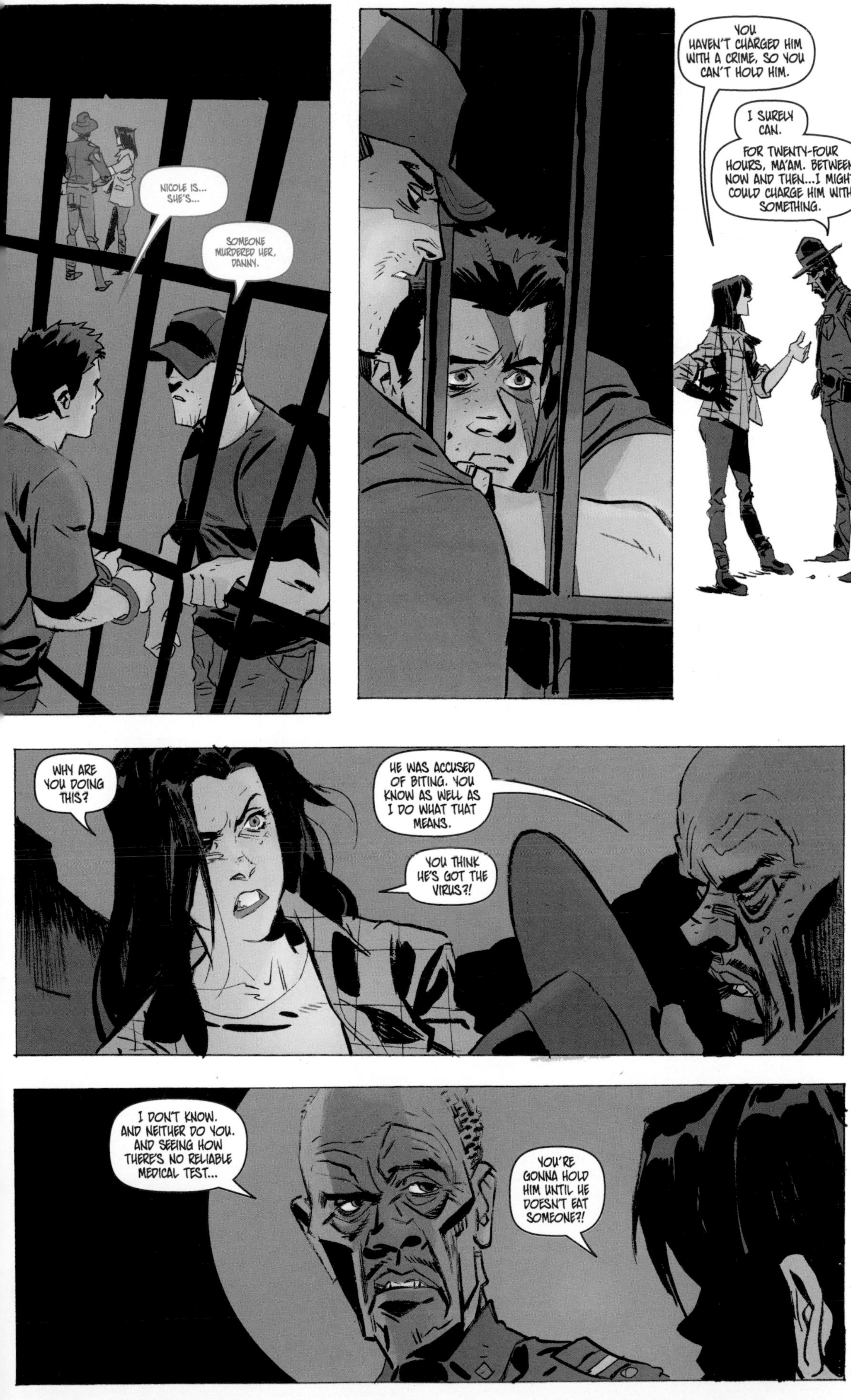
NICOLE IS... SHE'S...
SOMEONE MURDERED HER, DANNY.
YOU HAVEN'T CHARGED HIM WITH A CRIME, SO YOU CAN'T HOLD HIM.
I SURELY CAN.
FOR TWENTY-FOUR HOURS, MA'AM. BETWEEN NOW AND THEN...I MIGHT COULD CHARGE HIM WITH SOMETHING.
WHY ARE YOU DOING THIS?
HE WAS ACCUSED OF BITING. YOU KNOW AS WELL AS I DO WHAT THAT MEANS.
YOU THINK HE'S GOT THE VIRUS?!
I DON'T KNOW. AND NEITHER DO YOU. AND SEEING HOW THERE'S NO RELIABLE MEDICAL TEST...
YOU'RE GONNA HOLD HIM UNTIL HE DOESN'T EAT SOMEONE?!

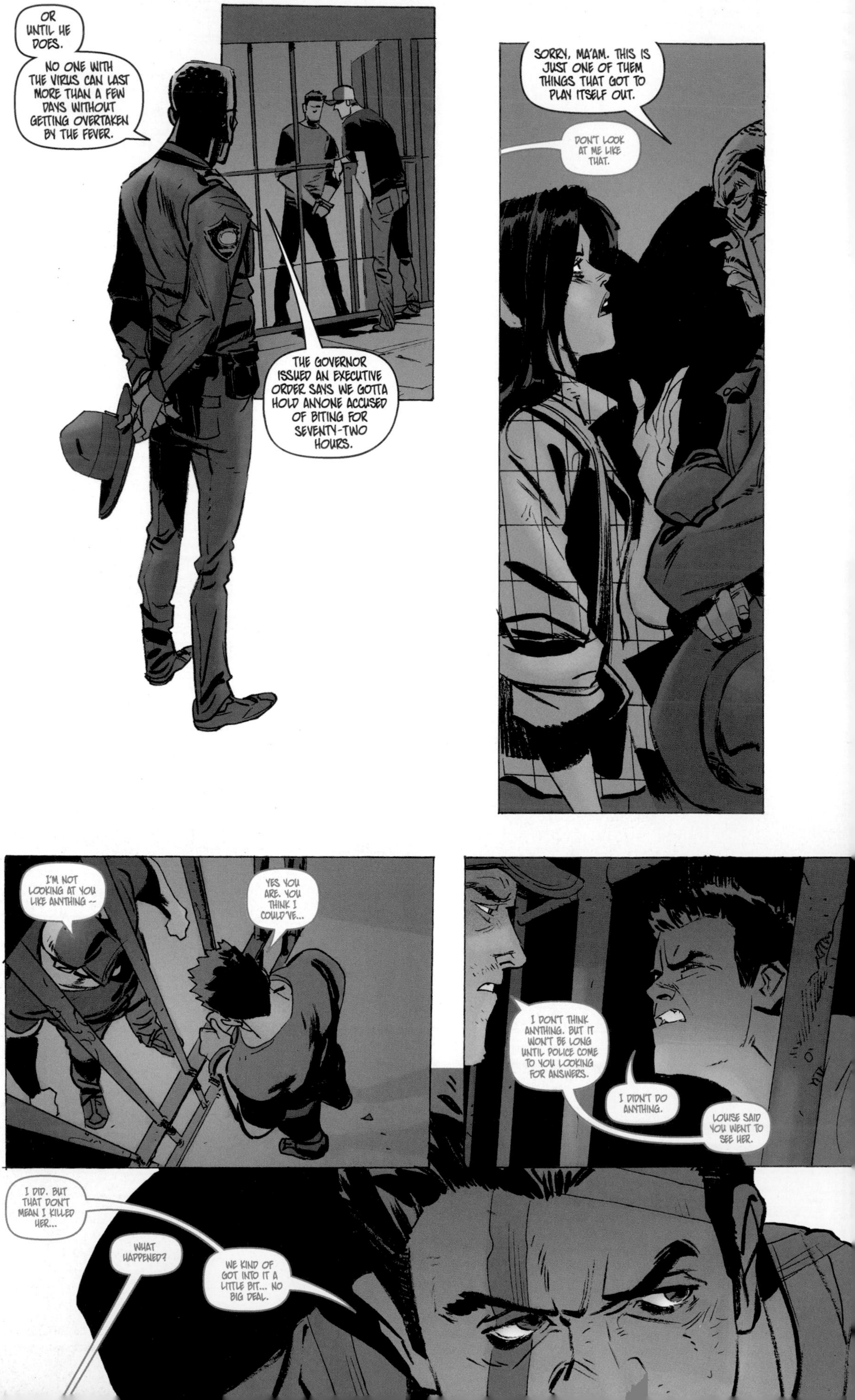
OR UNTIL HE DOES.
NO ONE WITH THE VIRUS CAN LAST MORE THAN A FEW DAYS WITHOUT GETTING OVERTAKEN BY THE FEVER.
THE GOVERNOR ISSUED AN EXECUTIVE ORDER SAYS WE GOTTA HOLD ANYONE ACCUSED OF BITING FOR SEVENTY-TWO HOURS.
SORRY, MA'AM. THIS IS JUST ONE OF THEM THINGS THAT GOT TO PLAY ITSELF OUT.
DON'T LOOK AT ME LIKE THAT.
I'M NOT LOOKING AT YOU LIKE ANYTHING --
YES YOU ARE. YOU THINK I COULD'VE...
I DON'T THINK ANYTHING. BUT IT WON'T BE LONG UNTIL POLICE COME TO YOU LOOKING FOR ANSWERS.
I DIDN'T DO ANYTHING.
LOUISE SAID YOU WENT TO SEE HER.
I DID. BUT THAT DON'T MEAN I KILLED HER...
WHAT HAPPENED?
WE KIND OF GOT INTO IT A LITTLE BIT... NO BIG DEAL.

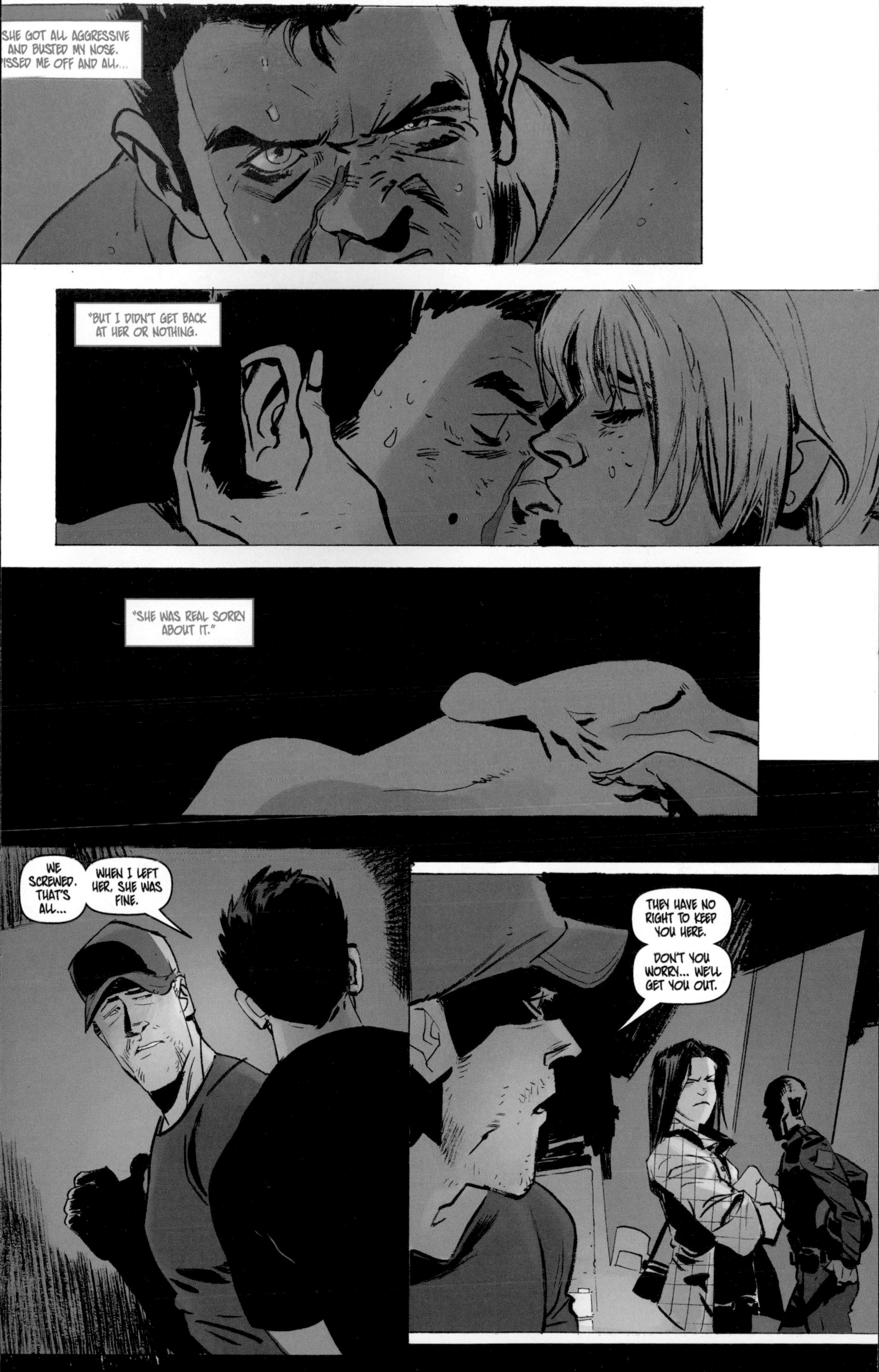
SHE GOT ALL AGGRESSIVE AND BUSTED MY NOSE. PISSED ME OFF AND ALL...
"BUT I DIDN'T GET BACK AT HER OR NOTHING.
"SHE WAS REAL SORRY ABOUT IT."
WE SCREWED. THAT'S ALL...
WHEN I LEFT HER, SHE WAS FINE.
THEY HAVE NO RIGHT TO KEEP YOU HERE.
DON'T YOU WORRY... WE'LL GET YOU OUT.

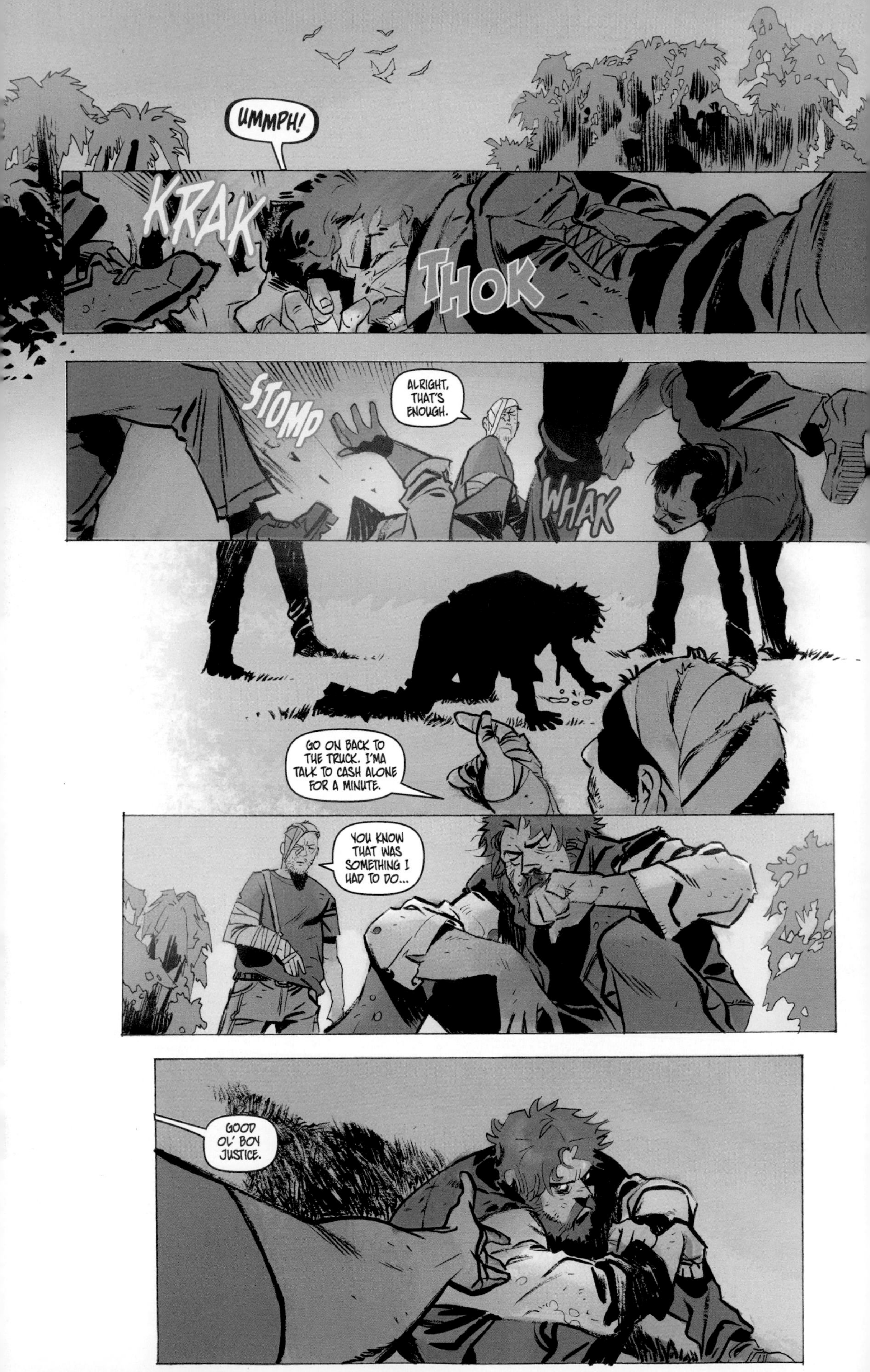
UMMPH!
KRAK
THOK
STOMP
ALRIGHT, THAT'S ENOUGH.
WHAK
GO ON BACK TO THE TRUCK. I'MA TALK TO CASH ALONE FOR A MINUTE.
YOU KNOW THAT WAS SOMETHING I HAD TO DO...
GOOD OL' BOY JUSTICE.

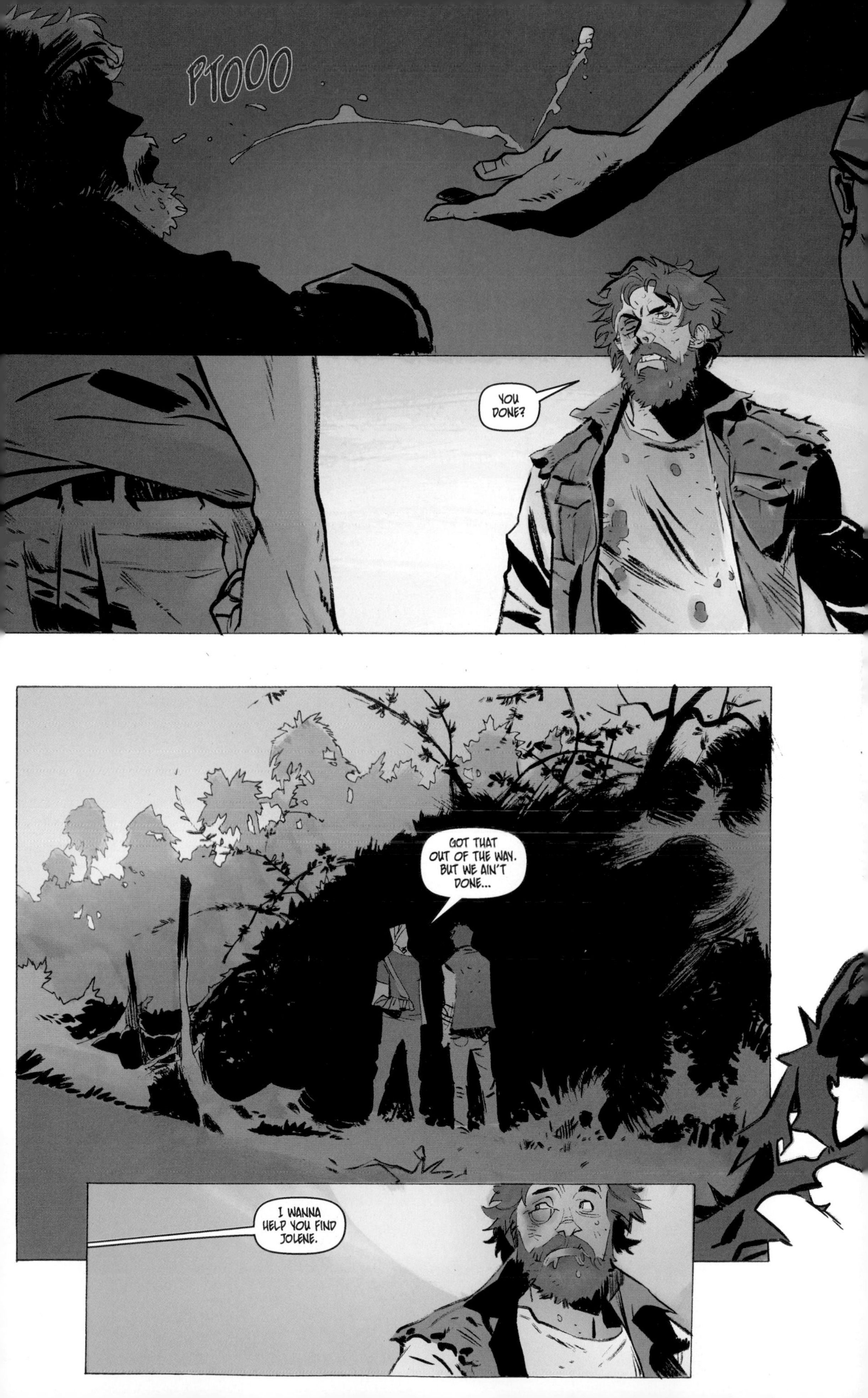
PTOOO
YOU DONE?
GOT THAT OUT OF THE WAY. BUT WE AIN'T DONE...
I WANNA HELP YOU FIND JOLENE.

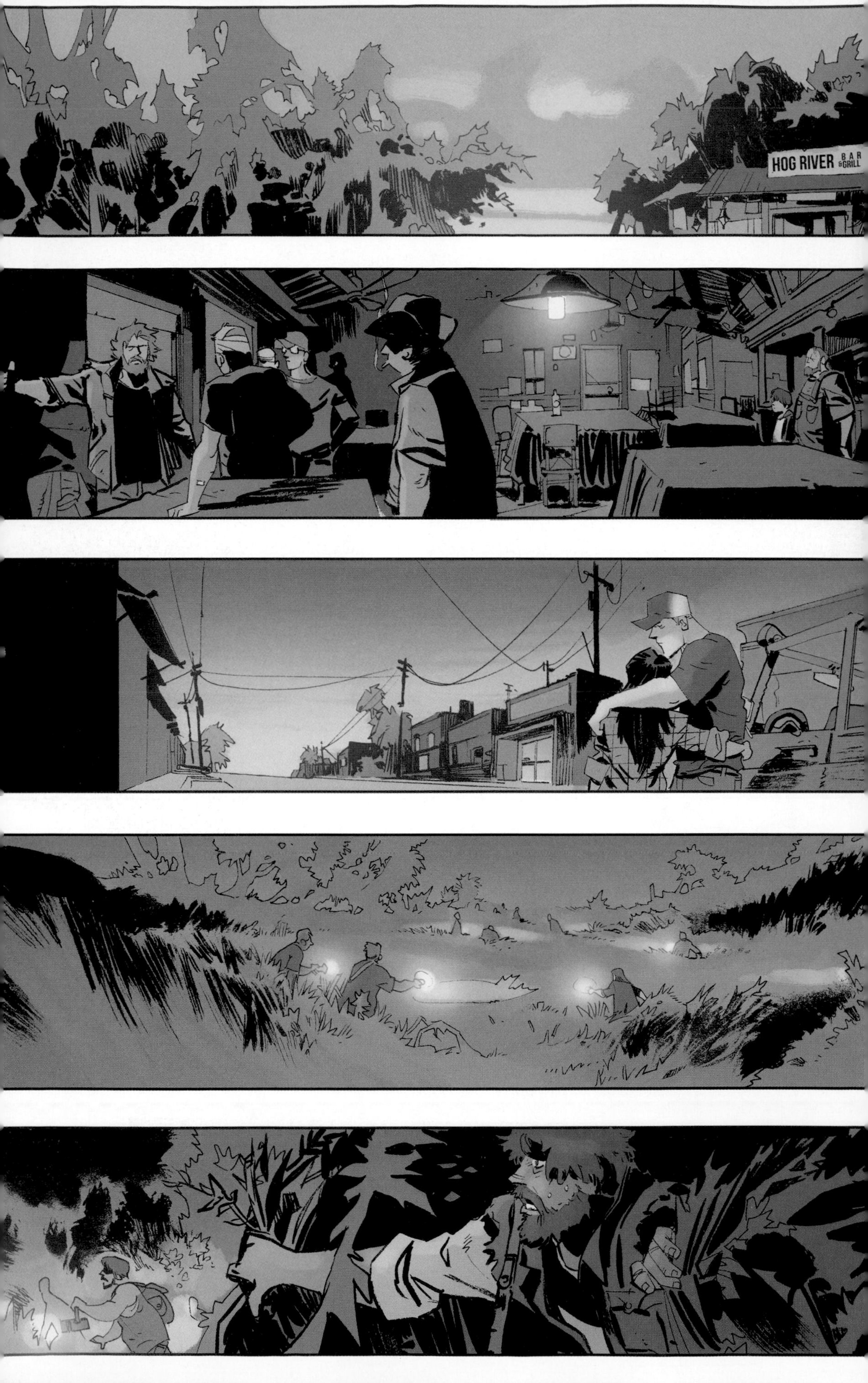
HOG RIVER
BAR & GRILL

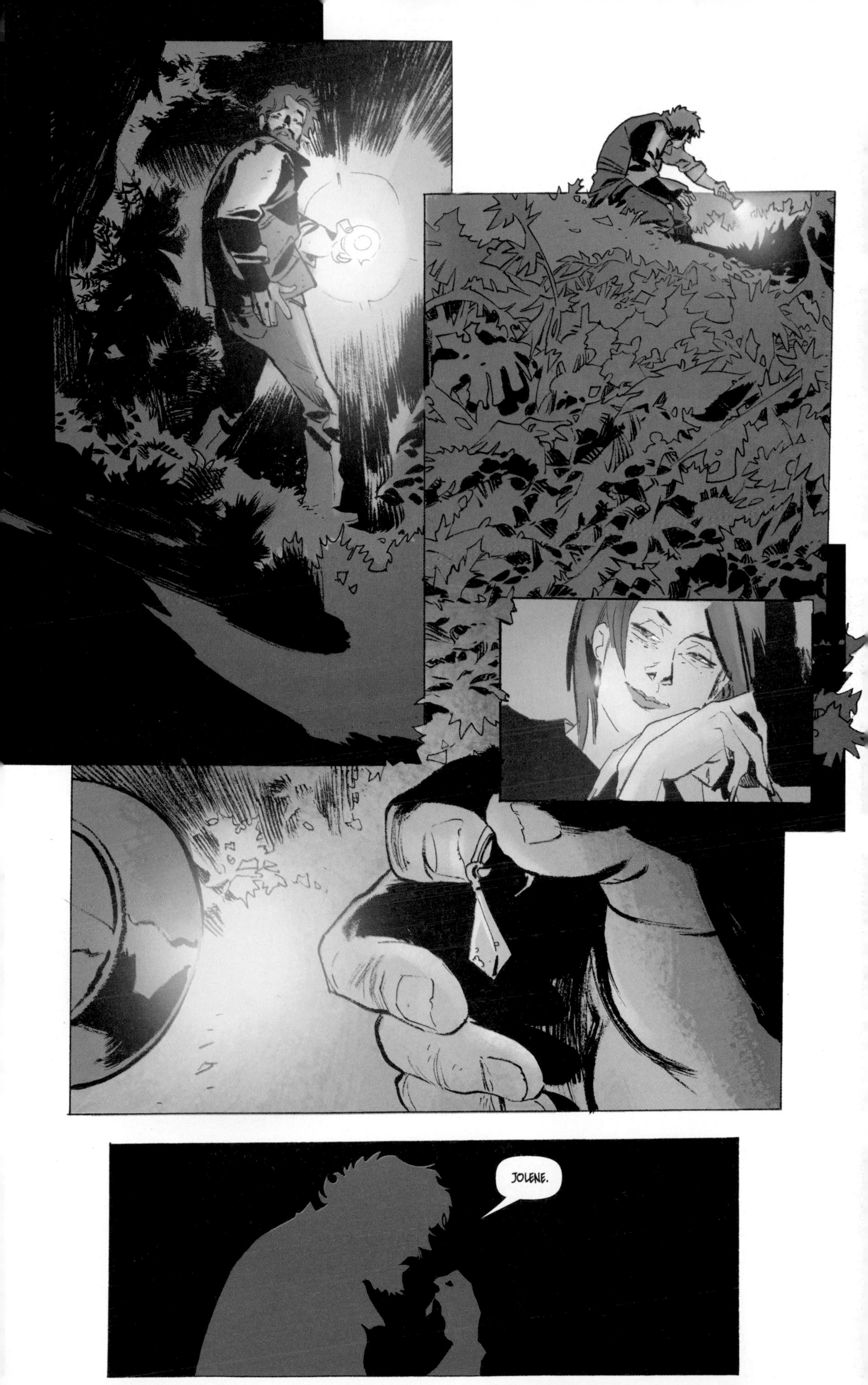
JOLENE.

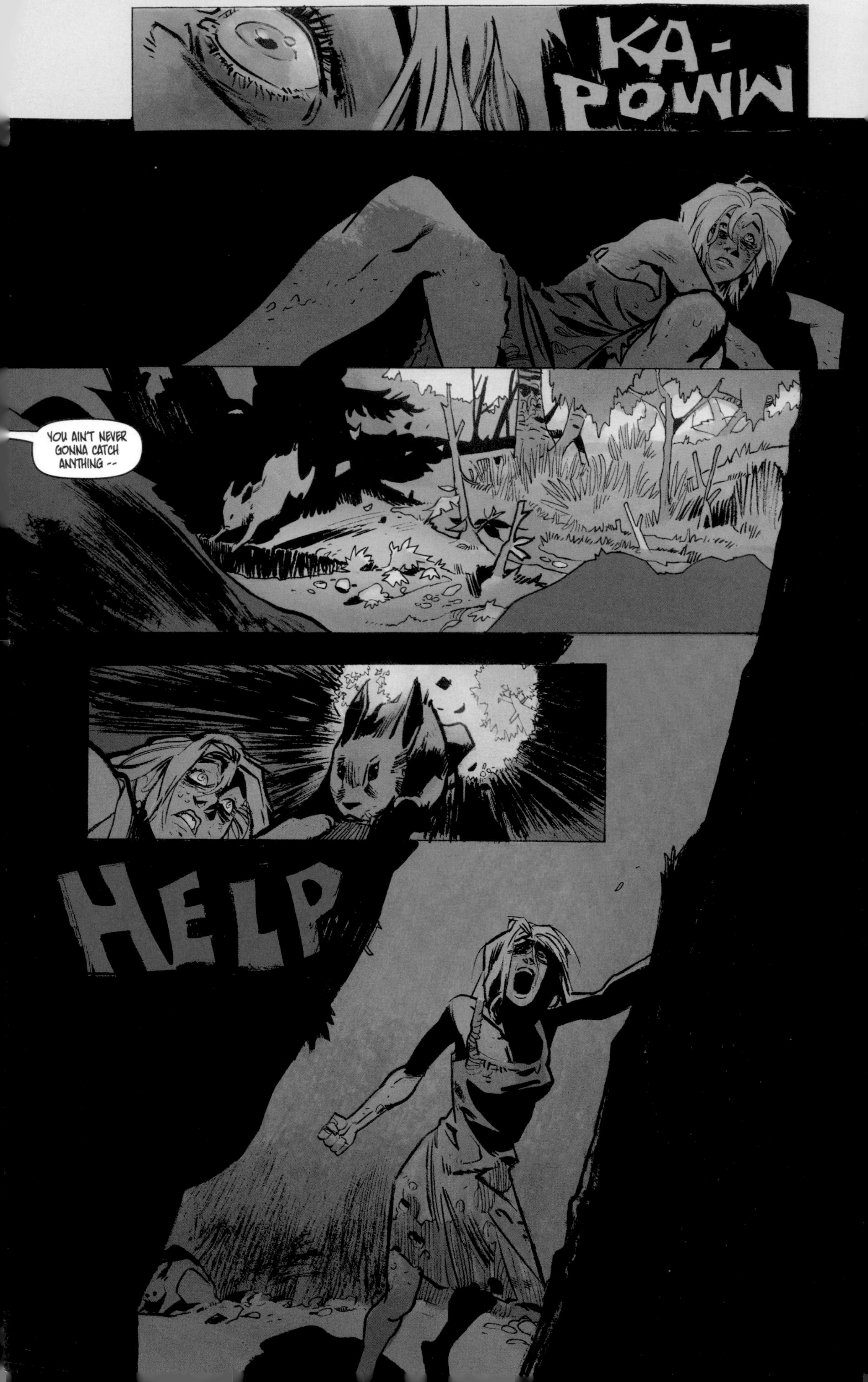
KA-POWW
YOU AIN'T NEVER GONNA CATCH ANYTHING --
HELP

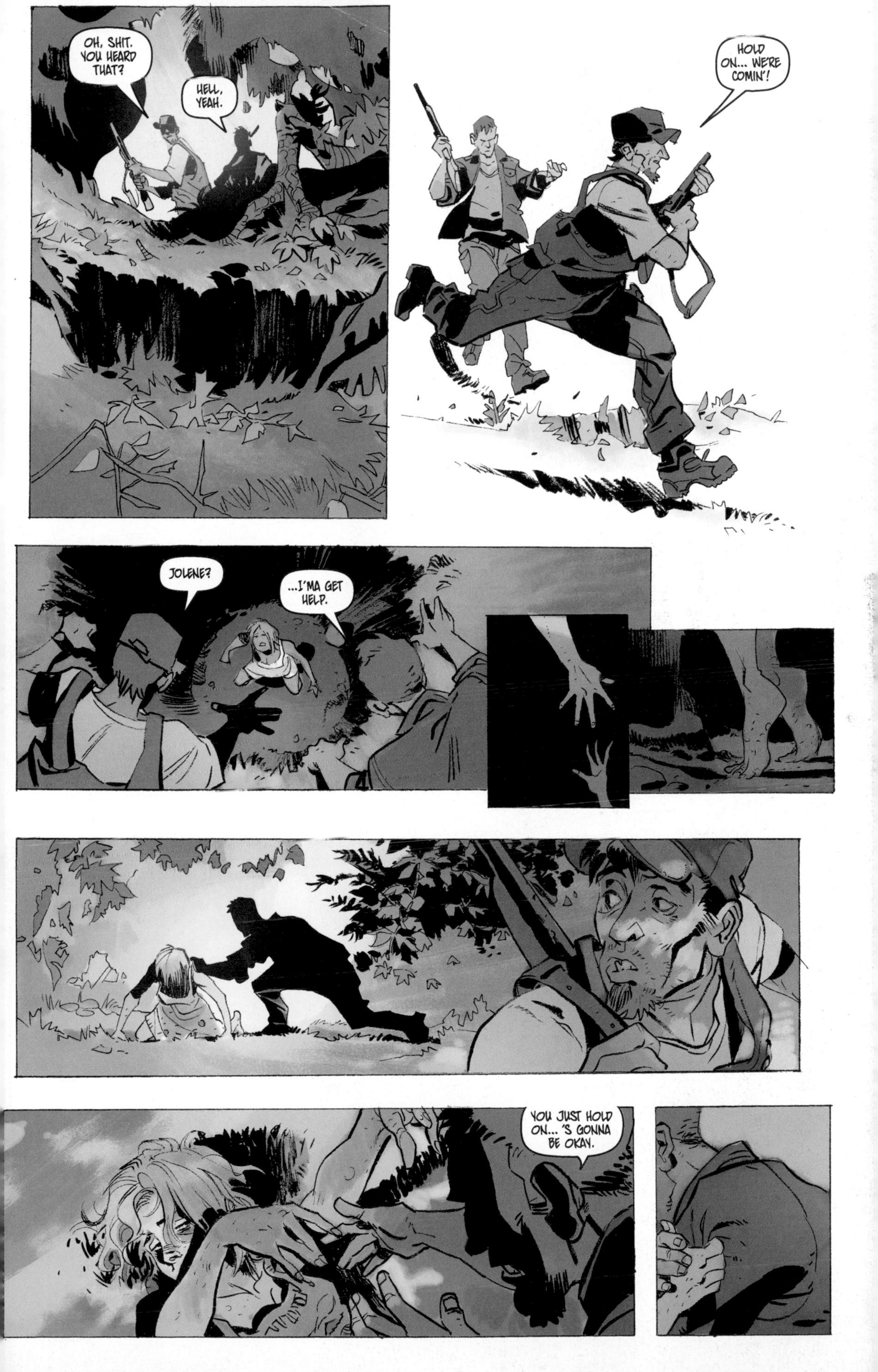
OH, SHIT. YOU HEARD THAT?
HELL, YEAH.
HOLD ON... WE'RE COMIN'!
JOLENE?
...I'MA GET HELP.
YOU JUST HOLD ON... 'S GONNA BE OKAY.

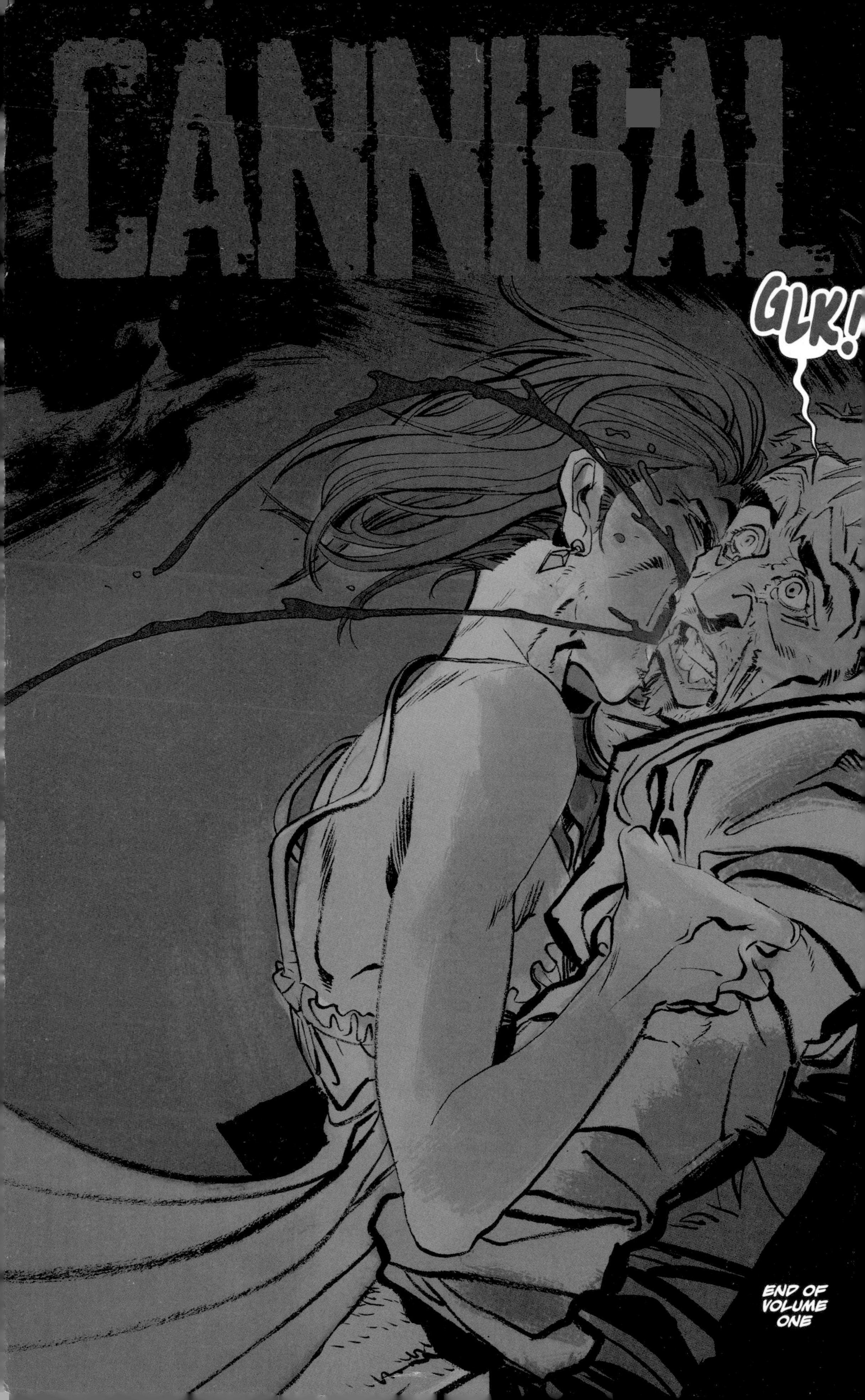
CANNIBAL
GLK!
END OF VOLUME ONE